The Magnificent Wilf

GORDON R. DICKSON

FICTION

THE MAGNIFICENT WILF

A Baen Books Original

Baen Publishing Enterprises
P.O. Box 1403
Riverdale, N.Y. 10471

ISBN: 0-671-87664-3

Cover art by Ruth Sanderson

First printing, June 1995

Distributed by SIMON & SCHUSTER
1230 Avenue of the Americas
New York, N.Y. 10020

Library of Congress Cataloging-in-Publication Data

Dickson, Gordon R.
    The magnificent wilf / Gordon R. Dickson.
        p.   cm.
    ISBN 0-671-87664-3 : $21.00
    I. Title.
    PS3554.I328M34   1995
    813'.54—dc20   94-46999
                                              CIP

Printed in the United States of America

Chapter 1

The spider on the wall made a sharp turn to the left.

"No, you idiot!" said Tom Parent. "Right! Turn right! You're going away from it, now!"

The spider stopped and made an abrupt turn. But it was not the complete about-face which would have headed it back toward the ventilator grille, on the wall of the waiting room of Albert Miles, Tom's immediate superior. That was the only way out for it, to escape from this twenty-seventh story of the All-Earth Federation Building. The ventilation ductwork could provide a pathway down to ground level. There, presumably, it ought to be able to find its way outside, at last, to where a spider could make a living—off aphids, flies, or whatever a carnivorous insect this size would consider takeable prey.

What it had done instead had only given it a forty-five degree change of direction that sent it straight up the yellow-painted wall, past the wall clock there, and entirely past the ventilator grille to which Tom had been trying to direct it. It was now headed toward the ceiling; to which it had already been three times in the past hour and a half, since he had been sitting, coaching it, for want of anything better to do.

It had now reached the ceiling again, and stopped

1

abruptly. Now it was standing there, motionless. It had done that before for minutes at a time.

Tom gave up. He sighed, and looked once more at the wall clock. It was just above a walnut colored door and behind a desk. The desk had an Alien-made Computer/Manager built into it. It was the personal instrument of Albert Miles, First Assistant (1S/SCAL) to Domango Aksisi, Secretary for Alien Affairs of Earth (S/SCAL).

The Computer/Manager noticed him looking at it now; and the red light in the front of the panel that was its single eye softened to a tender pink.

"I love you Tom," it said softly.

"I know," Tom said. "I love you too, Dory. But as you know, I'm already married."

"Oh, that's all right," the C/M said.

It was the usual interchange between them, when Tom found himself in Miles' waiting room.

Tom had a soft spot for Dory, and always thought of the C/M as "her" rather than "it." The name actually was an acronym, short for "*Desk-Oriented Route Yielder*"—which was how its alien designation translated. Miles should actually never have been given such a sensitive piece of machinery. Dory could handle just about everything under the sun of Earth, and do so with all of them simultaneously; from taking care of employees of the Secretariat temporarily on the other side of the world to managing whatever should come up in this office. She was actually much smarter than Miles.

But there was one problem. It was that, in addition to the tremendous capacity for work that Alien science had built into her, Dory also had a component that made her capable of understanding and affection for whomever she belonged to.

Actually, she had been designed to manage Miles as well, in all but his professional decisions. Miles,

however, was too self-centered and insensitive to recognize this; and treated her as nothing more than a
machine. Meanwhile, Dory's operating system required
her to measure her success in being of service by the
affection and dependence that her efforts should
engender in a human breast.

It was Tom's opinion that Miles had no breast. At
least, not one that felt anything. The result was that
Dory was totally unable to make any kind of emotional
connection with him; and was therefore completely
unable to satisfy the circuit that required her to measure how well she was helping him.

Tom, on the other hand, had treated her like
another human being from the first; and Dory's sensi-
tive/affectionate component had responded by falling
in love with him.

This was quite harmless, as Dory herself had
pointed out. If Tom had not been there, she would
have fallen in love with the next available human sub-
stitute. She was no competition in any real sense for
Lucy, Tom's actual wife and real love; but she did her
work much more effectively with the response that
Tom had quite naturally given her.

He was aware of this and usually made an effort to
acknowledge it. Today, however, he had been so full
of his own thoughts he had hardly spoken to her.

"It's a shame he makes you wait this long," Dory
said now, breaking in on Tom's thoughts, "he—"

She hesitated for a nearly imperceptible moment,
as her affection components came into conflict with
her loyalty circuit; then went swiftly on, "I mean, he's
been busy of course, but it's a shame he has to be
busy like this while you sit outside for an hour and a
half. You deserve better, Tom. You're much better
than anyone else here in the Secretariat; and he keeps
you at that low AS/SCAL rank, as if you were no different than any other Assistant Third Secretary. You

aren't even treated like an ordinary Third Secretary should be. You're treated more like an errand boy. But you won't be always."

"Oh, it's not that bad," said Tom, privately admitting to himself that Dory was absolutely right.

"Actually," Tom said, truthfully, "I'm glad to be part of the Secretariat here on any terms."

"Are you?" said Dory, filing this information on him in her private data bank.

"Yes," said Tom. "You see, I'd always believed that there were plenty of intelligent Aliens out in our galaxy; and that it was just a matter of time until they'd get into open contact with us. Everybody used to laugh at me. But now that Aliens have shown up and actually made open contact with us, you can't find anyone who doesn't claim they always knew it, too. But I actually did—even before the first Oprinkian official showed up here to tell us we were finally going to be accepted— probationary status only, of course—into the civilization of this Galactic Sector."

"I know," said Dory. "I've got your complete history on file, just like I've got everybody else's as well. Once you've been given the chance, you'll show your ability so clearly no one can help knowing how capable you are. And you'll be given that chance. You'll see. I'm helping."

"I know you are, Dory," said Tom. "And I appreciate it."

Dory went back to handling affairs for Miles, and Tom returned to his thinking.

Not that there was anything she could do, he told himself. She had been designed to advise, but only if asked—and Miles would never ask.

Still, what she said was true about Miles. But then, he treated everybody but his superiors like errand boys. He had been put in his present position back when this Secretariat was not a Secretariat at all, but only a minor Department, hastily thrown together after the first Oprinkian landed.

It had only been after a number of visits by the Oprinkians, and a growing realization that other intelligent Races like them were far, far advanced over humans, that the All-Earth Federation of Earth woke up. The realization dawned on them, finally, that dealing diplomatically with such Aliens called for an organization comparable in dignity to those they would be dealing with—and the Department became a Secretariat.

The only unfortunate part had been that Miles had made the change along with it. He was still in charge of everything; and ranked just under the Secretary for Alien Affairs, Domango Aksisi, himself.

The truth was, Tom told himself, Miles was sick with a desire for power. He was thoroughly convinced he should have been in Domango's place. But the Secretary had necessarily needed to be chosen by the All-Earth Federation in open Convocation. So Miles had stayed on as merely chief bureaucrat, just what he had been to begin with.

Tom looked back at the spider.

The situation had changed. It was now on the move again, slanting toward the ventilator grille from only a couple of feet above it. It was clipping right along. Finally, it seemed to have noticed the grille, and made it the goal to be reached.

Tom felt a slight warmth of self-congratulation. That was the answer to dealing with different species and Alien Races, he thought. Patience—and confidence. Undoubtedly these would be some of the important criteria in dealing with intelligent Aliens too. Always be patient, and never allow yourself to be baffled or surprised by anything they—

The spider stopped short about an inch and a half from the edge of the ventilator; as if the thought had suddenly occurred to it that the ventilator might be some sort of trap.

Calm down, Tom told it mentally. Don't get excited or angry. Remain patient, confident and optimistic at all times, the way I always do—

The spider suddenly zipped to the ventilator and through the nearest hole, out of sight into the blackness of the duct work beyond.

"Tom," said Dory, "you can go in. He says he's ready for you, now."

Tom got up from his chair and headed toward the maple-colored door. Ordinarily that "ready for you now" would have rasped annoyingly on his nerves after being kept waiting so long; but right at the moment he was too full of a feeling of triumph over the spider's escape. He came very close to whistling happily, as he touched the latch button of the door below the clock. The door itself slid back and he entered the inner sanctum of Albert Miles (1S/SCAL).

"Well, here you are!" said Miles, looking up from his desk.

He would not have been an unpleasant looking man, if it had not been for the now-permanent expression of ill-humor etched on his features by constant practice, the tight lips and the accusatory frown line between his slightly graying eyebrows. The bright noon sunlight of spring, coming through the nearest of the cathedral-shaped windows—not as tall and narrow as Miles would have liked (he had indented for recutting them, but Buildings and Grounds had so far refused permission)—at the moment unfortunately cast a halo around Miles' receding gray-black hairline.

What hair he had otherwise, plainly needed a haircut. It was standing up untidily. Curiously, he had unusually broad shoulders, which should have redeemed his appearance from being that of a small, vinegarish man; but instead gave the impression that he was hunched uncomfortably behind his desk. After a short pause, he added, "Well, I suppose you better sit down."

He nodded to a chair—a reasonably padded chair, but nothing to compare with the high-backed, cushioned throne he himself sat in. The facing chair was a little to one side of the center of his desk; and he turned slightly to frown at Tom like a judge who is already making up his mind about the prisoner in the witness box.

Tom waited. When dealing with Alien species, he reminded himself again, patience. Be calm. Remain optimistic.

"I suppose you want to know why you're here," said Miles, disagreeably.

As a matter of fact, Tom already knew. The news had been passed generally, from one person to another through the Secretariat for the last three days, that there was an important Alien visitor due on Earth. Another Oprinkian, an official representative of one of the forty-three ruling Races in this sector of the galaxy—in fact the very one that had watched over the growth of the human race into civilization. He was due here on a special mission to get to know the human race better, individual-to-individual. Undoubtedly, Miles had called Tom in because there was some errand or duty concerned with seeing that the visitor had a good time; and Tom was picked for it.

"It's a very important Oprinkian that's coming," Miles was going on. "An Oprinkian of the ninth level."

Tom blinked.

An Oprinkian even of the fifth level would have startled him. Nothing higher than one of fourth level had visited Earth so far. The idea of nine levels was mind-boggling. He might be only an Assistant Third Secretary, but theoretically he was supposed to know Alien ranks as well as anyone else in the Secretariat.

"Knocks you speechless, doesn't it?" said Miles. "And you may well wonder why someone like you should even be told about it. But for you it's only a matter of running an errand for me. I tell you this much only so you'll understand how important it is you do at least that right. There mustn't be any slip-ups. This ninth level Oprinkian is far beyond our dictating to him what he wants to do."

Tom could believe this. The first Oprinkian to visit Earth and acquaint it with the fact that it was being finally accepted—on probation only—into the Confederacy of Alien Worlds, had encountered some human who mentioned to him the problem Earth currently had with nuclear weapons and the storage of nuclear waste.

The Oprinkian had only tut-tutted on hearing this and gone on to other matters. But in succeeding weeks, all around the globe, those concerned with nuclear weapons and nuclear waste had suddenly discovered that the dangerous element in these artifacts of human technology had been neutralized. All such material had become inert.

Since that time, people had developed a certain wariness about all Oprinkians. Certainly the Oprinkians were a kindly race and well intentioned. They were the ones who had Earth within their own sphere of influence. They had directly studied the Human Race, evidently hoping that it would graduate to their own present, educated level; and recommended humans for probationary civilized status—though how Oprinkians defined the word "civilized"—except that it had nothing to do with technological achievements—was unclear.

Still, few humans nowadays would want to tell an Oprinkian he or she couldn't do something.

"All right, now!" Miles was going on, "this particular Oprinkian wants us to call him Mr. Rejilla. What Mr.

Rejilla's come here to find, he says, is the experience of everyday life in the case of a mated couple of humans. Particularly, a couple with a pet. It seems Oprinkians have been particularly taken with the fact that some of us—I don't, myself—keep specimens of a lesser species in their homes on a family basis. They seem to think that's advanced behavior for people like us."

Miles paused.

"Naturally," he went on, "all those things narrow our freedom to deal with him the way I'd like to. To begin with, we don't want to risk exposing him to any-one who isn't in the Secretariat—someone who, natu-rally, might make mistakes."

"Right," said Tom.

"Right!" said Miles. "Now, we don't want to expose him to anyone outside the Secretariat. Now, for who should host this Rejilla—the Secretary himself, of course, is out of the question; so am I—though the Secretary and I did talk briefly about me and my wife being the ones to entertain Mr. Rejilla."

He stopped and glared at Tom for a moment as if daring Tom to suggest any other couple could possibly be considered first.

"Of course," said Tom.

Miles went on.

"Anyway, we haven't got a pet. My wife would like a cat, but—" said Miles, once more sneering a little, for he considered any such disabilities a personal indulgence and evidence of weakness of character, "—she's supposed to be allergic to cats, or we'd simply have borrowed one for the occasion. In any case, Mr. Rejilla ruled it out. He'd asked which were the two most popular lesser species kept as pets by humans; and after doing a quick world survey, we came up with dogs and cats. He chose dogs—but my wife's also allergic to them—because, he says, they're socialized wolves. He thinks it's fascinating a socialized variety should be part of the lives of so many ordinary humans; when the wild variety's regarded as a dangerous predator. He's got some other, Oprinkian types of reasons, too, that he didn't explain clearly. There'd be no point in my telling you about them."

Miles paused; more to get his breath, Tom thought, than anything else.

"That's very understandable, sir," said Tom, to fill the gap.

"Of course it is," said Miles. "Well the upshot was that I dug into our list of Secretariat employees who fit the bill, and came up with the five best candidates for the Secretary to choose from—don't worry," said Miles, looking at Tom, "you and your wife and dog aren't on the list."

"I hadn't been expecting—" Tom was beginning, when Miles cut him short.

"Well, you aren't, anyway," he said. "You and your wife, Judy—"

"Lucy," said Tom, coldly.

"Oh yes, Lucy," said Miles. "Met her at one of our annual New Year's parties, I think. Young woman, reddish brown hair—there's a name for that kind of hair, but I can't think of it . . . well, it doesn't matter. The point is, Mr. Rejilla will be spending a day or two overnight with whichever one of the five is chosen, to see what Humans and pets are like, together. The Secretary's about to decide who. He was going to talk it over once more with me this afternoon so I could fill him in on any information that isn't in the dossiers, from my personal experience; but I've been subpoenaed to appear at a hearing in the Committee Conferences Building, now, so you're going to have to talk to him instead."

"I am?" said Tom, surprised.

"That's what I said—he asked for you when I

couldn't make it. I've got the dossiers on the chosen hosts here. They're Jennings, Ninowsky, Ormand, Jondu and Wilts. You know them all and you can tell him whatever he wants to know. Dory's made up extra copies of their dossiers for you to have with you when you talk. If he wants more info about some of the points in the dossiers, you can fill him in. Dory's got the copies outside now. Go get them and come back here—don't waste time."

Tom didn't.

He came back into Miles' office, juggling the rather heavy pile of thick dossiers in their slippery brown covers, to find Miles impatiently waiting by a small brown door in the far wall of his office. As Tom passed the desk on his way to join him, he saw what seemed to be another, similar dossier in Miles' wastebasket. He went on to Miles, who punched a button; and the brown door slid back to reveal the inside of a small private elevator. They stepped in and were carried up one floor, from which they emerged into the inner reception room of the office of Secretary Domango Aksisi.

Chapter 2

"Is the Secretary expecting—" a thin, young man behind the desk in the reception room began as, in the lead and without a word in answer, Miles marched past with Tom following. Miles led the way through the self-opening door behind the receptionist and into the Secretary's office.

The door shut behind them.

"Ah, here you are," said Domango Aksisi, looking up from some papers spread on his large desk.

He had a soft voice, husky with age. His dark face was surprisingly unlined, though his hair was gray and thinning. He had obviously been a big man once, but age had pared him down, making him look frail and thin.

"Sit down, sit down Tom," he said. "I needn't keep you, Albert."

"I was just going to mention," said Miles, "that Parent here can answer any questions you have about the candidates. He's been around here longer than any of them."

"Yes, yes, I know about Tom," said Domango, smiling at Tom as he came forward to the desk and sat down in the chair the Secretary had indicated. Tom balanced the pile of dossiers precariously on his knees. "As I say, Albert, you needn't wait. I know how the

13

pressures are on you. You'll want to get going to that hearing."

"Well, I—" said Miles, and checked himself. "Yes, Mr. Secretary."

He stepped back into the reception room, which got its automatic door open just in time to let him pass, and then closed upon him. Tom and the Secretary were alone.

"Ah, Tom," said Domango, "we've seen each other more than a few times, but we've never really had a chance to talk, have we?"

"No, Mr. Secretary," said Tom.

They had indeed had a few words on a number of occasions, but these were always official occasions where there was never the opportunity for the Secretary to say more than a few words or Tom to answer, other than briefly.

Domango was in many ways the exact opposite of Miles. He was the Secretary for Alien Affairs mainly because he was the one person for the post upon whom all the delegates to the All-Earth Federation could agree. He had not really wanted the job; but had thought it his duty to take it because he had such general backing, which might be of benefit to Earth in his discussions with off-Earth Alien races.

Actually, as Tom knew, what Domango really wanted to do was to retire. He was well past the age of retirement; and he had had a life that certainly entitled him to it. Of his fifty adult years, a total of thirty of them had been spent at one time in jails, or under detention. He had been tortured, mishandled and exiled for years; also separated from his family, of which his first wife and most of his family had been killed or died, so that only one daughter was left out of an original nine children.

Yet as Tom looked at him now, it did not seem to have soured him either on life or on humanity. His large, calm face was peaceful. Tom found himself warming to the man even more than he had previously.

"I understand you've had no extended contact at all with any of the other Aliens who've visited Earth?" asked Domango.

"None, Mr. Secretary," said Tom. "Just brief meetings at official affairs."

"Well," went on Domango, "I think you'll find the Oprinkians are among the best you'll ever encounter—possibly the best there are, at least in our Sector of the galaxy. Mr. Rejilla, now, is of a very ancient Alien Race. His people have not only been civilized, but in space, for tens of thousands of years."

Domango broke off.

"But I imagine you know that," he said.

"I knew they'd been in space for some time," said Tom, "but I'd no idea it'd been that long."

"Mind-bending, isn't it?" said Domango, smiling. "We were still hiding in caves when they were out among the stars. If all the forty-three Races who have seats as Representatives on the Council for our Galactic Sector, on Cayahno, were as mature, as helpful, and as—according to the Sector Charter, at least—as civilized as the Oprinkians are, our being in the same Sector wouldn't be as worrisome as it could be, now. The fact of the matter is the Council contains a few of what the Oprinkians would politely consider barely civilized Races. That description applies to us, too, of course; and these others have been admitted to knowledge of galactic civilization simply because once in a millenium inevitably some problem occurs where all the Races in that Sector have to work together."

"Yes," said Tom. But he was becoming more and more bewildered. Why was Domango telling him all this—unless he was just lonely for someone to tell it to?

"But I'm afraid it's a fact." Domango sighed—a little wearily, Tom thought.

"You may well eventually run into what you'd consider some very savage types of Aliens, if you ever end up having to do with some from many other worlds," Domango went on. "Indeed some seem very savage, even by our standards; and, like us, they're just recently into space. But some have already conquered and dominated other worlds with intelligent but even more primitive races on them. However, that doesn't concern you at the moment; I only mention all this to make sure you understand ahead of time that you'll find Mr. Rejilla a remarkable Being to know—and his people do want to help us as much as they can."

"Pardon me, sir," said Tom, feeling a mild sort of desperation, "I'm afraid I haven't completely understood. Am I to meet Mr. Rejilla?"

"Be rather difficult otherwise, don't you think?" said Domango, with a chuckle. "Yes, of course, you must meet him as soon as he arrives. You'll have some security people with you; but that's beside the point. Now, let me just check a few things on your dossier."

He reached out and unearthed from among the other papers on his desk what seemed to be an exact duplicate of one of the bound personal histories Tom was balancing on his knees.

"It says here that Albert Miles' Computer/Manager loves you," said Domango, staring at a page. "Can that be correct?"

"Well . . ." Tom struggled for a way of answering that would save him both embarrassment and any possible reflection on Dory, "she said so. I think it's something about her circuits, or her programming, or something like that."

"Possibly," Domango frowned at the page he was looking at. "It also says everybody else, with a few rare exceptions, loves you." He lifted his eyes to meet those of Tom. "That's rather a strong statement, don't you think?"

"Yes sir," said Tom, "it is. I don't quite know how I happen to be described that way."

"Further," went on Domango, looking at the page again, "am I to understand that, just in the last couple of hours, you made a strong effort to direct a lesser species of this world to escape from this building into the open air, where it would be happy and safe? Can this be correct?"

Once more he looked at Tom. Tom was beginning to sweat slightly.

"I was sort of talking out loud to a spider in Miles' reception room," he said. "You know how you can do something like that?"

"Not all of us do it," said Domango. "But I'm interested to hear that it's a fact. The spider, then, did escape?"

"Yes, as far as I know, anyway," said Tom. "It disappeared into a ventilator grille connected with the duct work of the building. It should be able to find its way to the ground floor and out the fresh air intake into the grass and the sunshine. I don't really believe it understood the directions I gave it to find the ventilator grille. It was probably just coincidence."

"Still," said Domango, "surprisingly few people take that kind of interest in a spider. However, leaving that aside—you are married, of course. In fact I think I met your wife—a charming young woman. Her name is Lucy, isn't it?"

"Yes," said Tom. "She was in the Linguistic section of our Secretariat here. But she'd climbed the promotion ladder very quickly; and Miles persuaded her to—er, take a temporary leave of absence of about six months. She's been writing a book on linguistics with her time off. It's almost done."

"Indeed!" said Domango. "Not one to let grass grow under her feet, I take it? Come to think of it, didn't she have a second name as well?"

"Yes sir. Thorsdatter—her maiden name. It's Scandinavian in origin. Thor was the Norse God of War; and 'datter' would mean she's his daughter."

"Is that so?" said Domango. "You mean her own family gave her that name originally? A rather powerful name, isn't it?"

"Yes. But it fits her. Small, but unstoppable."

"Well, well," said Domango, looking back at the pages in front of him, "also, you have a dog, a Great Dane named Rex, it says here."

"Yes indeed," said Tom, brightening. "He's the great grandson of Rex—the Great Dane with the English-accented bark, who used to help Sherlock Holmes in so many films, some years back. But, come to think of it, sir, you might never have heard of Rex Regis."

"I certainly have," said Domango. "I think I've seen every one of his films, most of them as recordings. I particularly liked the one where he saved the people who were trapped in the trans-atlantic tunnel, when it was thought there was no hope of rescuing them. And then there was that other great one in which he solved the mysterious case of the missing Empire State Building; and the one in which he sought out and brought back in handcuffs the world's master criminal, Wallaby Xanzadau."

"Yes," said Tom, carried away by his own enthusiasm for the films made by Rex's great-grandfather. "The people who handled him said that he could do everything but talk, but didn't need to do that because he could read people's minds."

"I didn't know that," said Domango. "But I can believe it. Yes, it's thoroughly believable. So you've got a dog like the original Rex, have you?"

Tom's enthusiasm evaporated suddenly, leaving a cold, uncomfortable feeling in his stomach.

"Well, not exactly," he said. "In fact—our Rex isn't

really anything like his great-grandfather, as far as being that remarkable. But he's an awfully good dog. He has a good heart."

"That," said Domango, "is an important thing in any Being, human, animal or Alien. Well, in any case, that's all I was going to ask you. It really was a matter of satisfying my own curiosity about these little things mentioned in your dossier. If you're that lovable it could be an asset for someone dealing with Aliens of all types and varieties, but especially the Oprinkians. And your attitude toward the spider trapped in a building like this, also shows compassion for a different life form. Not that any of this was absolutely necessary. I think I would have chosen you anyway, out of the six candidates I had Albert submit to me, to play host for Mr. Rejilla. Lucy and Rex were the only necessary qualifications."

He closed the folder before him. Tom was staring at him, and reaching for words.

"Sir?" he said. "You mean me? You mean you chose me to be the host for Mr. Rejilla, in his experience with a human family and pet?"

"Of course," said Domango, looking at him. "Nothing against the other five who had dossiers submitted, but you and your family will be just ideal."

"But—" Tom hesitated. "There weren't six candidates, sir. Miles said there were only five. I've only got five folders here with me, so I could refer to them if you had specific questions about things in them that I could enlarge upon for you. They were all dossiers on five other people."

"Your own dossier must have fallen out then, somehow," said Domango. "I certainly asked Miles to give me half a dozen to choose from and he sent up a stack for me to look at—"

He frowned slightly and turned back to the front page of the dossier in front of him.

"Though it's true," he went on in a thoughtful voice, looking at it, "one of them must have been missing from those he sent me, because it was sent up separately directly from his C/M machine—the one you call Dory—a few moments later. One of the original stack must have dropped out. How many do you have there on your knees?"

Tom had never actually counted them. He did so now.

"There's six!" he said.

"I thought so," said Domango. "See if your own dossier isn't one of them."

Tom hastily flipped through the first pages of each one and, sure enough, the third one down was his.

"You're right, sir," he said, holding it up.

"I thought so," said Domango. "Evidently there must have been some small mix-up somewhere. Strange, when Albert's usually so efficient and correct."

Dory was the one who was efficient and correct, thought Tom, but he did not say the words aloud.

"On the other hand," said Domango, looking again at the first page of his copy of Tom's dossier, "have you looked at this first page of yours closely?"

"No sir," said Tom. He did so now.

At the top of the first page in block letters was the legend (REPLACEMENT COPY—DIRECT FROM D.O.R.Y.)

"Oh," he said.

A memory of the folder in Miles' wastebasket flashed in his mind. He could imagine Miles barking at Dory.

"Here! Find me six candidates to meet this Oprinkian, for Domango to look at!"

—Then forgetting all about it until Tom's dossier turned up as one of the six.

"Well, in any case," Domango was going on now, "if you hadn't realized that you were the one chosen to play host to Mr. Rejilla, I suggest you take the rest of the afternoon off and get in touch with Lucy Thorsdatter right away. Mr. Rejilla will be coming to your particular suburban area on this evening's helicopter; and I imagine Lucy will like some time to get things ready, if she's anything like my wife. By the way, here's my private phone number at where my wife and I'll be staying over the weekend. Call me if you run into a real emergency."

Chapter 3

Tom was not allowed to move. He sat in the large, red overstuffed chair in the living room, with his feet drawn up out of the way. From the back of the house came the plaintive single bark of a Great Dane who is tired of being shut in the bedroom, out of the way.

"Rex wants out," said Tom.

"Well, he can wait a little longer," said Lucy, rapidly running her Single-Swipe cleaning wand over the living room walls.

"It's time for his food, too," said Tom.

"He won't starve," said Lucy. She put down the wand and went back into the little annex they called the library, to bring out the dust collector and set it in the middle of the living room. She turned it on. It hummed comfortably; and everything from dust motes down to large molecules that were floating around in the air or clinging to any surfaces in the living room, rushed to it; as if it offered their only hope of survival. Tom felt the device's attraction plucking at microscopic foreign bodies in his clothing.

"I would have said," Tom said, "that it'd be completely impossible for anyone to do a complete equivalent of a spring house cleaning of a house this size in two hours. I think you decided to do the whole thing just because any ordinary person would know doing it was impossible. That's also why you don't let me help. You're always starting things like that; and the irritating thing is you end up managing to get them done. It's not normal."

"Of course not," said Lucy from the dining room, having picked up her cleaning wand and gone on, "it could be, but most people won't make the effort; and as for helping, you just get in my way. That's the difference between us, you and I."

"Only because you always decide to work where I'm working," said Tom.

"No, it's because I catch up to you. You day-dream until you have to do something. I block everything else out. I make a sort of tunnel vision for myself, in which there's only this one thing to be done; and then I have all my forces to devote to it. When I concentrate like that, there's nothing to distract me."

"I know," said Tom, sadly, "least of all, me and Rex."

"Oh, stop it," said Lucy from the dining room. "This house is going to be in shape for Mr. Rejilla, whatever you say. If you have to do something, you can go take Rex into the kitchen and feed him. It's time for him to be fed, anyway."

Released, Tom unfolded from the chair, went carefully to the bedroom and likewise released a happy Rex. He led the dog to the kitchen. Lucy had started up the dust collector in the dining room now; and Tom, suddenly realizing this offered a handy excuse to break the usual rules, closed the door between the kitchen and the dining room.

He tip-toed to the Serve-all. Rex followed with ears pricked up, eyes bright and nose twitching. Quietly Tom eased open the door; and there was the hamburger—two pounds of it—he had picked up on the way home. He took it to the sink, still followed by Rex; put it on the drain board, unwrapped it, and—

picking up Rex's food bowl from the end of the kitchen counter—began to slice off some of the ground meat for him.

"Oh, no you don't!" said Lucy's voice behind him. "You aren't feeding Rex raw hamburger!"

"But it's an important occasion!" said Tom. "He deserves a treat, anyway, with Mr. Rejilla coming—"

"Well, his treat isn't going to be raw hamburger!" said Lucy, diving behind him, capturing the hamburger, rewrapping it and putting back in the refrigerated compartment of the kitchen Serve-all. "It's got to be cooked if he's going to eat it at all; and we don't have time to do that. Besides as far as he's concerned this is no different from any other day. He can eat his dog food, like any ordinary canine."

"But he isn't any ordinary canine, honey. Remember his famous ancestor. Rex Regis was a genius among dogs; everybody said so. And he lived on steak tartare—which is really nothing but high-class hamburger. What if it's Rex's diet on that dry dog food that's been holding him back? Maybe with a hamburger-tartare diet he'd begin to show some of the brilliance of his grandfather. Wouldn't that be something, with Mr. Rejilla coming?"

"It would certainly be something," said Lucy. "But what makes you imagine changing his diet would make that much of a difference in him?"

"Well—" Tom reached for a reason.

"Don't stretch yourself," repeated Lucy. "You know as well as I do what our Rex does best. This steak-fancying, vase-smashing, over-grown lump off the old block. Nothing! That's what our Rex does best!"

"Owooo," said Rex, mournfully to the floor between his paws.

"There you go," said Tom, "now he thinks you're mad at him."

"Well I'm not!" snapped Lucy at the huge canine.

"And you aren't going to get anywhere trying to play on my sympathies this time, Rex. Tom, you'd better be getting your best jacket on, because we're going to have to leave for the copter port in ten minutes."

Tom went sadly out the door, and Lucy resolutely poured dry dog food into Rex's bowl, added some water to it and put the bowl down on the floor for him.

Rex abandoned his expressions of despair and waded into its contents.

Daneraux, the Security Chief of Operation Oprinkian Visit, and a hard-faced man named White, from the Internal Security Branch, were waiting at the copter port when Tom and Lucy got there. The copter was not in yet, but expected any minute. The sun was already down, and a light, misty rain was falling. The lights on the landing pad were glowing through it.

"All right now," said Daneraux. He was a small man who had a habit of going up on his toes when he got excited. He was very much up on his toes now. "Now listen, both of you. You'll be completely covered at all times—"

"Right," said White.

"Right. And what we want is that you two just act normal. Just normal, you understand?"

"Sure," Tom replied.

"Remember, Rejilla's the representative of a greater race than any we've encountered to date. They may have all sorts of abilities. We absolutely can't afford to take a definite line with them until we find out just what their potentialities are."

"Right," said White.

"Right. In Security, we understand these things better than you desk-jockeys. We have a feeling, now— in fact, it's practically a certainty—"

"Check," said White.

"—that all these Aliens are as much in the dark

about us as we are about them. That's why Rejilla's
asked for this chance to spend twenty-four hours with
a typical human couple in a typical human household.
Theoretically, it's just academic interest. Actually, he
probably wants to learn things about us the Oprinkians
can turn to their own advantage. But we're ready for
him. Now, you remember the taboos?"

"No television while he's visiting," said Tom. "No
drinking. No fresh plants in the house. He's not to be
disturbed once he's shut himself in our spare bedroom,
until he comes out again. Keep the dog out of his
room—" Tom sighed. "That's wrong. Rejilla particularly wants to meet Rex."

"That may be," said Daneraux, "but Rejilla is Security's responsibility. Scrub sending the dog away, then.
Keep it. Act with perfect normalcy."

"Perfect," said White.

"All we ask is that you spend an ordinary twenty-
four hours. Just remember we suspect that the Oprinkians
outnumber us and that—this is restricted information,
now—they may be only pretending to be more
advanced than we are, technically—and furthermore—"

"Damn it!" said Tom, beginning to lose his temper.
"I know a lot more about Oprinkians than you ever
will. And furthermore—"

The announcer's voice broke in on him, overhead,
from the metallic throat of the loudspeaker there.

"*Please clear the stage. Please clear the stage. Eastbound copter landing now. Eastbound copter now
descending for a landing.*"

"How come they didn't send him out in a private
ship?" Tom just had time to ask as they all moved off
to the stage entrance.

"He didn't want us to," replied Daneraux. "He
wanted to ride out to your community here just like

any ordinary citizen. Ha! Every seat on the copter except his is taken by Security agents."

They brought up short against the chest-high wire fence that enclosed the stage. A gate had swung open and a flood of passengers from the copter was streaming out. Rather curiously, in their exact midst, emerged the tall, thin, black, furry-looking form of the Oprinkian Alien.

He was swept forward like a chip in the midst of a mass of river foam and deposited before the four of them.

"Ah, Daneraux," he said. "It is very good of you to meet me."

He had a slight, lisping accent. Aside from this, he spoke English very well.

"Mr. Rejilla!" exclaimed Daneraux, exuberantly. "How nice to see you again! This is the young couple that will be your host and hostess for the next forty-eight hours."

He stood aside; and Tom and Lucy got their first good look at the Oprinkian.

He was indeed tall—in the neighborhood of six feet five—but very thin, almost emaciated. Tom guessed him at less than a hundred and thirty pounds. He wore no real clothing in the human sense, only an odd arrangement of leather-looking straps and bands that covered him in what appeared to be arbitrary rather than a practical fashion. Evidently his curly thick black body fur, or hair, gave him some protection from the changing temperatures, since the early April night was in the low forties and the damp, chilly air seemed to leave him unaffected.

"May I present," Daneraux was saying, "Tom and Lucy Parent. Tom is a staff member of Alien Affairs Secretary Domango Aksisi, whom you know."

"I am fully acquainted with Domango Aksisi," said

Mr. Rejilla. "He is a large Human Being—great Human Being, I mean."

"He is indeed," said Daneraux. "You're very perceptive, Mr. Rejilla—but then we expect that from one of your race. Lucy Parent, Tom's wife here, is also one of our people. She was in our Linguistics Department, but is currently on leave."

"Hay-lo," said Rejilla to Tom and Lucy. "To you both, hay-lo. Do we shake right hands now?"

They shook right hands. Rejilla's furry grip was fragile but firm.

"I am so most indubitably honored to be a guest within your walls," commented Rejilla. "The weather, it is fine?"

He looked up into the misty darkness of the night.

"Very fine," Daneraux agreed, before Tom or Lucy could say anything.

"Good. Though perhaps it will rain harder. That would be good for the crops. Shall we go?"

"Right this way," said White.

The Security men led Tom, Lucy and Mr. Rejilla to the Parents' car. White slid behind the wheel in the front seat, Daneraux beside him. Rejilla insisted on sitting between Tom and Lucy in the back.

"I understand," he said to Lucy, as Daneraux pulled the car away from the parking area, "that you have two lovely grandparents."

"Well—" said Lucy, "as a matter of fact I have three, still living."

"Three!" cried Mr. Rejilla joyfully. "How wonderful! I dote myself on grandparents very much. I write them poems. Yes." He turned to Tom. "And you, Tom?"

"Ah—one grandfather," said Tom, "only."

"The ways of Providence are mysterious," replied Mr. Rejilla, putting a comforting hand on Tom's knee.

"Uh—thanks."

"How black the night," commented Mr. Rejilla, gazing out the window of the speeding car.

"We're almost there," White said.

"This is your structure then," said Mr. Rejilla, looking around their living room, after White and Daneraux had departed. "It is most interesting and friendly."

"I'm glad you think so," said Lucy. "Is there anything—have you had dinner?"

"I am not in need of feeding," said Mr. Rejilla. "Dinnering me is not necessary. You will want to dinner yourselves, however. If you will direct me to the enclosure within this structure that is for my use, I will retire to it. Ah, there's your wolf—I mean, socialized wolf. Dog."

Rex had come out of the kitchen into the dining area and was examining Mr. Rejilla with some uncertainty from a distance. He sniffed in Mr. Rejilla's direction.

"He's really quite friendly," said Lucy. "Here, Rex, come meet a friend of ours. Come, boy!"

Rex advanced a few steps tentatively and then stopped. Then he backed up a step.

"There is no need to hurry a subordinate Being," said Mr. Rejilla. "Time brings wisdom, does it not? Such a subordinate does not often wish to rush into anything, acquaintance or otherwise. There will be time. But you were going to show me my enclosure?"

"Oh yes," said Tom, "this way, please."

"I'll take him to his room," said Lucy. She led off, with Mr. Rejilla following. Left alone together, Tom and Rex looked at each other.

"He said we should go ahead with our own dinner and everything else, just the way we usually do; and he'd see us tomorrow," Lucy said, returning. Tom was now looking at the mail. It was all ads and charitable solicitations.

"What do you suppose he's going to be doing in that room of his between now and tomorrow morning?" she asked him.

"I don't know," said Tom. "I'm not sure whether Oprinkians sleep or not. It stands to reason any living creature, alien or otherwise, would probably need some kind of rest period. At any rate, it's nothing we need to worry about; and he specifically said that we were to do just what we'd do ordinarily. So why don't we eat?"

They did. Mr. Rejilla did not show up.

"He isn't anything like I imagined," Lucy said later, while they were getting ready for bed. "I expected someone who would be more . . ."

"More what?" asked Tom, tossing his jacket at an armchair near Lucy, from which it slipped off on to the floor. He began to pull apart the cling-strips that fastened the front of his shirt, in the process of taking it off completely.

Lucy absently reached down, picked up the jacket and put it on a hanger in the right hand compartment of their bedroom's open closet, where Tom's things hung. She was busy studying her various night clothes at the other end of Tom's compartment, to which they had crept by way of overflow from her own compartment.

"I don't know," she said. "I expected something more impressive, in a way."

"You can't tell impressiveness from outside appearances."

"Well," said Lucy, "you know what I mean."

"The Oprinkians," said Tom solemnly, "are one of the forty-three races of Aliens who are entitled to a seat on the governing Council of this Sector of the galaxy. Only a few Races in our Sector are entitled to a seat on that Council; and some of them have conquered and dominated as many as dozens of other worlds where intelligent aliens live. The Mordaunti, for example, rule twenty-seven other races over an empire hundreds of light years in diameter. Then there's the Jaktals, who I think have even more—I can't remember how many other races they dominate."

"Forty-three?" echoed Lucy, startled for a moment out of her contemplation of her clothes. "The Oprinkians, these Jaktals, the Mordaunti, us—and who else?"

"We," Tom said, "are not among the forty-three. We were accepted into Sector civilization only because of the sponsorship of the Oprinkians, and that acceptance is only probationary. In the next three hundred years we must make a marked impression on this Sector's forty-three great interstellar powers, if we're going to get a majority vote from them to establish a seat in addition for us. Theoretically, of course, we could conquer some already seated race, then take over their seat. A race like the Mordaunti, say, but we've got as much real chance of doing that as we would have of trying to huff and puff and blow the sun out of the sky. You know, I wonder why that warning was tacked on to that part of my briefing that dealt with the Mordaunti—something about *'beware a Mordaunti when he starts to roll his r's when he speaks. Make a mental note of this and do not forget it.'* "

"The reason'll probably come back to you when you need to remember it," said Lucy, prying among the various hangers in his part of the closet. "Ah, I knew it was here!"

"But then," said Tom, beginning to put on his pajamas now, "our chance of seeing a Mordaunti in our lifetimes, the way we're seeing Mr. Rejilla now, are practically zero."

"I don't see why they'd allow a tyrannical race like that or the Jaktals to be on that Council!" said Lucy.

"Any Alien culture can present some dangerous points," Tom said, "just as it has to present some advantageous and congenial ones—" He continued talking as he dressed.

"How well you explain it," said Lucy, absently, disappearing with her selection from the closet into the bathroom. "I'll be back in a minute."

"Part of the briefing I had to take to reach Third Assistant status down at the Secretariat," Tom called.

"Tell me more," Lucy's voice floated out of the bathroom.

"Well, basically the Oprinkians just wanted to make sure we had a general picture of the civilized races in our Sector; and, more to the point, that we'd all taken the necessary briefing, so that we understood the languages spoken by the most important of the alien races . . ."

Tom was in his pajamas now. He tilted a couple of pillows together against the back of the bed so that he could sit up and reach into a bedside table for the book he had been reading the last few nights.

"If it hadn't been for this briefing I got today—"

"Briefing?" said Lucy, her head popping out of the bathroom doorway to look at him. "What briefing? When?"

"Today," said Tom, "after I'd had the talk with Domango about Rejilla coming to visit us. Domango authorized Dory to give me the same special briefing she'd been equipped to give to only someone in his position—or someone he authorized. I'm the only person he's ever authorized—and that was only at Rejilla's suggestion for whomever he was to visit."

"What did it tell you?" asked Lucy.

"I'm not supposed to tell anyone. But, for example, I can now speak nine hundred and twenty-seven Alien languages. It only took me five seconds apiece to learn them."

"Teach me one!" said Lucy. "How about Oprinkian? I'd like to learn a language in five seconds."

"I'm not allowed to," said Tom. "Not even Miles knows there was this special briefing capacity in Dory. Only Domango and me. Anyway, teaching you on my own, it'd take much longer—some minutes, at least. But anyway—I'm forbidden to."

"Why did you have to know so much?"

"So I'd understand the Civilization of our Sector and be able to deal with Rejilla during his visit."

"Oh," said Lucy. Her head vanished back into the bathroom.

"If it hadn't been for that," Tom went on, "it would've been too large a task to prepare me to deal with him, or any other possible visiting Aliens—oh!"

He climbed out of bed again and headed toward the part of his closet area where Lucy had hung up his jacket.

"What is it?" called Lucy, still out of sight.

"Some more Security nonsense, I guess," said Tom, rummaging in an inside pocket of the jacket and finding the long envelope he had just remembered. "Daneraux slipped it to me as we were getting out of the car."

He took the envelope back into bed with him, ripped it open and unfolded a thick, single sheet of paper.

" 'Information received by special courier on same copter as Rejilla,' " he read aloud. " 'Late advices from Oprinkian Surveillance and Study Group indicate Rejilla may be actively engaged in studying homo sapiens for weak points which may be exploited to Oprinkian advantage in inter-Alien diplomatic field. Be on lookout for any unusual activities on part of Rejilla and offer no information that you believe might be harmful to us in Oprinkian hands.' "

"Well," he said, "there's a typical general warning

from Security. Suspicious of everyone—a monster under every bed."

"You don't think Rejilla's planning on doing anything like that, then?" called Lucy. "Should we be careful anyway?"

"I suppose so. But what weak point? That's the problem."

"Well, we can just be careful, Tom."

"May be easier said than done."

"Well, anyway," answered Lucy, "there's nothing you can do about it tonight. Put that sealed order, or whatever it is, away in the nightstand drawer. Here. Now that's that for tonight. Sufficient unto the days are the cares thereof." She came out of the bathroom and posed on the rug before him. "What do you think of my new nightgown?"

Chapter 4

"—What?" said Tom, waking up. Sunlight was filtering through the closed slats of the venetian blinds of the bedroom. "Whazist?"

"Tom! Wake up!" whispered Lucy urgently, shaking him.

"What's the matter?"

"It's Rex. Rex!" she hissed urgently, clutching his arm.

"It's what Rex? Rex what?" demanded Tom, irritably. "Rex?"

He came all the way awake to realize that the Great Dane was standing by the side of the bed with his tongue hanging out apologetically. The bedroom door was ajar. The doors in this new house of theirs, unfortunately, had a push-button type of latch; and one of the few things Rex had learned was that pushing the button on the knob of an unlocked door with his nose made the door open. Tom had cited it to Lucy as an instance that Rex had, after all, inherited his famous great-grandfather's brain. Lucy had remained unconvinced.

"I love you," said an unmistakably masculine voice.

Tom blinked and struggled up into a sitting position. He glanced around the room. He leaned over the side of the bed and peered under it.

"Huh?" he said.

"I love you. Get up," answered the voice, while Rex tried hard to lick Tom's face.

"Lucy!" croaked Tom, fending the dog off. "Who is it? Where is he?"

"That's what I'm trying to tell you," said Lucy. "It's Rex! Our Rex—and he's right beside you, speaking to you."

"I love you. Play frisbee? Fun? Go walk."

"Rex!" Tom stared at the dog. "Lucy! He's—I mean he isn't, is he?"

With a sudden explosion of energy, Tom jumped out of bed, lunged across the room, closed and locked the door. Turning about with his back against its panels he regarded the canine orator before him.

"How can he talk?" he said thickly. "He hasn't got the vocal apparatus. Say something, Rex."

"Play frisbee? Nice Tom."

"See—" yammered Tom. "His mouth doesn't move—"

"Nice Lucy. I love you, Lucy."

"I don't care what you say!" snapped Lucy. "That's Rex and he's talking."

"Nice Lucy and Tom. I'm hungry."

The two humans stared at each other.

"I'm nice, too," said Rex.

"Well, there you are," said Tom insanely. "They always said he had his great-grandfather's brain—and Rex Regis could do everything but talk. Our Rex just decided to learn to talk. That's all."

"Don't be funny!" said Lucy, sharply.

"Who's being funny? You hear him, don't you?"

"Of course I hear him. But he didn't just *learn* to talk. That's impossible."

"How can it be impossible when he's doing it?"

"I don't care. How can he talk with the kind of mouth he has? You said that yourself."

"Well, he is." Tom looked grimly at the tail-wagging Great Dane. He ordered—"Rex, say something again."

But Rex's attention had wandered. He had sat down and was now nosing after what might be a flea or just a stray itch.

"Rex!" Tom ordered again, in a sharp, no-nonsense voice.

"I'm Rex! I'm Rex! I'm here too!" said Rex, looking up cheerfully with one leg on the floor and the other up in the air. "See me? Play frisbee? Nice Tom. I love Lucy, too."

"Wait a minute!" Tom snapped his fingers. "I've got it!"

"What?" asked Lucy.

"Frisbee?" asked Rex. "Ouch! Got flea? Flea! There flea. Take that! Bite, bite, bite, bite! Crunch flea."

"We really ought to get a new radiant flea collar. The old one could be worn out," said Lucy, thoughtfully. "I'll run down to the pet shop after breakfast—"

"Will you listen?" Tom demanded. "Listen, Lucy!"

"Another flea?" queried Rex, checking his other hind leg. "Where flea?"

"Lucy, it's telepathy."

"Telepathy?"

"That's right. Look, his mouth doesn't move and he speaks English, doesn't he? You're right, he couldn't just do that overnight. But if he had been thinking these things for a long time in our language—and now suddenly he's able to broadcast them to us so our own minds are putting them automatically into words—"

"Tom," said Lucy, "that's downright silly!"

"Why?"

"Telepathy doesn't exist," said Lucy, "and if it did, how could he go telepathic all of a sudden?"

"We don't know telepathy doesn't exist. The only thing is, he picked one hell of a time to do it. With Mr. Rejilla here."

"That's right!" said Lucy.

"Pet me," said Rex, nuzzling up against Tom's pajama jacket.

"Down, Rex! Not now!" Tom said, pushing him away.

Ears drooping, tail sagging, Rex hung his head and burst into heart-breaking telepathic sobs.

"Tom! How could you?" snapped Lucy. "He was just trying to get your attention."

She was out of bed in a flash and threw her arms around the dog's neck.

"Poor Rex! There, that's all right. Tom didn't mean it. No, he didn't."

"Love Tom. Love Lucy," gulped Rex. "Good Rex?"

He looked up hopefully and flicked out a long, wet tongue, which Lucy almost dodged. It got her on the left ear.

"You might have expected that," said Tom, passing her a paper handkerchief. "Lucy, how he feels right now isn't the important thing—"

"Well, you made him think he'd done something wrong," said Lucy.

"I only—in any case, he's forgotten about it now you've made a fuss over him," said Tom. "As I was saying, the important thing is what we're going to do with him."

"I see what you mean," said Lucy, holding Rex off with one arm, while she wiped her ear with the paper handkerchief in her other hand. "We can't have him going around talking to the neighbors. He might say anything to them. We'd have no privacy."

"That, too," said Tom. "But it's not the important thing. Have you forgotten Mr. Rejilla's here?"

"If you want to keep his telepathy a secret from Mr. Rejilla," said Lucy, "I don't see how you're going to do it. Mr. Rejilla particularly wanted a couple with a dog, remember? Which undoubtedly means he wants to get to know Rex. And I can't think of any way on Earth to keep Rex from talking to him telepathically, if they do get together."

"That's the thing," said Tom.

He sat down on the bed and rubbed his nose thoughtfully.

"But something's got to be done," he went on. "Rex here, is now probably the most valuable piece of property on Earth at this moment, from every standpoint, including the military. To say nothing of science— they'll want to investigate him—and maybe they can find a way to make all sorts of dogs telepathic, so they could go into enemy territory and come back and report in words."

"I thought that now that we were part of the civilized races in this sector of the galaxy, and we've set up our own All-Earth Federation, that there's not supposed to be any such thing as enemy territory any more."

"Tell that to the Defense Departments around the globe," muttered Tom. "In any case, it doesn't matter. Daneraux and his people would make enough fuss on their own if any one else knew about Rex—particularly an Alien."

"But Oprinkians—"

"Yes, I know," said Tom, "they've sponsored us among the other interstellar Civilized Races, and done nothing but help us ever since the first one appeared here; but there's still thousands of people on Earth here, still looking at them suspiciously. For our sakes—our own sakes—we've got to decide what to do with Rex."

"Well, for now," said Lucy, decidedly, "we can begin by shutting him up in our room here. Meanwhile, you can try and get in touch with Daneraux. You could phone him right from here."

"No, no," said Tom. "He'd undoubtedly be sure that

Mr. Rejilla knew how to listen in on anything I said over a telephone from our place, whether he actually could or not. I'd better run out and phone from the copter port."

"Go walk?" asked Rex.

"Sorry," Tom told him, starting to dress hurriedly. "Later—if we're lucky," he added.

The copter port was almost empty, as it should have been a little before nine o'clock in the morning. Tom phoned. Daneraux's office informed Tom that Daneraux had not come in yet.

"Hell!" said Tom.

He went back home.

When he got there, Lucy was drinking coffee in the living room, in a rather frilly black dress that was one of Tom's favorites. Mr. Rejilla was seated opposite her in the red wingback armchair, playing a flute.

"Good morning," said the Oprinkian as Tom came in and lowered his instrument. "Take a condolence, please."

"Uh—I beg your pardon?" asked Tom. He dropped down on the living room sofa. Lucy got up and handed him a full cup of coffee. He took it gratefully.

"I was just telling Mr. Rejilla how sick Rex is," she said, giving Tom a glance that spoke volumes. "And how you had to go for the veterinarian. Did you get him?"

"He wasn't in his office yet." Tom took a healthy swallow from his cup. "Ow!"

He breathed violently out through his open mouth.

"Well, you might have known it was hot," said Lucy.

"You find yourself internally dismayed by hot liquids?" inquired Mr. Rejilla. He looked up at the ceiling of the living room. "Note number one for this day," he told it.

He lowered his head and found Lucy and Tom staring at him.

"I am noting myself to remember pertinent facts," he explained to them.

"Oh. Certainly," said Tom.

"I am endeavoring, you see, to understand humanity even better than heretofore, as a means of establishing the bonds between," further explained Mr. Rejilla. "That is my mission here. Do you like music?"

"Oh, yes," said Tom. "Of course!"

"Then I will play you a small composition," said Mr. Rejilla. He did so, on the flute. The tune that came out sounded like anything but a tune. "Does it provoke you?" he inquired proudly.

"Absolutely," said Tom. "It's very original," volunteered Lucy, speaking in the same moment.

"Indeed. Eighty percent original," said Mr. Rejilla, proudly. "That is, using your human measurements. It is a theme upon one of your native melodies."

"Oh?" questioned Tom, searching his memory for something in the way of music to connect it to.

"A Chinese melody, I am so told," said Mr. Rejilla, driving his point home.

"I'd like some more coffee," said Tom to Lucy. "What would you like to do today, Mr. Rejilla?"

"I would like to peep," said Rejilla, as Lucy passed the self-heating pot of coffee from the chair-table beside her.

"I beg your pardon?" said Tom, puzzled.

"Peep in on your lives. How fascinating the living process in all creatures; but particularly so in those of intelligent civilized proportions! Don't you agree? You are inbound so many things that on Oprinkia are unthought of. This pet of yours, now in malady. Has he existed a number of years?"

"Five, I think," said Tom.

"No," said Lucy, "Six. Six years ago February third. I remember it because Groundhog Day was just one day before; and I made a joke about getting a groundhog for a pet. We'd been talking about a dog for some time."

"Oh yes," said Tom. "February third."

"Has he offspring?" Mr. Rejilla wanted to know.

Tom sipped cautiously at his second cup of coffee, which was beginning to get down to a tolerable temperature finally.

"Not only that, but his offspring has offspring."

"A grandfather!" breathed Mr. Rejilla.

"Yes, he is that," said Tom.

"How noble!" said Mr. Rejilla enthusiastically. "I will make a special effort to remember him in my thoughts. Now I must not detain you both. There will be housing affairs to demand your attention, no doubt. I would wish that you concern yourselves as customarily. Pay no attention to me. I shall merely peep as you go about your daily activities."

He stopped and looked at them expectantly.

"Well—" said Tom. "That's right. I suppose I'd better, well, cut the lawn back to size. Weren't you going to bake a cake or something, Lucy?"

"A cake?" asked Lucy, staring.

"A cake."

"Oh, a cake! Why, as a matter of fact I was. I was going to make a cake the old-fashioned way," explained Lucy to Mr. Rejilla. "None of this business of simply telling the kitchen Serve-all what I want, and taking whatever it delivers to me."

She got to her feet.

"Tom, I'll get a list of specifications from the kitchen for things you should buy me for it," Lucy said. There was a gleam of real interest in her eye. "Yes, a home-made cake. You won't mind going to the supply center first, before you cut the lawn, will you, Tom?"

"Not at all," said Tom. "I've got to *swing by the copter port* anyway, I can do that while I'm down at the store."

Tom got to his feet and Lucy went off to the kitchen.

"Superb!" said Mr. Rejilla. "So this is how the human day inaugurates. I am complete attention. But Tom, the concept of 'lawn' escapes me. What is a lawn, and why must you cut it? It appears to me as something possibly hurtful?"

"Not at all," said Tom. "A lawn is that area of short green herbage that surrounds our house here. It's like human hair. It keeps growing, and you have to cut it every so often to keep it from getting too long and keep it looking neat."

Lucy returned from the kitchen with a slip of paper with a list printed on it. She gave it to Tom.

"Get these things," she said. Tom tucked the slip into a shirt pocket.

"I'll go right away," he said.

"And I will go talk to your lawn," said Mr. Rejilla. "It will be interesting to get its viewpoint on being kept looking neat."

They went their separate ways. Once more at the copter port, Tom phoned Daneraux at his office and found he was out. He gathered all the things that were on Lucy's list, although he had to enlist the help of the store's operator to order some of the more rare ingredients for the cake. Then, he tried phoning Daneraux's office again. Daneraux was still out. He took back to Lucy all the things he had bought; and an hour and a half later, he was out pruning some rose bushes, with Mr. Rejilla watching.

"—And the lawn told me," Mr. Rejilla was saying to him, "that in its wild state it would object to being cut. But here, it takes pride in its appearance and does not object at all. It wishes to look better than other lawns."

"It said that, did it?" replied Tom. He reached for something interesting about lawns to add to his response; but was saved at that moment by the appearance of Lucy, who had just come out and got into their neighborhood gyroscopic three-wheeler.

"I'm going back down to the supply center myself for a few more things!" she called to them. "This cake making from scratch is interesting. I should have tried it before!"

The three-wheeler backed out of the driveway and was gone in a moment.

"Next," Tom said to Mr. Rejilla, "I should probably prune the hedge. Would you like to watch that?"

"It would charm me," said Mr. Rejilla.

Within fifteen minutes the three-wheeler was back and Lucy left it to go into the house, throwing an encouraging smile at the two of them.

Tom talked Mr. Rejilla into trying his hand with the pruning shears and hurried off to the kitchen. Lucy was standing before a cluttered worktable, with flour up to her elbows and even a dab of it on her nose.

"Tom, this is actually fun! I'm sorry, honey, but you'll have to run back to the supply center once more and get me some coloring—pink—for the icing," she said as Tom came in. "We should never eat anything but real home cooked meals made from scratch."

"Daneraux didn't phone here, did he?" asked Tom. "I didn't have any luck reaching him from outside."

"I called him from here, as soon as I got back. I thought I might as well," said Lucy. "They told me he hadn't come in yet. Did you try that red button on your service phone he told you to push?" asked Lucy.

"Half a dozen times; but that doesn't work either," said Tom. "I can't go for this coloring of yours. I've got Mr. Rejilla on my hands. What's to be done about him?"

"He can come watch me cook," said Lucy.

"All right," said Tom.

At the supply center, this time, Tom finally got the Security man on his service phone.

"Daneraux!" he barked. "Where have you been?"

"Late meeting last night," said Daneraux, a little hoarsely. "What is it?"

"What is it?" echoed Tom. "Listen—"

He outlined the situation.

"You're imagining things," said Daneraux, coldly.

"I tell you it's the truth!" snarled Tom. "Come out here and see for yourself!"

"I have no intention of coming as long as Mr. Rejilla's there," said Daneraux, even more coldly.

Chapter 5

Tom stared at Daneraux's face in the phone screen.

"Not coming!" he said. "I just told you there's an emergency here, and you're not coming?"

"I am not," said Daneraux. "The Oprinkian's request was that he be left alone with you two people. Under these conditions I'm not permitted to come; and let me tell you it would take several weeks to get permission."

Tom thought with the alacrity of someone facing a charging rogue elephant.

"Where are you?" he asked.

"In my office, of course," said Daneraux. "Where else would you expect to find me?"

"Well, stay there!" barked Tom and broke the connection.

He hunted through his wallet for the piece of paper that held the emergency private phone number that Domango Aksisi had given him. Finding it, he read it aloud to his phone, meanwhile holding up his identification card to the screen before him. There was a brief wait while the security circuit at Domango's end examined it. Then a voice answered from the other end.

"Yes?" said the voice.

Tom let out a sigh of relief. It was Domango's voice. This must be a purely personal phone link.

"Sir?" he said. "This is Tom Parent. I've got an emergency situation here at my house with Mr. Rejilla; and I've just been talking to Daneraux and he says that he can't come out because Mr. Rejilla said we were to be left alone with him. But it's desperate—"

He went on to tell the Secretary of Alien Affairs essentially what he had told Daneraux. He wound up with, "—can't you call him and order him to come out here?"

There was a pause at the other end.

"Of course, I could," said the mild, calm tones at the other end. "Yes, perhaps it would be for the best if he came. Very good, Tom. I'll give Daneraux a call right now. Do you know where he can be reached?"

"In his office, he told me," said Tom.

"I'll call."

"—Oh," added Tom, hastily, "and would you have him call ahead and tell me he's coming so I know he's on the way?"

"I'll do that too," said Domango.

Tom went home and took refuge in the utility room. He waited. After thirty-five minutes he began to pace back and forth.

Finally the tension grew too great even for pacing. He left the utility room and walked through the house to the kitchen.

"Ah," he said, "how are things going?"

Lucy and Mr. Rejilla looked at him cheerfully.

"We are ecstatic!" answered Mr. Rejilla.

"The first one didn't quite work out," said Lucy. "But this one's going to be just fine."

"Good, good," said Tom.

He withdrew his head and went back to pacing around the house again. Finally he made himself sit down in a chair in the living room, close to the front door. He waited. The phone did not ring.

But the doorbell chimed after a space of time. Tom jumped to his feet, took three steps to it and opened it. Daneraux stood there.

"You didn't phone to say you were coming!" said Tom.

"Your line was busy," said Daneraux. They glared at each other. "Well," Daneraux went on, "do you want me inside or not?"

"Yes," said Tom, in a low, dangerous voice. "Come with me to the utility room."

"There's no dog here," said Daneraux, when they got there.

"Of course not," said Tom. "I want to talk to you first. I talked to Domango and Domango talked to you. Now are you convinced about the seriousness of this situation?"

"No," said Daneraux. "I don't believe your dog went telepathic all of a sudden."

"But you're here," said Tom. "Didn't the call from the Secretary convince you?"

"No," said Daneraux. "But he ordered me here; so it's no skin off my nose. What's it matter whether I'm convinced or not? I'm here."

"That's not enough," said Tom. "Rex can telepath. You've got to realize the seriousness of this situation. It goes far beyond the Secretariat. Rejilla's going around taking notes and Rex is locked in our bedroom, ready to blab his head off. Don't you realize what it would mean if we've got even a *dog* that could telepath? I'm not thinking just about Rejilla, I'm thinking about the whole world if this news gets out. Rex ought to be covered with Security men ten deep, until they find out how he does it. He shouldn't be able to breathe without a man on each side of him. Now what I think

we've got to do is smuggle him out of this house without him saying anything—"

"You could wind a scarf or something around his
muzzle," said Daneraux, "then he couldn't talk."

"He doesn't telepath with his mouth!" said Tom.
But Daneraux had hardly heard him. The other man
was actually looking thoughtful.

"You know," said Daneraux, in a totally different
voice, "on the wild chance there's some truth to this—
you're probably right about the seriousness of it. He's
your dog; can't you think of some way of getting him
out of the house quietly?"

"It's simply because he's my dog," said Tom, "that
I know him well enough to know that he's bound to
speak—I mean telepath—the moment he sees you,
me, or anyone. Don't you have some way of making
his unconscious without hurting him? I won't stand for
his being hurt!"

"There're probably ways," said Daneraux. "We'd
have to get in touch with—no that wouldn't work."

"What wouldn't work?" asked Tom.

"What I was thinking of would mean contacting
some other department with the means to do what
you suggest," said Daneraux, "But that would let the
cat out of the bag. I think you have to be an expert
to use that kind of a tranquilizer gun."

"They'd shoot him with a tranquilizer gun?" said
Tom. "I've heard that's dangerous unless they know
exactly the weight of the animal and the species
they're tranquilizing."

"Well, do you know his weight?" asked Daneraux.

"No," said Tom.

They were both silent for a long minute.

"I have it," said Daneraux. "Let's talk to your wife
about this. Maybe she's got some ideas. Where is
Rejilla right now?"

"She and he are in the kitchen," said Tom. "Stay

here. I'll try to go and get her out by herself and make sure Rejilla stays there while she's gone. On second thought, come with me."

He and Daneraux went off to the kitchen door. Tom opened it and stepped inside.

"Lucy," he said, "Daneraux is here with a private message for us from the—"

He broke off.

Lucy was alone in the kitchen.

"There you are, Tom," said Lucy. "I'm afraid the second cake didn't come out very well either. But I figured out what was wrong. The cake falls if it gets any sudden jar. If you slam the oven door, for instance. I'd forgotten that part of it; and with both cakes, I had to look after a while, to see whether it was done. So I—"

"Where's Mr. Rejilla?" interrupted Tom.

"Mr. Rejilla?" said Lucy. "Why, he's back in our bedroom, isn't he—oh!" Lucy broke off suddenly.

"The bedroom the dog is in?" demanded Daneraux.

"Yes," said Lucy, grimly. "What with the cake and all, I forgot Rex was there. You know how he likes to sleep under the dining room table; and somehow I was thinking he was there instead of in the bedroom—"

The last of the sentence was lost, as all three of them headed swiftly for the bedroom, Tom leading, Lucy right behind him, and Daneraux as close as he could get.

When they reached the door of the bedroom and burst in, they discovered Rex lying on the floor and Mr. Rejilla tightening what seemed to be a thin strap around the dog's neck.

"Stop!" yelled Tom and started to make a dive for the Oprinkian, only to be brought up short by some complicated sort of wrestling hold which Daneraux had clamped onto him.

Mr. Rejilla rose with a surprised expression. Rex got

to his feet with the strap dangling unfastened and wagged his tail.

"He's the accredited Representative of an Alien Power!" hissed Daneraux in Tom's ear, and let him go.

"I beg your pardon?" Mr. Rejilla was saying. "Am I in violation of some custom? Observing that this grandfather appeared to enjoy the wearing of collars, I was impelled to decorate him with another as a token of affection and get-well-quick."

"Like furry man!" said Rex, happily and—it seemed to Tom—much louder than necessary, flicking a tongue in Mr. Rejilla's direction. "Play wrestle?"

"All right!" said Tom, before Daneraux could stop him. "Go ahead. Deny it if you can, Mr. Rejilla. You've found out Rex could project his thoughts—telepathy. For some reason we're not supposed to have telepathy yet, I suppose. So you came here to shut him up permanently!"

"Fight?" queried Rex, doubtfully.

"No, no. Shut up, Rex," said Tom. "Now—"

He was interrupted by Daneraux grabbing his arm and shaking it.

"Parent," said Daneraux, "did I understand you to say that this dog of yours was telepathing right now?"

"Of course," said Tom. "Didn't you hear him? Now, Mr. Rejilla—"

"No," said Daneraux.

"No?" demanded Tom, turning to stare at the other man.

"No, I did not hear Rex say or broadcast anything," said Daneraux, deliberately.

"Rex? I'm Rex," announced that individual.

"Well, there you are! Just now," said Tom. "What are you talking about, Daneraux? You heard him that time all right—how could you help it?"

"I," said Daneraux, "heard nothing."

"Pardon me," interrupted Mr. Rejilla, "but do I

understand your implication, Tom, to the effect that this grandfather is broadcasting his intentional statements by non-auditory way?"

"Of course he is!"

"And you too, Lucy, are receiving the grandfather clear and strong?" Rejilla asked her.

"Why, yes—" said Lucy. "Don't you?"

"Woe," said Mr. Rejilla. He turned about and walked away from them out of the bedroom into the living room, where he dropped into a chair and fanned himself with a magazine from the coffee table nearby.

The humans had followed him bewilderedly.

"I don't understand," said Daneraux.

"How unguestly of me!" said Mr. Rejilla. "I have made a violation of hospitality. Unintentional, purely, but that does not excuse it. Nevertheless, my deepest apologies to you Tom and to you Lucy. How mysterious the ways of grandfathers! Ah, well. I am not unhappy at this termination, being by nature enthusiastic and optimistic where the movement of all species toward civilization is concerned."

"Sir," said Daneraux, "could you perhaps explain it all a little more clearly?"

"With great pleasure," Rejilla said. "Basic facts of individual life and movement toward civilization dictate certain necessary actions. What is of all universal relationships most important? Responsibility of teacher to teach, pupil to learn. Consequently grandfathers, percolating wisdom down to younger generations, are venerated. Oprinkian nature and sociological development cast us in role of teacher at present. But what if pupil prove not fully developed? By stern duty, I compelled myself to investigative procedure, while here on Earth. Spy. You understand."

"I'm afraid not yet," said Daneraux, ominously. His face had hardened at the word "spy."

"During unconsciousing hours of nighttime for fine

young couple here, I investigated them exploratora-
tively. This is the result."

"Tom!" said Lucy. "He means he read our minds
last night while we were asleep!"

"You Oprinkians have that ability?" demanded
Daneraux.

Mr. Rejilla nodded.

"Matter of training only," he said. "Astonishing as
last night's results were, yet I defer action until, first,
amazing chemical investigation of Lucy leading to
rediscovery of almost extinct art of cake-baking, and
now this. Lucy, Tom and Rex plainly overwhelming
average citizens in pupil-ability."

"Well—" began Daneraux, uncertainly.

Mr. Rejilla held up his hand and continued.

"Affection basis for instruction. Consequently, I am
informing Oprinkia no need to suspect humans unteach-
able. So we will set in motion mechanism of science
to guide future path of humans among other galactic
races. Myself, I intend to follow duty here with continuing peep; plus instruction of chosen representative
pupils, Tom and Lucy Parent—with their permission,
only, this coming night, of course; now that full revelation of purpose stated."

"I don't know about that," said Tom, slowly.

"If agreeable, this will be on contributing to golden
future of human race on Civilization's track," urged
Mr. Rejilla. "Original planetary survey this world presenting a four point two capability of absorbing and use
of such instruction. But you, Tom—and you, Lucy—
startlingly reveal at least seven point two, personally.
Due to good feelings and tender hearts, undoubtedly—as substantiated by happy attitude of grandfather Rex."

"We could talk it over first, Tom," said Lucy.

"You'd better get permission," said Daneraux.

"We'll see," glowered Tom. "Anyway, what's all this

got to do with Rex broadcasting his thoughts? The thoughts—" he glanced at Daneraux "—our friend here claims can't be heard."

"He is correct," said Mr. Rejilla.

"Correct?" said Tom.

"Correct," stated Mr. Rejilla. "The grandfather, though venerable and praiseworthy, has discovered no unknown talent. His simple emanations always in existence. Only now, new sensitivity of your and Lucy's minds, triggered by my mental investigations last night, render you capable of reception and interpretation of only his well-loved, simple animal statements."

Everybody else stared at Rex. There was a moment of peculiar silence.

"Play frisbee?" suggested Rex.

"You mean—" croaked Tom finally "—it's *us*?"

"Yours. You. Yourself and Lucy."

"But—" said Tom.

"With training I supply you with ability to eventually receivi-translatable more complex intelligence racial and Oprinkian thoughts."

"Just a second," said Daneraux. "You're saying that these two people here are the ones who are now telepathic?"

"You understand," said Mr. Rejilla with courteous approval.

"Don't move," said Daneraux to Tom and Lucy. "Don't leave this house. I'm going to arrange for a complete twenty-four-hour security coverage of this house and lot. I can guarantee you'll have agents around this house ten deep. Stay right where you are, all of you. I'll be back."

He left them. A moment later they heard the front door bang shut.

"And to think," said Lucy, "all this time we thought it was Rex."

"Rex? I'm Rex," telepathed the Great Dane, attempting

to lick Tom and Lucy alternately. "Love everybody. Pet me."

"A most magnificent grandfather," said Mr. Rejilla admiringly.

Tom and Lucy stared at each other. They looked at Mr. Rejilla and Rex. Then Lucy concentrated on Mr. Rejilla.

"Would . . ." she began hesitantly, "would we feel anything tonight if we let you—er—peep? And would you be looking into anything, well, personal?"

"Certainly not!" said Mr. Rejilla. "And another 'certainly not!' To both questions. Manners of first importance, of course. Invasion of personal life unthinkable. No, your private thoughts will be unpeeped; and only awareness of this in future will be to make your lives more interesting."

"We'll do it then!" said Lucy.

Tom made a strangled sound, like a word half-uttered.

"Tom—?" said Lucy.

"You didn't wait to hear what I think about it."

"Well," said Lucy. "What do you think about it?"

"Oh damn it!" said Tom. "I guess we might as well."

"Future generations of your human race will bless you," said Mr. Rejilla, solemnly. "The future now opens before you and lovable grandfather."

Chapter 6

"It does look like a remarkable opportunity," said Domango Aksisi. "Mr. Rejilla and I had a long talk about it before he left. He said he was highly impressed with what he discovered in his two nights of examining you both. He suggested you be given every opportunity to meet any Aliens who visit this planet of ours. Naturally, that'll require you being raised in rank, Tom, so you can be present at every one of the functions where an Alien is present. Then there's the necessary secrecy, or 'security' aspect, as Albert would no doubt put it, if he was here."

Albert Miles, pointedly, was not there. It was Tom and Lucy alone with the Secretary in his office.

"But," Domango went on, "I think that part of it can be covered best by the three of us simply keeping it a secret among ourselves. The only person who has any notion of Mr. Rejilla's discoveries where you are concerned, is Daneraux; and I think he's been given adequate grounds for forgetting it—as the result of a possibly unfair rebuke and a reversal of his order to bring in Security people around your house."

A twinge of conscience struck Tom, momentarily.

"He's been told, officially," Domango went on, "that it was completely unnecessary. But I explained to him privately that this would not go on his record; that it

59

was an action taken only to avert media attention from Mr. Rejilla, who apparently felt you should be rewarded for his visit with you—which will also explain your being promoted. I think a new position as Alien Technical Advisor, Grade One to the Secretariat will suit very well."

"Grade One?" said Tom. "I mean, thank you Mr. Secretary! Thank you very much."

"No need for thanks, Tom," said Domango. "It's the sort of promotion that'd be entirely understandable after a strong request by a visiting dignitary, like Mr. Rejilla. Also, one which usefully takes you out of the direct line of authority here and gives you and Lucy both a freedom of action at official functions. Then, too, it'll justify your future appearances at such situations when Aliens are present. Meanwhile, it looks very much like giving you an essentially meaningless title, to go through the motions of satisfying Mr. Rejilla. How does this all strike you, Tom?"

"I'm very pleased and flattered, sir," said Tom. "I'll be particularly happy if Lucy and I don't have to talk about Mr. Rejilla's visit; and I take it I won't be responsible to Miles or have to talk about my work at all with anyone but you?"

"That's right," said Domango. "And you, Lucy?"

He turned his attention to her.

"Do you have any comment or objection to any of this?" he added. "I want it to be something you're both happy with. For one thing, Lucy, you'll be considered with Tom as on full-time duty for the Secretariat. If you have questions or doubts, let me have them now. Because, to be frank with you both, I'm hoping Mr. Rejilla was right; and, somewhere along the line, what he discovered in you may make it possible for you to give us much greater insights into the other Alien races we come into contact with."

"I think it's a fine idea," said Lucy. "Do I understand

you right, Mr. Secretary? You do want me working along with Tom?"

"Absolutely," said Domango. "You were equally praised by Mr. Rejilla, and apparently have equal potential to be helpful to the Secretariat. I'm sorry, though, that I don't have the authority from the Oprinkians right now to expose you, as well, to the same special briefing that Tom has had."

"I understand," said Lucy reassuringly—but thinking a little wistfully all the same about access to whatever it was that had enabled Tom to absorb nine hundred and twenty-seven languages in a little over an hour and a quarter, so that he spoke each like a native.

"Mr. Rejilla's going to try to arrange for an exception in your particular case," went on Domango, "so you can get that training eventually; since the technology was given us with the understanding that it was for our whole world, eventually; but it was to be kept under certain strict controls to begin with."

"I really don't mind waiting," lied Lucy.

"It shouldn't be too bad, meanwhile," said Domango. "Since you and Tom will ordinarily be together when you're in touch with Aliens. Also, if your work takes you off-Earth, you'll be on worlds at least like ours— that is at least on probation to be rated as civilized— and you may be omni-lingual at some time, we hope, in the near future."

"Good!" said Lucy.

A dulcet chime sounded on the air. Domango pressed a button on his desk unit.

"Who is it?" he asked.

A feminine voice answered.

"Albert Miles to see you, sir."

"Tell him to wait," said Domango. He punched the button again and turned his attention back to Tom and Lucy. Tom's earlier twinge of conscience about Daneraux's fate, was now replaced by a warm, pleasant sensation at the thought of Albert Miles outside, cooling his heels in the Secretary's inner reception office, with not even a spider to look at while he waited.

"Well, I think that covers everything," said Domango. "Tom, as Technical Advisor Grade One, you'll naturally have to have an office to yourself. We're a little short on space, as you know, but we've arranged to have you take over one of the conference rooms on a temporary basis; until Building and Grounds finishes building a new wall to cut off some of Albert's space and make a separate room for you."

"Thank you," said Tom, smiling.

"The construction is already underway," Domango went on. "In fact, Albert has been having a little difficulty getting things done, he tells me, with all the work going on. That may be why he is here now. You may already be aware of it, but an Alien is due to arrive— the Ambassador of the Jaktal Empire is going to be here in ten days for an official visit. He'll be bringing some of the Empire's barbarian subject Races, with him. The private and special information on them, too, has now been released to add to your briefing, Tom. You two must be ready for that visit."

"Yes sir," they both said.

"Then that takes care of everything, I think," said Domango. "Since we've only got those few days between now and then, Tom—and since you've also got clearance generally in this matter of Alien technology—I suggest you concentrate on exploring the details of as much general Alien culture and conditions as the briefings made available to us, so that you actually can perform as a Technical Advisor on Alien galactic Races."

"I'll do that, Mr. Secretary." Tom was, in fact, impatient to explore this earlier peripheral information. He had a boundless curiosity; and had gone through some

rather elaborate struggles to get a position on the Secretariat staff.

"I know," Domango said, "this will probably be
rather like asking you to memorize the *Encyclopaedia
Britannica,* even with the incredible speed with which
these Alien devices work—"

"I can do it," said Tom, bravely.

"If you can, I will be very greatful," said Domango.
"Now, if you'll forgive me, I think I'd better let Albert
in to see me."

He stood up behind his desk and shook hands with
first Lucy, and then Tom, with the utmost courtesy.

"Goodbye for the moment then," he said.

"Goodbye sir," said Tom and Lucy both; and went
out. Albert glared at them briefly on his way in.

"Isn't there any more to it than that?" asked Lucy,
as Tom lifted his burden into the official automated
Secretariat limousine, lent them by Domango for their
use during the next ten days. The Secretariat owned
five such limousines; and they were primarily for trans-
porting important Alien visitors.

"Yes," said Tom, putting the laptop-sized device
down on the floor of the limousine's back seat, as the
vehicle itself pulled away into noon rush-hour traffic.
"I was surprised when I first saw it, myself. But as
Domango explained to me, most of these Alien devices
have been refined over hundreds, if not thousands, of
years, so that they're very compact."

"The traffic is somewhat thick," came the automated
voice of the limousine. "Should I turn on my siren?
Or would you prefer to fly instead, sir?"

"Oh I think, fly," said Tom, with a wave of his hand.

"Yes, sir," said the limousine. It lifted into the air
and soared away above all the confusion on the ground
toward Tom and Lucy's home, a hundred and fifty
miles west.

"What an excellent way to travel," said Lucy, gazing out the window at some clouds they were passing by. She looked again at the device Tom had brought into the back seat. "I don't suppose I could just listen in from time to time, when it's teaching you something?" she said.

"You could, of course," said Tom. "But it would be a betrayal of my trust. You heard Domango. On the other hand, maybe it'll only be a matter of a few weeks before you're authorized to use it yourself."

"There's that, I suppose," said Lucy, looking out at the clouds again.

"On the other hand," said Tom, "I'm specifically allowed to share absolutely necessary information with you. That effectively means I can tell you about anything I find that is interesting—that's quite permissible. Since the device will automatically note and store what I tell you, however, even if we aren't in the same room with it, what I tell you can't add up to any full revelation of any single area of information."

They exchanged the kind of glance between them that only married couples of experience can exchange.

"It will be very interesting to hear what you tell," said Lucy.

"You're going to set it up in the library?" she asked, when they got home. The library was actually a little nook off one corner of the living room, but it had loaded bookshelves and a curtain that could be pulled, to separate it off from the living room—although usually it was left open.

"Go walk?" telepathed Rex, eagerly, coming in.

"I'm afraid not now, old son," said Tom. "Work."

Rex's ears drooped. His tail drooped.

"No walk?" he asked.

"I'll go out for a little while with you, Rex," said Lucy. "But just for a few minutes. I'll leave you when

you start sniffing around after things. You've got lots
to look at and roam around in."

It was true. Their home was not in any way an
extraordinarily large and expensive house. But it was
lucky enough to have a backyard that ran up against
a section of parkland that was as yet uncleared. Essentially this parkland was full of bushes, spruce and fir
trees and such like.

There were small paths all the way through it. In
addition, there were three magnificent trees in the
backyard itself, that were a heritage from the time of
the farmhouse that had occupied this site, before it
had been turned into a residential area.

What with the park's fencing and their own, Rex
had an enclosed area of about five acres to roam in
and investigate. These five acres were peopled by
squirrels, a raccoon or two, rabbits and other small
creatures, as well as birds in season. There was a bird
feeder in the backyard and a bird bath, but neither of
these attracted Rex as much as the uncleared area.

That space had been the strongest part of Tom's
argument in getting Lucy to agree to their having Rex
as a puppy. Tom had always wanted a Great Dane.
On the other hand, Rex—although he had not known
it as a puppy—needed a kingdom, not a city lot; and
this was it.

Lucy and Rex went out and Tom settled down with
the device. Apparently, its only controls were the single touch-point that turned it on or off. The device,
he remembered, was sensitive both to his touch and
voice.

"Details of Races represented on the Council for
our Galactic Sector," he said, and laid his finger on
the touch-point. Immediately, the house was nowhere
around him. He was off among Alien worlds.

This time he seemed to be under water.

If it was not water he was under, then he was in

some other dense medium which made it difficult to see anything at a distance, although the medium was transparent. That is to say, most of it was transparent. Very close to him was a large black area, about the size of the front end of a cross-country truck.

"Welcome, visitor," said what seemed to be two voices speaking at once, one incredibly deep and one almost as high-pitched as the chirping of a bird. They spoke in unison, and it was only their tones that identified them as separate voicings.

There was also no apparent movement in the black area he was seeing, but the voices seemed to be coming from it. He looked more closely at the large black area, leaning his head out a little to one side; and saw that it was not just a black area close up, but the front end of what seemed to be a large dark body stretching away until its further end was lost in the blurring effect of the medium that surrounded them.

"Since you are watching this particular material," the voices went on, "you are, relative to me, a creature from a small race. Therefore I, from a relatively large race and with an undoubtedly greatly different environment than the one you are familiar with on your own homeworld, have deliberately been chosen to be your Answerer in this instance."

"Why?" asked Tom, still craning his head out to see if he could not at least glimpse the further end of this creature.

"To emphasize the fact," said the two voices, "that there is no comparability between races. If you consider yourself large in your own terms, somewhere there is an Alien race much larger. If you consider yourself small in your own terms, then somewhere there is a civilized race much, much smaller."

This Alien, Tom thought, was like nothing so much as a whale—but an enormous whale. The mother of all whales.

"Now," the voices were going on, "further conversation is up to you. It has been determined that what is best absorbed by any civilized mind is something about which that mind is curious in the first place. Therefore we do not instruct, we merely answer any and all questions. Do not feel that you might ask any question that would be emotionally distasteful or unkind to me. We are too dissimilar for any question of yours to produce any such emotional reaction. Now, I leave it to you. Ask what you wish."

Tom could feel his heart beating fast with excitement in his chest. A wealth of questions presented themselves to his mind, and he grabbed blindly at one that was closest.

"How big are you?" he asked.

"The part of me here—that which you see—" answered the Answerer, "would be, in your most familiar terms . . ."

There was a infinitesimal pause.

"—several hundred feet in what you would call length; and proportionate to that, in other dimensions. Those are the figures of course, as I say, only of the part of me that you see. The rest of me is elsewhere."

"I don't understand," said Tom. He waited for some kind of explanation, but the Alien said nothing. Apparently the other would answer only to direct questions.

"You keep talking about yourself as an individual," said Tom, getting more and more interested, "but I distinctly hear two voices from you. Do you have two parallel mechanisms for speaking—or what?"

"No," said the Answerer. "What you think you hear is the best possible translation of the fact that I speak over a much larger range than you do—now, that's assuming that our communication methods are the same, which they aren't—but for a practical answer to your question at the moment, let me just say that what I have—in terms of how you communicate—is a much larger vocal range. So that at any given time I'm speaking both in supersonic tones above the range you can hear and in the sub-sonic range, below. The result of this is that you are—or seem to be—hearing two voices speaking at once. But actually there's only one."

"But," said Tom, "you also talked about part of yourself being elsewhere. Does part of your body detach itself and go off and do something else?"

"Not exactly," said the Answerer. "It's more the way you can think of one thing and your mind be busy with it while doing something else. I suppose it is, in fact, a sort of detachment; only, translated into the physical terms you would think of using."

"I suppose," said Tom. The Alien Being's answer did not quite make sense, but that was probably all the answer he would get.

He continued asking questions, becoming more and more interested as he did so. In the case of some of these, he thought he understood the answer very well indeed—in others, not. In the end he sat talking to the Answerer for some time.

". . . You're getting tired," said the Answerer, finally. "I suggest you take a rest now, and let our conversation rest in the back of your mind. Little by little, it will begin to fit together—not only with your own experience and view of the universe, but with other things you will discover from other Answerers you will talk to. So I will say farewell for now."

"Farewell," said Tom—and woke up to find Lucy shaking him.

"Tom!" Lucy was saying. "Tom, wake up! Are you all right?"

Tom sat up and blinked. Outside the windows of the house, it was late afternoon.

"I'm fine," he said. ". . . I think."

"Well it's time for dinner," said Lucy. "I've been fixing it. I came in, saw you looking concentrated there, and decided that I wouldn't disturb you. But it's down to the point where the food's ready; and every time I come in, I see you looking exactly the same way. Finally, I got worried."

"I was talking to an Alien," said Tom.

"An Alien? What kind of an Alien?"

"I'm not sure," said Tom, still trying to sort out his memories of the conversation. "It's something like the three spirits that come and visit Scrooge in Dickens' *Christmas Carol*. I met someone, but whoever it was was rather hard to describe—what he had to tell me was even harder to understand."

He shook his head, physically trying to put what he had just been through completely out of his mind.

"Never mind," he said, getting to his feet. "Now that I think of it, I'm starving!"

He did his best to put the whole experience with the Answerer out of his mind for the moment, and by bedtime he had just about succeeded. That night he slept very soundly, but there were occasional dreams in which he was back in the underwater-like environment talking to the enormous Alien. If this was a sample, he thought, waking from one such dream with it still vivid in his mind, what would it be like with the other Answerers—or whatever they would call themselves—in the device he had brought home?

During the rest of the ten days he found out. In fact, by the seventh day he had exhausted the variety of Answerers he met in the device, and started back through them to get a clearer idea of what he had experienced with them before. He discovered first, to his surprise and then his intense interest, that each time through he could ask a completely new set of questions. In that respect the equipment seemed to have no limit.

By the time the Jaktal Ambassador was due to arrive on Earth, however, Tom had been introduced only to a small fraction of the nine hundred and twenty-seven

Alien races whose languages he had been taught by the same device; he began to realize what an impossible task it would be for him to familiarize himself completely, even with just the important Races. Each different type of Alien could take a lifetime of study to know.

Nevertheless, as the first Answerer had predicted, he found what he learned from one of them beginning to make sense in context with what he learned from another, so that he did grow in understanding of the ones with which he talked. More than that, he began to get an idea of how alien an Alien had to be to exist on a totally different world.

Meanwhile, he had met Aliens the size of ants, Aliens like skinny kangaroos, Aliens that were perfect spheres—more like bowling balls than anything else, except that they seemed to be capable of growing any number of tentacles practically instantaneously—and many seemed also able to levitate themselves and drift around on the local winds. These, and many more, had broken some kind of interior glass barrier of notions in him, about Aliens in general.

But the day for the reception of the Jaktal Ambassador, put on by the Jaktal visitors themselves, finally arrived. Tom and Lucy rode to it in another of the Secretariat's special limousines, with Tom feeling that he was much more prepared to meet in the flesh those Aliens who had come, like Mr. Rejilla, to his own native Earth.

"How shall I dress for it?" Lucy had asked.

"Oh—you know," said Tom. "However you like— something formal. These are Aliens, remember. They don't know anything about Human clothes."

"Hmph!" said Lucy.

Chapter 7

"The Jaktals certainly picked an impressive place for their Embassy," said Lucy, as they rode the gently rising escalator that wound like an extended pathway through the garden, alive with all the colors of summer flowers. It was not quite sunset, and the broad portals of the entrance were only a short distance ahead of them.

"It ought to be," said Tom. "They paid ten tons of gold for it."

"Ten t . . ." Lucy stared at him.

"I'm not making it up," said Tom. "They actually did pay ten tons of gold for it. Bought it."

"They bought it?" said Lucy. "Just for one night?"

"That's right," said Tom. "They sent a Spandul—that's one of their subject races, who was acting as their advance representative—around looking for a place they'd like. He saw this one, traced the person who owned it, and asked him what was the most important medium of exchange on the Human world. Whoever it was said 'gold.' The Spandul asked him, 'how much gold do you want for it? We'd like to buy it.' The person who owned it thought they were kidding and said, jokingly, 'ten tons.' So, they gave him ten tons of gold."

"What's that worth in ordinary money?" asked Lucy.

71

"I haven't the slightest idea," said Tom. "But I'd think it ought to be enough to buy this place several times over. Even if it didn't, there's a certain amount of fame that would come from selling your home to Aliens for ten tons of gold. At any rate the Jaktal Embassy bought the place for one night's use—they'll be gone tomorrow," said Tom. "Ah, we're almost at the entrance now. The Spandul that greets us will already know who and what I am, so we don't need to go through any introductions. I know the proper words to say, anyhow, after my latest work with the briefing device. I'm full of Alien information, including 'Phrases of Custom.' "

"Do I say anything?"

"Not unless you want to," answered Tom. "Just be nonchalant. You do this sort of thing everyday. Ho-hum."

"But certainly the Jaktal Embassy must know you're an Alien Technical Advisor, Grade One, with the Secretariat; and suspect you of being here to study them?"

"We hope the title won't mean much to them."

"You sound nervous, honey."

"I am not nervous."

"Then why are you biting your nails?"

"I am not biting my nails," said Tom. "I never bite nails. I just thought I had something stuck between my front teeth, that's all. I don't know why you always keep talking about me biting my nails ... Ah, good evening Spandul," he said in English. "My card. I am Thomas Whitworth Parent, and this is my mate, Lucy Thorsdatter Parent. Beware the *zzatz*."

"You are welcome, sorr!" hissed the Spandul in the same language. It was about three feet high, black, lean as a toothpick and had a mouthful of vicious-looking needle-sharp teeth. It stood just within the golden glow of the light from the arched inner door-way. Its large, green eyes glittered at Lucy. "Welcome alssso, Lady. Enter please. Here you will be safe from *zzatz.*"

It took their cloaks; and they proceeded on through the entrance into a long, high-ceilinged hall, already well filled with humans and aliens of all varieties. Most of the other men there were either in evening dress or business suits. All of the women were in floor-length, formal gowns. Lucy had gone shopping, the day before they came here, after asking him about what would be worn, and was now wearing a long, dark blue dress, nipped in at the waist, that fitted her beautifully. It was low-cut at the neck to show off a small but brilliant necklace of blue sapphires she had inherited from her great-grandmother. Her hair was up.

"Ha!" said Lucy, seeing what the other women were wearing.

"What?" asked Tom.

"Nothing," said Lucy. "What's *'zzatz'*?"

"Means 'a most unfortunate fate'," muttered Tom back. "Ah, good evening, Monsieur Pourtoit," he said in French. "I don't believe you've met my wife."

He introduced Lucy to a tall, thin gentleman with a sad face and a broad red ribbon angling across his white dress shirt under his dinner jacket. The gentleman acknowledged the introduction gracefully.

"Elle est charmante," he said to Tom, bowing to Lucy.

"Why, thank you, Mr. Ambassador!" said Lucy. "I can see—"

"However, if you'll excuse us," said Tom, catching Lucy by the hand, "we must be going."

"Of course," said Mr. Pourtoit, with irreproachable politeness and only one slightly lifted eyebrow. Tom towed Lucy off.

"Well, all I was going to say was—" Lucy started to whisper, in Tom's ear.

"Ah, Brakt Kul Djok! May I present my wife, Lucy Thorsdatter Parent?"

"Well, well, honored I am positive!" boomed a large Alien, looking something like a hippopotamus with a stocking cap on, but no other clothes. "A fine young lady, I can see at a glance, hey, boy?"

The walrus-sized elbow joggled Tom almost off his feet.

"See you coming up in your world, hey? Hey? Alien Technical Advisor, Grade One, I hear! Wonder what type of entertainment and food this Jaktal puts out tonight, hah? Never tell about these Imperial-minded Alien types, hey, ho?"

Tom laughed heartily. He and Lucy moved on, Tom introducing her every few feet to some new human or Alien of the diplomatic circle. Finally they found themselves at the punch bowl, were given a couple of large flute-style glasses full of punch, and—going a little further—were able to find a small alcove out of the crowd.

"I'd been wishing there was someplace to sit down," said Lucy, once they were seated. "What I don't understand is how they can have a banquet for so many different kinds of people and Aliens. I should think getting the right food for everybody would be just about impossible."

"Well," said Tom, "they do have a number of different foods for those who can't eat anything but their own special diet. Of course, also, it's necessary to stay clear of what might offend anyone." He took a large swallow of the punch. "But you'd be surprised how much in common tastes are, among different intelligent, animal life forms. It's all animal flesh and vegetation, in every case. Of course, we can't digest most Alien dishes, and some of them would even—not so much poison us—as cause a massive rejection in our bodies. But looked at from the galactic point of view it's all pretty much the same."

"Still," said Lucy, making a small face, "some of them must taste . . ."

"Some, of course," said Tom. "But a lot of Alien foods are quite tasty, and even can be digested by the human body with profit. I've been surprised myself, these last few weeks, at the diverse items I've encountered."

"Oh!" said Lucy.

"What's wrong?"

"What do you think's in this punch?" said Lucy, examining her glass with suspicion.

"Fruit juice and alcohol. Earthly fruits, of course. Now," said Tom, "let's just run over the schedule for the evening. First, we'll be having entertainment."

"Oh, Tom—wait a minute," said Lucy, looking past him. "Listen. How sad!"

"What?" he said—and then he heard it, too. A voice from just around the corner of their alcove, and through a small archway leading away somewhere, was pouring out a thin, heartbreaking thread of melody.

Tom stiffened suddenly.

"Wait a minute," he said, "I'll see."

He got up and went around the corner. At the other end of an empty room, he could see a further doorway from which light was showing. He went forward and looked into the lighted room beyond. At this moment Lucy bumped into him from behind.

"I told you to wait for me!" he whispered angrily at her.

"You did not. You said, 'wait a minute.' Anyway," whispered back Lucy, "there's nothing here but that big jelly mold on the table."

She pointed to an enormous, three-tiered mass of what seemed to be gelatin, with pale colors of blue, yellow and green washing progressively through it. It sat on a silver box set on a white tablecloth—itself on a table with wheels. The table was the only furniture in the room.

"You know what I meant!" said Tom. "And somebody was singing here."

"It was I," said the jelly mold in sweet and flawless tones of English.

They stared at it. But Tom made a swift recovery.

"May I present my wife?" he said. "Lucy Thorsdatter Parent. I am Thomas Whitworth Parent, Alien Technical Advisor, Grade One, of the Secretariat for Alien Affairs, here on our human world."

"I'm awfully pleased to meet you," said the jelly mold. "I am Kotnick, a Bulbur."

"Was it a Bulbur song you were singing?" asked Lucy.

"Alas," said Kotnick, "it is a Jaktal song. A little thing I composed myself; but sung, of course, in Jaktal—though unfortunately with a heavy Bulbur accent."

"But you sing so beautifully!" said Lucy. "What would it sound like if you sang it in Bulbur?"

"Alas," said Kotnick, "there is no Bulbur to sing it in. There is only Jaktal."

Lucy looked at Tom, questioningly.

"It's a manner of speaking," Tom said to her, hastily. "There are a number of intelligent races that have been subjugated by the Jaktal but come from different planets. The Jaktal, however, are the ruling ones. The language and everything else takes its name from the rulers."

"Indeed, yes," said the Bulbur, with an odd little sound very like a choked-back sob. "And properly so."

"I knew about Spanduls, Gloks, and Naffings," said Tom, looking at it. "But we haven't heard about you Bulburs, along with the rest of the subordinate races of the Jaktal."

The Bulbur turned pink all over.

"Pardon my immodesty," it said, "but I have been brought by our overlords especially for the occasion."

"How nice," said Lucy. "We're very happy to have you."

The Bulbur made the odd little choked sound again. Meanwhile, Tom had stepped closer to it and lowered his voice.

"Ah?" said Tom. "Perhaps, then you can tell me—"

"Did the Sorr and Lady wisssh somesing?" interrupted a sharp hissing voice.

Tom and Lucy turned abruptly to see a Spandul like the one that had admitted them to the Embassy. It was standing in the doorway. Beside it was a sort of four-foot long worm reared up like a cobra, with its mouth open and fanglike teeth curving down from its upper jaw.

"Oh!" said Tom. "No. Nothing. Nothing at all. We heard this Bulbur singing and wandered in to meet it."

"It ssshould not sssing!" hissed the Spandul, looking at the Bulbur, which quivered and went almost colorless.

"Well, it wasn't really singing," said Tom. "Sort of just humming. Well, we'll have to be getting back to the punch bowl. Glad to have met you, Kotnick."

Still talking, Tom took Lucy's arm and led her back past the Spandul and the worm-like being; and out into the shadowy area giving on the entrance to the Reception room. The worm-like being slithered past them into the room and the Spandul fell in beside them, its needle-like teeth glittering at them.

"Guestsss," it hissed, "will find it mossst comfortable in main hall area."

"I imagine you're right," said Tom. "We'll trot on back. Nice of you to show us the way. See you later, then. May there be no *zzatz* beneath this roof, tonight."

"There *will* be no *zzatz* beneasss sssiss roof tonight!"

replied the Spandul, fixing them with its green eyes as
they moved out again into the hall.

"Well," said Tom, "how about another glass of
punch, Lucy? I could use one, myself."

"I should say not," said Lucy. His eyebrows wig-
wagged at her angrily. She looked at him, puzzled, for
a moment. "Why yes, on second thought, a glass of
punch would be just the thing."

"Yes," said Tom, "and we can sit down in our
alcove."

They got new flutes full of punch and took their
seats in the alcove.

"Ah, Lucy," said Tom, "how wonderful it is, here at
this amazing Jaktal reception, and the two of us sitting
together, out of the crowd. It reminds me of the first
night we met, and how I fell in love with you at first
sight."

Lucy stared at him again.

"But you didn't," she said. "And anyway it wasn't
anything like this. I was in the row behind you at the
homecoming game when we were at college, and some
of the coke I was drinking just happened to fall on
your program with its list of players—"

"I mean before that," Tom hastily interrupted. "The
night with the full moon, at the homecoming ball a
year before. I saw you for the first time. You were
wearing something like—well, like you're wearing
now—and I thought you were the most beautiful
woman I'd ever seen. I got all my nerve and came up
to you, but you didn't even seem to notice me. So I—"

Lucy put her hand up and felt his forehead.

"Cool," she said, thoughtfully. "So, that was where
we really met, was it?"

"Yes," he said, a tense note in his voice. "I remember every moment of it. I remember how I finally did
get the nerve to speak to you. I asked you to dance.

And we danced. It was like floating on air. Lucy—why don't we dance now?"

"Yes," said Lucy, "why don't we?"

They left their drinks on a small table in the alcove and walked out into the center of the floor. A band had been playing very politely and quietly on the far side of the room, and just a few couples were beginning to dance to it. Tom slipped Lucy into his arms, and they also began to dance.

"Just what is going on?" she demanded in his ear, under the sound of the music.

"I had to talk to you some place where we couldn't be overheard," said Tom, speaking into hers. "Even though they've been here only a couple of days, the Jaktal Embassy will undoubtedly have had this place completely bugged. Undoubtedly they're trying to listen to us now, since we discovered that Bulbur. But I'm hoping the music will cause too much interference."

"Then you did know about Bulburs before we found him—or whatever it is," said Lucy.

"They were at the bottom of the list of the subordinate races conquered by the Jaktals," said Tom. "But the presence of this one here confirms what the Secretariat has been suspecting. At least, Domango Aksisi and I have been expecting it; since we're the only ones who've had the full briefing from the devices the Oprinkians delivered to us from the Sector Council on Cayahno."

"I take it Domango is worried about these Jaktals?"

"You couldn't be more right," said Tom. "For certain diplomatic reasons the Oprinkians couldn't give us a direct warning; we just got a general impression that we ought to keep our eyes open where the Jaktals were concerned. But until six months ago, we hadn't had any contact with that Race at all. Since then they've been steadily increasing their contact with us; and they have a large and powerful spatial empire."

"They could take us over easily?" said Lucy.

"That's right. They'd need an excuse, of course; but they seem to have a conqueror psychology, as indicated not only by the data supplied us by the Oprinkians on the other races who are on the Sector Council, but by the history of their expansion at the expense of intelligent, if barbarous, Races like the Spanduls, Naffings, and Gloks."

"Was that one of them? That worm-like thing with fangs?" Lucy asked.

"Yes. A Naffing," said Tom. "They aren't much more intelligent than an adult chimp, actually. But dangerous. However, to get back to the important part of the business, recent information seems to indicate that even with our Alien allies, we'd be at the mercy of the Jaktal Empire, if they decided to move against us right now."

"Would they?" Lucy shivered.

"We don't know. That's just it. Their Ambassador talks peaceful relations; but we can't make this match up with the character he and his subservient races show. You'll see what I mean when you get a look at Bu Hjark, the Ambassador."

"But what's it all got to do with us—with you?"

"Well, you remember how Domango thought we did a good job with that Oprinkian? Well, we'd heard that there was a Bulbur being brought very quietly into the Embassy here, at the time their Ambassador arrived. The Bulbur—he, she, or it; we don't even know that much yet—seems entirely different from the rest of the Jaktals' conquered Races. So what does it mean? What's the Bulbur's place in the organization? What does it showing up here mean in terms of the Jaktal attitude toward us and our Alien allies?"

"I can see where we need to know more," whispered Lucy. *"Ouch!"*

"What happened?"

"You just stepped on my toe."

"Oh. Sorry."

"Quite all right. Nothing I like more. Go on."

"Well," said Tom, as they whirled around together, "it's hard to concentrate on two things at once. As I was saying, Domango thought we might be able to get the information—you and I, that is—where official and unofficial other methods might fail."

"And why wasn't I told about this before we came?" asked Lucy.

"Our intelligence and analysis people had to have their chance first," said Tom. "If they got the answer, I was simply to forget it, myself, and not mention it to you at all. But we've now passed the deadline for getting that word to me. It ended when we entered this embassy."

"You could at least have let me know what you knew," said Lucy.

"Domango specifically asked me not to mention it to another soul until I got word—or failed to get word—from the intelligence people," said Tom. "But we're clearly on our own now; and already you've found out for us where the Bulbur is—I was guessing it would be under lock and key, somewhere. Now we know it's in that empty room without a crowd around it. The next step is up to me. I have to have a chance to talk to it alone."

"Oh, I see."

"Not that I wouldn't like to have you along," said Tom, hastily. "But I need you to help in another direction. It's a good thing there's two of us, because we can't each be both places at once."

"We could trade places."

"Not very well. I've got what data we've been given

on Bulbur psychology and that indicates it may be nervous about talking openly to more than one human at a time. Also, I'll need help."

"What for?" asked Lucy, "if it's a one-person job?"

"Do you think you can get that Spandul out of the way while I have a talk with the Bulbur? I can gas the Naffing. It can't talk and report what's been done to it. But the Spandul could, if I gassed him."

"Well," said Lucy, biting her lower lip, "I don't know. It isn't as if the Spandul was a man, or something. Haven't you any suggestions?"

"The Spandul has to be polite to you—especially if you can get him out where people can see him. You'll think of something."

"I hope," said Lucy.

"Sure you will. Let's go." Tom started to lead the way off the dance floor and suddenly noticed that she was limping. "Ohmigosh, I didn't realize I'd stepped on you that hard!"

"It's all right," said Lucy, bravely. "Maybe I can use it as an excuse to make him stay with me."

"That's an excellent idea," said Tom. They were off the dance floor now and he lowered his voice. "I'll tell him I want him to take care of you while I go for a doctor to make your foot more comfortable. Then when I leave you with him, you get him away from the entrance there any way you can."

He broke off suddenly. A fanfare of something like trumpets had just silenced all the talk in the room. The crowd was splitting apart down the middle, leaving the center of the floor clear. Luckily, Tom and Lucy were already on the side of the room they had wished to reach.

"I wonder what's happening?" said Lucy. "I wish we had Rex with us."

"Rex!" said Tom. "What good would it do to have him along?"

"He could keep us in touch with each other."

"How? Just because we picked up enough telepathic sense from that Oprinkian to understand Rex doesn't mean he'd be any use to us now. What I wish is that we'd been able to go one step further and understand people's thoughts. Even each other's thoughts. That's what we need now."

"If Rex was with you and trouble came," Lucy said, "he'd start broadcasting excited thoughts, and then I'd know you were in trouble."

"But what good would that do?" said Tom. "You couldn't do anything about it, probably. No, believe me, Rex would be just what we needed to bollix things up. Besides, I'm happy to have a rest from those inane canine thoughts of his. *Nice Tom! Good Lucy! Play frisbee?*'—all day long."

Tom broke off suddenly. The trumpets had sounded again—a wild, violent shout of metal throats. Now, bounding down through the open lane in the middle, they could see an Alien fully eight feet tall, approaching and bellowing greetings to people in the crowd.

"It's him," said Tom. "The Jaktal Ambassador, Bu Hjark. Just look at him!"

Chapter 8

Bu Hjark was a huge lizard-like Alien with a heavy powerful tail. Elbows out, large hands half-clenched, he danced down the open space like a boxer warming up for a bout in the ring. Brilliant ribbons and medals covered his silver tunic and shorts. Into a gem-studded belt was fastened a heavy, curved-bladed sword.

"Ho! Ho! Welcome! Welcome all!" he roared. "Great pleasure to have you all here! Great pleasure. Greetings, Brakt Kul Djok, evening, Mr. Vice-President! Great evening, isn't it? Find yourselves seats, respected Beings, and let me show you how the Jaktal entertain."

"What does he need a sword for," asked Lucy in a low voice in Tom's ear, "with those teeth and nails?"

"And that tail," said Tom. "The sword may be just part of his costume, however. Wait until the entertainment starts. Then we can slip off while everybody's watching him."

Naffings were hastily producing small gilded chairs. Apparently, however, there were only enough of these for the chief dignitaries—a couple of dozen, perhaps. The rest of the crowd was left standing behind those fortunate enough to be seated, Tom and Lucy well to the rear of the standees.

"Positions, everybody!" shouted Bu Hjark back the

way he had come, and added something in Jaktal. A crowd of ape-like beings in full metal armor trotted in and formed a protective wall in front of the audience. Laughing hugely, Bu Hjark took off his sword belt and sword and tossed them to one of these.

"Gloks," explained Tom in answer to Lucy's inquiring gaze, nodding at the ape-like beings in armor. "A little brighter than the Naffings, not so bright as the Spanduls. Sort of low grade human-level intelligence. But extremely strong for their size."

"First," Bu Hjark was crying, "let in the Bashdash!"

There was a moment's pause, then a gasp from the far end of the room, drowned out by a sudden bestial bellow.

Something in the general shape of a rhinoceros, but not so large, charged down the aisle full tilt at Bu Hjark; who met it with flailing hands and tail and a deep-chested shout. Amid roarings and snarlings they rolled on the floor together.

"Repulsive!" said Lucy. "I refuse to look."

She turned her head away.

"It's all right, it's all over," said Tom, a few moments later. "He wrung its neck. See, some Gloks are carrying it off."

"Now, for the armed Wlackins!" shouted Bu Hjark. A moment later a herd of five small, centaur-like creatures, clutching sharpened metal stakes, galloped down upon Bu Hjark, who joined battle with them briefly.

"Everybody's watching," whispered Tom. "Let's get going."

"Yes, let's," said Lucy with a shudder. They threaded their way through the back of the staring crowd to the shadowy corner which led back to the room where they had discovered the Bulbur.

"Limp a little more!" muttered Tom. He guided her toward the lighted doorway. "Hey! Spandul!"

The Spandul they had seen earlier emerged from the room. Its eyes burned suspiciously upon them.

"What isss the masser?" it hissed. "Guessstsss will be more comfortable in main hall."

"My mate has hurt herself. I insist you give me a hand here," said Tom. "I need help."

"Help?"

"I must get a doctor. Right now!" said Tom. "You understand? Find her a chair. Look after her while I find a doctor!"

"Doctor?" hissed the Spandul. It glanced back into the room behind it, and then out again at Tom and Lucy.

"A chair . . ." moaned Lucy, clinging to Tom.

"What're you waiting for?" snapped Tom. "Is this the way you do things for guests here at the Embassy? I'll speak to the Ambassador himself about this!"

"Yesss, yesss. I help," said the Spandul, gliding forward. It took hold of Lucy's other arm. "Chair, Lady. Thisss way."

"Good. Stay with her!" said Tom. "I'll go after a doctor." He turned and headed back toward the main room. Once he had joined the crowd there, however, he looked back, turned around and carefully made his way back to the room in which he had relinquished Lucy to the Spandul. The room was empty. He went into the further room where they had seen the Bulbur, taking what appeared to be a broad-tipped magic marker pen from his pocket as he approached the doorway.

Holding it, he peered inside. The Naffing, curled up in a corner, reared up at the sight of him.

He pointed the pen at it and pressed the clip. There was an almost inaudible pop. The Naffing wavered a minute and then sank down to lie still on the floor.

"What is it?" fluted the jelly on the table, paling to

near transparency. "Have you come to end me before my time?"

"No," said Tom. "I, and all other Humans are your friends."

Tom glanced behind him and saw the entrance and the room beyond still deserted. The crowd was out of sight, but he could hear the sounds of a combat still going on. He moved in to stand before the Bulbur.

"I want to talk to you."

"Take my worthless life, then," keened the jelly. "I have nothing worth talking about."

"Yes, you have," said Tom. "You can tell me about yourself."

"Myself?" a little color began to flow back into the Bulbur. "Ah, I see. It is not me. It is the high role I've been chosen to play here that makes me an object of interest to you."

"Oh? Oh yes, that of course," said Tom. "Let me hear you describe it in your own words."

The Bulbur turned pink.

"I am not worthy," it murmured.

"Tell me anyhow," said Tom. The Bulbur turned flame-colored.

"I am . . ." it began, and its voice almost failed it, "the . . . most important item . . ." At that point its voice failed completely.

"Go on," said Tom, drawing very close to it indeed.

"I cannot. The emotion involved is too strong."

The Bulbur had deepened its red color until it was almost black. Its voice seemed strangled and unnatural. Tom cast an uneasy glance to the doorway.

"All right," he said. "Let's talk about things you can talk about for a moment. Tell me about yourself— aside from what you're supposed to do here."

"But I am nothing," said the Bulbur, all its colors paling relievedly. "I am a mere blob. A shameful blob."

"Shameful?" said Tom.

"Oh, yes," said the Bulbur, earnestly. "A shameful quiver of emotions. A useless creature, possessing only a voice and the power of putting forth weak pseudopods to get about. A pusillanimous peace-worshiper in a universe at war."

"Peace?" Tom stiffened. "Did you say *peace-worshiper*?"

"Oh, yes. Yes," fluted the Bulbur. "It is the main cause of my shame. Ah, if only the worlds of the universe were oriented to my desires!"

Its voice sank, and took on a note of sad reasonableness, not untouched with humor.

"But obviously," it went on, "if it had been meant to be that way, all life forms would be cast in the shape of Bulburs and this, manifestly, is not the case. I am allowing myself to take a bulburmorphic point of view."

"Look," said Tom, glancing out through the doorway. Seeing the way was still clear, he went on, "I'm afraid I don't understand you. What do you mean by peace-worshiper?"

"If you will permit me," said the Bulbur humbly. "I might sing you a little melody?"

"Well, if it'll help," said Tom. "Go ahead."

The Bulbur turned a pale, happy pink. A thread of melody began to pour forth from it. Up until now, Tom had been too concerned to figure out how a three-layer aspic, even one of large size, could manage to talk and sing.

Now, however, looking closer, he perceived—palely-moving and pulsating within the body of the Bulbur—an almost transparent heart, lungs and other parts, including a vertical tube that might well be some sort of windpipe, leading to a small opening in the very top surface of the Bulbur. He was also suddenly aware of a row of pale, almost transparent eyes, ringing the upper tier like decorations on a wedding cake.

But almost as soon as he had seen this he began to forget all about it.

The wordless melody he was listening to began to pass beyond mere sound; began to pass beyond mere music. It moved completely inside him and became a heart-twisting voice speaking of peace, beyond any other voice that could possibly speak in opposition. He felt himself swept away, completely disarmed by what he was hearing. It was only with a sudden, convulsive effort that he broke loose from the emotional hold of that voice upon him.

"Wait! Hold it!" he gasped. "I understand."

The Bulbur broke off suddenly, once more, with that sound that was very much like a sob.

"Excuse me," it whispered. "It's shameful, I know; but I get carried away."

"Well, so did I," said Tom, surreptitiously wiping his eyes. "That's a mighty powerful vocal apparatus you have there. And I don't see why you think it's shameful, at all. I mean—there may be more to like about you than just that, of course. But I don't see why you think you have to be ashamed of feeling the way you do."

"Because," said the Bulbur, going a sad, translucent blue, "it is my mark—the mark of my difference from all the rest of you. I cannot stand to force my opinion on anyone else. I have no virtues. It is quite right that I should suffer."

"Suffer?"

"Ah, indeed—suffer. Oh," said the Bulbur, pinkening again, "it's a great honor, I know. I should be rejoicing. But I'm a failure at rejoicing, too."

And now it did sob, quite distinctly.

"Wait a minute," said Tom. "You seem to have

things all twisted up. What gives you the idea nobody but you prefers peace to fighting?"

The Bulbur turned completely transparent.

"You mean—you don't mean—others ... possibly you ... find peace to be a pleasant and desirable thing?"

"Of course we do," said Tom.

"Oh—you poor creatures," breathed the Bulbur. "How you must suffer."

"Suffer? Certainly not!" said Tom. "We like it peaceful. We keep it peaceful by talking."

"You *keep* it peaceful?"

"Well—most of the time," said Tom, feeling a touch of guilt.

"But how do you live with such Beings as the Jaktals, the Spanduls, the Gloks and the Naffings?"

"We—well, we stop them when they get unpeaceful," said Tom. "By force, if necessary."

"But force? Isn't that coercion?" said the Bulbur, turning pink, chartreuse and mauve in that order. "Isn't that fighting fire with fire?"

"Why not?" said Tom. "You should try it."

The Bulbur went slowly, completely transparent again.

"Oh, I couldn't!" it said at last.

"Certainly. That singing of yours is a strong argument. I'd think you could use it."

"Oh, no," said the Bulbur. "What if I was successful? That would make me a dominator of the Jaktals—and the Spanduls."

"To say nothing," said Tom, "of the Gloks, Naffings and so forth."

He stopped suddenly, wondering what had just alarmed him. Then he noticed that the sound of battle from the main hall had suddenly ceased.

"Why shouldn't you have things peaceful if you want them that way?"

"Why, it's not natural," said the Bulbur. "Look into the matter logically. If Beings had been intended to live in peace—"

"Goodbye!" interrupted Tom, sprinting out the door.

He had just heard the sudden chatter of voices and the sound of chairs being pushed back, people moving about, and other indications of general movement beyond the shadowy entrance and the further room. He made it once more to the fringes of the crowd in the main hall, just as the onlookers parted for a platoon of Gloks marching toward the room he had just left.

Tom slipped aside; and thrust his way through the crowd to the edge of a further open area in the center of the floor. A table had been set up there; and a Naffing, operating a sort of vacuum cleaner, was busy cleaning up a few last spots of pale blood.

Bu Hjark, wearing a few neat bandages, his sword replaced, was standing by the table directing the Naffing. Tom gained a ringside position; and all but bumped into Lucy, limping around the ring in the opposite direction.

"That Spandul finally insisted on going to get a doctor, himself," she said. "I came to warn you to get out of the Bulbur's room as fast as you could. But here you are. What happened?"

Before Tom could answer, there was another fanfare of trumpets. The crowd opened almost alongside them; and the platoon of Gloks, now bearing the Bulbur on its silver stand, marched out to the table. They set stand and Bulbur up in the middle of it. Bu Hjark raised his hand for silence and barked at the Naffing with the vacuum cleaner, which scurried hastily off.

"Respected Beings!" boomed Bu Hjark. "I now bring you the climax to the evening's entertainment and the commencement of the banquet itself. I have no doubt, respected Beings, that you have on occasion tasted rare and fine dishes. However, tonight I mean to provide you not merely with the best-tasting food you have ever encountered—a food which all Beings who have yet tried it consider to be better than any other they have ever absorbed. In addition I offer it to you with a certain preliminary, which is unique to the food itself and will also be more memorable to you than anything else you have encountered. After that, I shall, with my own hand, prepare and serve the dish to you."

He drew his sword and stepped a little aside from the table.

"And now," he said to the Bulbur. "Commence!"

"R-respected Beings," the Bulbur began with a slight quaver. It turned remarkably transparent then washed back to blue again.

"—It is a great honor," it went on in a somewhat stronger voice, "a great honor I assure you, to be the appetizer to your banquet tonight. We Bulburs are a worthless lot, fit only for pleasing the worthy palates of our betters. It is our one pride and pleasure, to know that you find us good to—"

The Bulbur swallowed audibly and then took up his speech a little more rapidly as Bu Hjark scowled at it.

"—eat. I cannot express the intense enjoyment—" it said rapidly, "—that it gives me to be here tonight, awaiting my supreme fulfillment as appetizer to you all. To ensure your unalloyed enjoyment of me, therefore, I will now," it said, speeding up even more under Bu Hjark's steely, lizard-like eye, "sing you a mouth-watering song to increase your appreciation of my truly unique flavor."

It broke off and visibly took a deep breath, turned pale, but came steadily back to a solid blue color.

"Tom!" Lucy clutched Tom's elbow with fingers that dug in. "It can't mean we're going to *eat* it? There's got to be something in that special briefing you got through the Oprinkians to stop something like this!"

"There isn't," said Tom.

"Well, something's got to be done!"

"What?" asked Tom, as a small beginning thread of golden melody began to emerge, growing in volume as it continued from the mouth of the Bulbur.

"I don't know! But it's got to be stopped!"

Desperately, Tom looked around for inspiration. He thought of how he had almost begun to convince the Bulbur that his attitudes were not unique in the universe. He thought of how effective the Bulbur's gift of song had proved in the room when the Bulbur sang to him.

"What we need," he said, "is another Bulbur to sing this one into resisting the Jaktal. And that's imposs—"

"Oh, for—" Lucy said, impatiently, broke off and abruptly began to sing, loudly and in French.

"Allons, enfants de la patrie—" she sang.

Almost with the first word, Tom understood what she had in mind. His best bathroom baritone chimed in with her. And her own clear soprano picked up the second line.

*"—Le jour de gloire—*sing!" she cried to Monsieur Pourtoit, who was standing only a little ways away across the open space from them. He looked a little puzzled. But, aside from being the Ambassador from France, there was the fact that he was a Frenchman down to his bones. He could hardly stand silent in a situation like this. He opened his mouth and joined a resonant, trained voice to Lucy's tones and Tom's.

"What is this?" roared Bu Hjark, spinning around to face Tom. His lizard face was agape, showing great dog teeth. He lifted the sword ominously in his hand. Tom swallowed, but continued to sing.

The *Marseillaise*, the National Anthem of France, was beginning to sound its battle cry against tyranny

from other confused but cooperative lips. The sword
swung up. The Gloks turned as one Glok toward Tom.
Suddenly a clear, pure note, two octaves above high
F, trilled through all the sound of the room, striking
everyone in the room motionless for a second. Then
they turned as one Being toward the table.

The fine, thrilling note was coming from the Bulbur.
It had stretched upward until it was now almost twice
its original height. From what well of knowledge it had
picked up the necessary information Tom was never to
discover, but it had changed color again. Its lowest tier
was now a dark blue, its middle white, and its top red,
the colors of the French flag. As those around it stood,
like soldiers at attention, it broke magnificently into
song to the tune of the anthem itself.

"Against us long, a tyranny," it sang in English, in
wild masterful accents, *"a bloody sword has waved
on high!"*

It was pitching its notes directly at Bu Hjark. Those
assembled saw the full power of the Bulbur's melody-
born emotional might driving through the savage ego
of the Jaktal like a metal blade through the tender
body of a Bulbur. Now the whole assemblage of guests
had joined in the song. Spellbound, a chorus of diplomatic and government personnel, Humans and Aliens
together, roared with the Bulbur to the tune of the
Marseillaise:

> *Too long have you kept us subject.*
> *With your Spanduls, your Naffings*
> *and your Gloks!*
> *Why shouldn't peace be sweet?*
> *Who dares a Bulbur eat?*
> *Have done! Have done!*
> *Let there be an end!*
> *It's beautiful PEACE—*
> *from this hour on, my friend!*

Then, as the last great chord of voices crashed into silence, the huge figure of the Jaktal ambassador could be seen to shiver through all its length; and, leaning more and more at an angle with eyes glazed, it toppled at last, to thunder upon the floor like some mighty ruined tower. And the voices of the Spanduls and the Gloks present rose in one great wail, crying *"Zzatz! Zzatz! Zzatz . . ."*

When their cries at last died away into silence, the Bulbur on the table could be seen to have taken on an all-over shade of perky pink.

"Jaktals," it mentioned, in mild but audible tones as it leaned slightly to look down at the fallen Bu Hjark, "are also supposed to be very good eating."

"—And that remark," said Tom, as he and Lucy were back home again and once more getting ready for bed, "will undoubtedly go down in the history books of our galactic Sector as the harshest statement ever made by an adult Bulbur."

"But what's going to happen to the Bulburs now?" asked Lucy. "Did you learn anything from that long, scrambled-phone conversation you had with Domango after we got home here?"

"In theory, the Bulburs should now take over the Jaktal Empire. I don't know exactly what's going to happen, though. Domango had a private talk with our Bulbur after all the fuss was over at the embassy. There's to be another private session at Domango's office tomorrow. The other Bulburs, our Bulbur said, would ratify any statement of his—if for no other reason than that they wouldn't want to hurt his feelings by disagreeing with him."

"They're that sensitive?" said Lucy.

"Yes," said Tom, taking a thoughtful swallow from the champagne that Lucy had insisted on opening in honor of the occasion, "but shrewd—Domango suspects.

And I agree with him. Domango told me there was one interesting thing the Bulbur said in the course of their conversation, without explaining it—'*Greater love hath no being than to take on authority as a duty rather than as a privilege.*'"

"You're right," said Lucy. "It's a very good thing to say, but there's a definitely ominous sound to it, all the same."

"Yes," said Tom, "and in any case, the Secretariat is in for one hell of an expansion. There's going to be a full department of Technical Advisors—but you and I aren't going to be a part of it."

"We're not?" said Lucy. "Particularly after tonight? What's Domango got in mind for us, then?"

Tom sighed heavily. Rex licked his hand sleepily. "Love Tom and Lucy," he telepathed softly.

"Domango wouldn't tell me," said Tom.

They fell silent and both drank some more champagne. In the quiet, they could hear the yells and shouts from a night soccer game, winding up under the lights of a nearby cleared area of the parkland and penetrating through their living room walls.

It sounded to both Tom and Lucy a little like Glok and Spandul voices in the distance, faintly and forebodingly crying, "*Zzatz! Zzatz!*"

Chapter 9

"This is a critical moment for the people of our world," Domango said to Lucy and Tom two days later, as they sat in his office, now flooded with morning sunlight through perfectly ordinary, but large, windows. Domango was behind his desk, and Tom and Lucy were in the comfortable armchairs facing it. "So forgive me if I ramble a bit as I tell you things. I was up most of the night talking not only to the Oprinkian representative on Cayahno, but some others on the Sector Council."

"You can talk between here and Cayahno?" said Tom. "That's hundreds of light years away from here."

"Alien technology." Domango gave a tired wave of his hand, barely lifting it from the desk. "I don't have the slightest idea how it's managed; but I do have a voice-and-picture link to Mr. Valhinda, the Oprinkian on the Council; and he put me in touch with several other members from even older, wiser, civilizations. The problem, of course, is compounded by the fact that the Bulbur wants to leave immediately for his home-world aboard the Jaktal Ambassador's space-ship—which is, of course, now entirely at his disposal. The Ambassador himself, incidentally, will survive, after all. But he is a broken Being. There is no physical defense against an emotional strength like that Bulbur

99

showed us. You might even say the Bulbur owns the Jaktal spaceship, now. To him, of course, leaving for Bulburnia immediately seems like a simple decision."

He paused and looked at Tom and Lucy, who were staring back at him. After a moment he blinked.

"I am rambling, aren't I?" he said. "At my age trying to get by with a couple of hours' sleep makes things difficult. Excuse me a moment."

He reached into a drawer of his desk and came up with a vase holding a single golden, tulip-shaped flower in it.

"This is one of the few native Bulburnian things the Jaktal Ambassador allowed the Bulbur to have. He passed it on to me, since he said he would have no great need now, himself, for it. He said if for any reason I was troubled or ill I should sniff it."

He put the blossom to his nose and sniffed. Immediately his eyes brightened up and a smile changed his face.

"Remarkable!" he said in a strong voice, putting it back in the drawer of his desk. "I should have done that before you came in. The effect only lasts for about an hour or two, but that will do for our conversation. I can't remember exactly what I've said so far. Did I tell you the Jaktal Ambassador has recovered from his defeat by the Bulbur?"

"You told us he's still alive," Lucy helped him out.

"Oh, yes," answered Domango. "I saw him being assisted on to the now Bulbur-owned spaceship, myself, a little earlier this morning. He was able to walk, with aid; but he was very unsteady on his legs. I understand what happened to him was analogous to the vital fluid—might as well call it blood, I suppose— freezing in his veins. But he thawed out without a problem, after the Bulbur sang a reassuring melody to him."

"I'm glad," said Lucy. "He's a horrible alien, but—"

"I know," said Domango, sympathetically, "I feel the same way. But he can't help being a Jaktal. All his instincts plus a lifetime of training have fitted him for one occupation—tyranny. But you'd hardly have recognized him. He even made a great effort and shook hands with me weakly, as he passed me on his way to the ship. I had to be there, you see, officially. He is, after all, still officially the Ambassador from the Jaktal race. He also tried to apologize to me in a faltering voice. I told him it was quite all right. No one had been offended."

"A white lie," murmured Tom.

"Exactly," said Domango. "It will do no harm in our future relationship with the Jaktals. But—back to the point I wish to talk to you about—the important matter confronting us right now. As I say, I took the advice of several of the more knowledgeable members on the Alien Sector Council on Cayahno and they thoroughly agree with me. Unfortunately, it has to be a handshake decision between me and the Bulbur, before he leaves. There's no time for our All-Earth Federation to discuss this matter and take a vote on it. That would take months at least; and by that time there would be no knowing what the situation would be with the Jaktal Empire as we know it at this moment. Other aggressive probationary civilizations might have tried to snap up parts of it."

"Excuse me, sir," said Lucy, "but you haven't yet told us what the decision's about."

"It's a little difficult for me to come to the point on it," said Domango. "It appears so simple and is actually anything but that. You see, our Bulbur here told me last night that his race would have no great desire to run the Jaktal Empire. He offered the authority over that Empire to us Humans; with the Bulburs committed to back us up in case our authority was challenged. All other Bulburs, he said, would ratify

that move, if they were contacted by us—if for no
other reason than that they wouldn't want to hurt his
feelings by disagreeing with him."

"Yes, Tom told me something about that last night,"
said Lucy.

"Did he? Good!" said Domango. "The Bulbur also
said he believed he was turning the authority over to
people who would regard it as a sacred trust."

"What a fine thing to say!" said Lucy.

"Isn't it?" said Domango. "If we all just—but back
to business. I wasn't in a position to disillusion him
with the information that we have more than a few
people on this planet of ours who are far from being
that trustworthy. But, you see, particularly if that offer
was passed on to the U.R. Assembly, it would be very
hard for many there to turn down the opportunity.
A ready-made galactic empire is a tempting thing to
many minds."

Tom and Lucy nodded solemnly.

"My own feelings, of course," went on Domango,
"are that not only are we not ready for such responsibility, but if we did, we would most certainly be in
the position of, bare-handed, catching a Jaktal by the
tail. To say nothing of the Spanduls, the Naffings, the
Gloks and the others among their subservient races.
The Bulbur will not turn down the responsibility to
oversee and discipline the Jaktal Empire, if we decide
not to take it on—the Sector Council on Cayahno
would have to approve our doing so, in any case. They
are—if I may say so—a far, far better Race than we
are. Accordingly, I told the Bulbur that we might not
feel equal to the task—and found that there was a
snag to that course."

"A snag?" said Tom, sharply.

"Yes," said Domango. "He told me quite frankly
that if that was the case the Bulburs would agree to
manage the Jaktal Empire—but only for a certain

length of time; until we humans proved that we were
able to handle it, and felt that we could."

"But there's no way we can do that!" said Tom.

"Well, yes and no," said Domango. "To begin with,
the length of time they would be talking about would
be up to several thousand years. But, nonetheless, to
come from our—between the three of us—very low
state of civilization to one with all the power, will and
authority to peacefully control something like the Jaktal Empire—we haven't got a moment to waste. In the
end, he and I agreed that in any case we should get
started on trying to achieve an interstellar profile as a
Race; and achieve a higher civilized status as quickly
as we're able to."

"How?" said Lucy.

"That's the thing," said Domango. "I used the same
word in questioning him; and he offered a suggestion—about the only practical suggestion that appears
to have any chance at all of being successful; and that
brings me to the reason you two are here talking to
me today. I assume you were both somewhat startled
to hear there was now to be a Department of Technical Advisors in the Secretariat, but you two were to
have no part in it?"

"That's right," said Tom. "I should think that if anyone has, we've qualified ourselves—"

"You have indeed," interrupted Domango. "In fact
you've qualified yourselves for more than that. The
Bulbur suggested that you two be sent out as Ambassadors-at-large to the other Races of our Sector; with the
announced mission merely of establishing contact with
other Races that have been admitted at least to a probationary stage of civilization."

"I don't see how that'll help," said Lucy, frowning.

"In itself, it'll do nothing at all," said Domango.
"Officially, it'll appear that you're merely on a sort of
goodwill mission. But, the Bulbur pointed out, backed

up by the very high report the Oprinkian had to give after investigating you two and your dog, under the cover of this mission you could gain a necessary familiarity with other important Alien races. At the same time, you could both get a general picture of the Alien situation in our Sector of the galaxy; and possibly find opportunities to establish the ability of humans to take control of situations involving other Aliens."

"What opportunities?" asked Tom, dealing with an itching earlobe by thoughtfully rubbing it between thumb and first finger. "That's the question."

"The Oprinkian representative on the Sector Council," said Domango, "told me that the Bulbur was quite right in his suggestion. On the larger stage of the Sector community, opportunities would present themselves, the counterpart of which you'd never run into, here on the small world that is our Earth. And by the way, Tom, I would advise you to refer to the briefing you've been studying and brush up on your racial gestures. That action with your ear, just now, is regarded as the most deadly insult to anyone of the Heffalumpia Race. They have very large ears, you see, about which they are extremely modest. Very like we Humans and—well, certain parts of our bodies."

"Would it be dangerous?" asked Lucy.

"I am afraid it might—at times," said Domango. "I'd want you both to go into this with your eyes open if you decide to take on the job. But on the other hand, it may prove the only key to the future of the human race as a power in this Sector of the galaxy—particularly since Humanity has so far been restricted to this one small world. It's not as if we were spread over a number of planets in a number of star systems."

"It does sound interesting," said Lucy, almost to herself.

Tom felt a tingle of temptation in him, also. It would be personally attractive to go out and visit these other

Aliens and their worlds. It would make being tourists in other parts of Earth ridiculous by comparison.

The older man was eyeing him keenly.

"You would be the first two humans ever to visit Alien worlds," Domango said.

"We'd have to leave Rex at the boarding kennel, though," said Lucy to Tom, "and he hates the kennel."

"Oh, by no means," said Domango. "Rex must go with you."

"Take him along, too?" Tom stared at the Secretary.

"Well, I suppose you wouldn't have to, every trip," said Domango. "Perhaps it would complicate your planet-hopping. But both the Bulbur and the Oprinkian seemed to think he'd prove to be an asset."

"It's hard to see why," said Lucy.

"Evidently, our Human relationship to our pets is unheard of among other Races in this Sector of the galaxy. The relationship would strongly impress the other Races you would meet," answered Domango.

"You mean Mr. Rejilla was impressed that way?" asked Lucy.

"Yes indeed," said Domango.

"How would we travel, then?" asked Lucy. "In a spaceship like the Jaktal Ambassador did; or like the one that must have brought Mr. Rejilla here?"

"Actually," said Domango, with a cough, "Oprinkians, like most of the older and more civilized Aliens, don't bother with anything as clumsy as a spaceship to travel around. But they can arrange to find you one— or perhaps find you passage on a spaceship going in the right direction and belonging to an Alien race that does use them."

Tom nodded thoughtfully and looked at Lucy and then back at Domango.

"Now," said Domango, "as I said, there's not a minute to lose. On the other hand, I understand something like this is really too important a step in your

lives to be decided on the spur of the moment.
Between the three of us, I should tell you, however,
it was the Oprinkian on the Council who first strongly
suggested that you should go out if at all possible. But
the Bulbur won't leave for another forty-eight hours;
and I should think I could give you that much time
to think it over, if you want."

Tom and Lucy looked at each other again.

"We better take the time," said Lucy.

"Yes," said Tom, "I was thinking that myself."

He wanted very badly to agree to the proposition—
to actually be out on Alien worlds, meeting the Aliens
themselves personally. But he was aware Lucy might
feel differently about it. In any case they would be
better off talking it over thoroughly between them.

The subject, however, did not seem to want to come
up on their way home. They drove back home relatively slowly, no more than a couple of hundred kilo-
meters an hour, in their family car, since this time no
official transportation had been provided. Actually, the
entire fleet of the Secretariat's official limousines was
now sitting empty in their garage, having been thoroughly polished and cleaned now that the reception
was over. It had not occurred to Domango, tired as
he was, to send one of them to pick Tom and Lucy up
for their interview; and perhaps that was just as well.

They were both the kind of people who liked to
think something over before talking about it.

Accordingly, they talked about other things. About
replacing the three regular-sized windows in their living room, which were getting old and letting the win-
ter air in; about buying tulip bulbs to put in this fall—
the front lawn, the neighbor children, and what might
happen to the lawn if those same children kept
insisting on using the tree there as second base for
their softball games.

All in all, small talk like this filled the rather long

time it took to get home. They pulled into their attached garage at last. The garage door went jerkily up in obedience to the signal Tom beamed at it from the car, and came jerkily down behind them once they were in.

"That reminds me," said Tom, as they were getting out of the car. "I've got to balance the tension in those garage door springs. I'll get on it right away."

"And I've got to balance the checkbook," said Lucy.

They went to work at their separate tasks, and continued with others, until by bedtime that night they had still not said anything to each other about Domango's proposition; and they were both thoroughly weary of thinking about it.

So they forgot about it for the night.

But the next morning, there it was waiting for them. Within a short time, both their residence and their domestic affairs were in better shape than they had been for many a week. Still, they each found more things that needed to be done. It was not until late afternoon that Tom wandered back into the living room and found Lucy collapsed in a chair.

"Where's Rex?" asked Tom.

"Out having a high old time chasing squirrels," said Lucy.

She stayed collapsed as she was, her arms flung out on the overstuffed arms of the chair, and merely stared at him.

Tom stared back with equal understanding and agreement. He flopped into another overstuffed chair facing hers. They gazed at each other for a long moment of silence.

"Well, I don't know," said Lucy, at last.

"Neither do I," said Tom.

There was a new silence and then Tom said, "I suppose we better discuss it."

"Yes," said Lucy, springing to her feet. "I'll go make some coffee right now."

But Tom was already on his feet and waved her back down again.

"This time I'll make the coffee," he said. "Be back in a few minutes."

A few minutes it was; since their kitchen unit gave water of any temperature on demand, and coffee only took a few moments to be delivered. Tom brought the two brimming cups back to the living room, gave one to Lucy, and sat down with the other himself.

"Well," he said.

"Yes," said Lucy. "In a way, there's everything to be said against doing it."

"That's what I've been telling myself," said Tom.

They talked about all the reasons for not being the first humans to go out to Alien worlds; finding themselves in perfect agreement. Then, almost without knowing they had done it, they found themselves beginning to compare these reasons with ones for going—on which they also seemed to be in perfect agreement.

They drank more coffee and talked.

Somewhere along the line, as the daylight was fading outside the living room windows, there was a brief break as Lucy went to the kitchen, and punched the kitchen unit for a pizza that they could eat while continuing to talk. She brought it back to the living room and they continued their discussion.

"Well," said Tom about three hours later, with the living room lights enveloping them in a golden glow, and the remains of the pizza forgotten on the coffee table, "it's settled then. We'd be crazy to do it."

"You're absolutely right," said Lucy.

There was a long pause.

"There's a couple of slices of pizza left," said Lucy, "would you like some?"

Tom shuddered.

"No thanks," he said.

Lucy looked with disfavor at the cold and aged slices herself.

"You know," she said, "if you were single—if you'd never met me and we hadn't gotten married—would you want to go out yourself on this Ambassador-at-Large business?"

"As a matter of fact," said Tom, "yes, I would. To tell you the absolute truth, I would."

There was another moment of silence as they gazed at each other.

"And if you were single," he said, "and had never met me. Would you go out?"

"You bet I would," said Lucy.

They sat and stared at each other for one last long moment.

"Well, that's it," said Tom wearily. "I guess we go."

"Right!" said Lucy—and suddenly, somehow, they were hugging and kissing each other.

"—After all," said Lucy, rather muffledly, "we're only young once."

Chapter 10

"I suppose you think of it, sometimes," said Lucy, as their Mordaunti spaceship descended on the capital city of Bug'raf, the world of the Lefazzi, a hospitable, jolly race that looked a little like three-dimensional gingerbread men and were reportedly both energetic and hospitable. In fact, it was said they had turned their world into something of a tourist attraction for other Aliens, and as a result its main cities and open areas were usually well populated with visitors.

"Think of it?" said Tom, instantly alert. He and Lucy had been standing side by side in their personal spaceship-suite, watching the city below growing larger on a viewing screen. "Think of what?"

Lucy did not answer at once; and Tom's mind raced to anticipate what she might have been referring to. So far things had gone well enough. The spaceship they were on was owned and operated by the Mordaunti Race, and so far those aboard had been very agreeable, if also very decidedly Alien. They had politely asked Tom and Lucy to keep to their own quarters aboard the ship; and effectively barred them from having much social contact with anyone else among them but the captain of the vessel himself. His name was Arknok; and he had explained to them that it would be necessary for the ship to let down here at

111

the city of Bug'raf to realign the drive control chamber.

"Think of what?" asked Tom once more of Lucy.

"Oh, what it would have been like," said Lucy, "if we hadn't been married and you had been offered the chance to go out like this all alone. It might have given you more freedom of action; and, come to think of it, I'm not really all that necessary. I never did get the briefing you got, or even the training in all the different alien languages. You could do very nicely without me."

"What gave you that idea?" said Tom.

"Oh, it just occurred to me," said Lucy. "I just saw you looking down at the city now with a sort of eager, half regretful look on your face, as if you were thinking of all the things you could do if you didn't have me along."

"That's nonsense," said Tom. "You entirely misread the look on my face. I wasn't feeling or thinking anything like that; so it couldn't possibly have shown on my face."

"If you say so," said Lucy.

"Lucy, if you don't mind—" Tom was interrupted by a nudge at his knee. It was Rex, holding his frisbee in his mouth and looking up at Tom with the soulful eyes of a neglected canine.

"Play frisbee?" telepathed Rex.

Trying to eradicate a false assumption on Lucy's part, and correct one on Rex's at the same time, was too much. Tom chose the simpler of the two problems.

"There isn't room, Rex!" Tom said.

Rex smiled happily, dropped the frisbee at Tom's feet, and bounced over to the far wall of the sitting room of their suite in three giant leaps.

"Play frisbee! Play frisbee!" he telepathed happily.

"What do you want me to do?" Tom demanded. "Throw it through the wall?"

But, of course there was no point in arguing with Rex—for that matter there was no point in arguing with Lucy. Tom picked up the frisbee, walked over to where Rex stood against the wall, and dropped the frisbee on the floor. He pointed a stern finger at it, lying between his toe and Rex's nose.

"Rex's frisbee!" he said sternly. "Guard! Guard, Rex."

"Guard?" said Rex. "Frisbee? Guard!"

He dropped down to lie with one paw on the frisbee and gently nibbled the edge of it. "Guard!" he told himself sternly.

"That's right," said Tom. He went back across the room. "Now, Lucy—"

The gentle chiming of the entrance bell to the door of their suite in the far end of the living room tinkled. Rex's head came up immediately.

"Come in," said Tom.

A seven-foot tall humanoid looking like a satanic Tarzan in purple robes stepped into the room. Rex growled, putting both paws on his frisbee; but stopped as Tom glared at him.

Tom turned back to the newcomer. A weapons harness covered the visitor's robes, with various types of weapons depending from it. He touched pale green fingers to his winged skullcap.

"Good morning, Captain," said Tom, touching his own eyebrow in the proper Mordaunti response. "May your Race live forever."

"And yourrr own *rrrace* also," replied the Captain, rolling his r's like a Scotsman. His black eyes glittered as he added affably, "I thocht I'd let you know that there'll be ample opportunity for you to stroll around the capital city of Bug'raf below, if you wish. We'll be on the ground at least half a day."

"Oh? Yes! Yes, that'd be fine!" said Tom, happily. "Yes. We will. Thank you so much, Captain."

"Not at all," replied the other. Touching his head again he went out.

"Bark now?" Rex asked.

"Certainly not!" said Lucy, so severely that Rex hung his head, though he remained on guard over the frisbee.

"You go by yourself, Tom," went on Lucy. "I think I'll just stay here with Rex."

"No! Rex stays; but you've got to come!" Tom hissed. Lucy turned and stared at him. Tom shook his head and put his finger to his lips. Lucy still stared.

Half an hour later, the ship was down and the captain came to escort his two human passengers to the exit ramp. Rex was left in the suite, still keeping a watchful eye on his frisbee.

A small wheeled device took them from the ship to a sort of terminal; and from there they wandered off into the winding, colorful streets that looked as if they had been lifted out of illustrations of an old book of fairy tales.

The streets were aswarm with a hundred other Aliens, besides the locals. Once they were well away from the airport, Tom started walking at a pace that had Lucy almost trotting to keep up.

"Tom!" she grabbed his arm. "Slow down. There's no reason for us to be in that kind of hurry!"

"Just around this corner," said Tom, dragging her around it and down to something like a sidewalk cafe, where they found seats at a table. A robot—a simple tank on wheels with a speaker grille near its top—rolled up to them.

"Alcohol, human-style, scotch flavoring, and cold distilled water, two," Tom said in the local language. The robot rolled away. "Lucy, I couldn't talk on the ship."

"Why not, for heaven's sake?" said Lucy.

"Did you notice how the Mordaunti Captain was talking to us this last time?"

"Not particularly," said Lucy. "He was talking English—with an accent . . ." She looked thoughtful.

"But I think he gave himself away, not knowing that I might suspect. Remember that line from my briefing that I quoted to you, back at home on Earth, before we ever thought that we might actually be out on alien worlds—'*Beware a Mordaunti when he starts to roll his r's. . . . Make a mental note of this and do not forget it.*' "

"Hmm," said Lucy. "You're right. He was rolling his r's. In fact, I did notice it at the time, but I didn't pay any attention to it. But maybe the Mordaunti just slip into that accent from time to time, without meaning any harm."

The robot rolled up and deposited two squeeze-bulbs before them. Tom produced his identity papers with the Secretariat's seal from Earth upon them. The robot punched a hole in them and went away.

Tom had not answered until the robot was well away. Now he leaned across the table to Lucy.

"I only told you about that one line," he said in a low voice. "You remember I wasn't supposed to talk about my briefing to anyone. But there was more to what I just quoted to you than that. It seems that the change in the way they talk is a definite, instinctive reaction in the Mordaunti to the fact that they are meditating something mischievous or evil. They can't help doing it, just like we humans give away the way we're feeling with our body language, without realizing it. According to the rest of my briefing, a Mordaunti talking like that could be a signal that our lives were in danger."

Lucy stared at him, her gaze suddenly sharpening.

"In danger?" she repeated, in a voice as low as Tom's. "That was why you didn't want to talk to me

on board the ship, in case they had some way of listening in on us?"

"Yes," said Tom, "and I think Rex sensed it—the
way dogs do, you know; and was trying to warn us."

"Oh, and I snapped at him," said Lucy.

"I don't think he'll worry about it," said Tom, "but
since we've been alerted to possible danger, if anything
happens to me, you'll have to carry on by yourself—"

"Tom!"

"I don't know that anything actually is going to happen," said Tom. "But just to be on the safe side, there
are things I ought to tell you; and never mind that the
briefing was given me with the understanding I'd
never divulge it to another human being. At that time
no one had any idea we'd be going out to Alien worlds.
It was simply informing me so I'd know how to deal
with Aliens who came visiting Earth."

"But something in the briefing's suddenly become
important to me?" asked Lucy.

"Exactly!" said Tom. "You see, it wasn't just a casual
suggestion, the Secretary advising us to go first to Cayahno. Another section of the briefing had already
informed him—and me—that while gatherings of all
representatives from those forty-three great powers are
held at regular intervals, emergency meetings can also
be held, without warning. There's one starting right
now on Cayahno, with forty-two of the forty-three representatives present. The Jaktal representative, of
course, has now been expelled. You can guess why."

"Because the Jaktal Empire is suddenly up for
grabs? Is that why this emergency meeting is going to
be held?"

"That's right," said Tom. "Now, at the time when
Domango asked us if we'd go out to the stars, I
believed myself still bound by my obligation not to
mention what was in the briefing to anyone else—even
you. But now the situation's changed drastically, since

the Bulbur suggested humanity take control of the Jaktal Empire. Domango didn't have to put it into words for me. My being sent out as Ambassador-at-Large would give me the credentials to be heard at that meeting, though of course until Humans are given a seat at that Council I couldn't consider myself a member. Not surprising, since I'm only a representative of a near-primitive race on one small world. But of course, it's vitally necessary that there be someone at that meeting who can give them the Human point of view, when they come to discussing their official attitude to whoever takes over the Jaktal Empire."

"Well what's the Mordaunti captain of the ship to do with all this?" asked Lucy. "You aren't getting to the point."

"I'm not sure there is a point," said Tom. "But because the Mordaunti unconsciously lapsed into that accent, I suspect him of somehow being connected with the Jaktals, or with one of the other races that would hope to take over at least a part of the Jaktal Empire. So, I think we should both be on guard."

"You're right," said Lucy, decisively. "So, what's your idea about what we ought to do?"

"Well, one thing I was planning to do, but hadn't mentioned to you," said Tom, "was talk to the Oprinkian representative when we get to Cayahno and see if he can't speed up the authorization for you to have the same sort of briefing I had. I'm almost sure he can, and will. So, if anything should happen to me— that's what you should do. Find the Oprinkian representative, once you get to Cayahno; explain you're the sole Human Ambassador-at-Large now, and what's happened to me; and that you'll need that briefing to shoulder the whole burden from here on."

"You're sounding pretty cold-blooded, the way you're talking about something happening to you!" said

Lucy. "I'm more worried about you than I am about Human politics on Cayahno!"

He calmly reached across the table and squeezed her hand.

"I love you, too," he said. "However—"

He broke off suddenly, looking up. A hush had fallen over the street and suddenly it was very empty. Every Being earlier in sight there had disappeared, even the serving robot and those at the other tables. Without warning, around the corner floated a metal platform with two odd-looking Aliens of different species on it.

The first was a stubby humanoid individual wearing a harness draped with what must surely be weapons. There were pistol-like things, tubes, a strange corkscrew-like device with an aperture at its far end, and other objects. He wore nothing else but the harness; and was completely hairless, with leathery brown skin. His face looked something like a bulldog's.

The other Alien, beside him, was about three feet tall, wearing a white robe, a sort of magician's cone-shaped hat and a long white beard, above which showed a bulbous nose and two large, purple, trusting eyes.

"Greetings!" boomed the harnessed individual, in the local Lefazzi language, bringing the platform to a halt at their table. As it settled to the ground he took a device from his harness and looked through it at Tom.

"Magnificent!" he said, switching effortlessly into English. "Just as advertised! Point seven two on the ferocity scale. Congratulations, my boy. I am Drakvil, Master Assassin—and you are my apprentice."

"Apprentice?" said Tom.

"Such good fortune is hard to believe, I know. But you are. I just picked you."

"Pardon me," said Tom. "But overwhelming as the honor is . . ."

"Tut-tut," said Drakvil. "Say no more."

"—I must decline—"

"WHAT?"

Drakvil suddenly paled all over his body until he was almost white. Gradually his color came back. He slowly extended a hand and pointed at Lucy.

"So," he said, "I think I see. Does that wilf belong with you?"

"I certainly do!" said Lucy.

Drakvil's arm dropped.

"Wilf-ridden!" he breathed. "I get an apprentice with one of the finest aptitude ratings ever recorded; and it has a wilf! But don't worry, my boy—"

He got down and began to rummage inside the back edge of the platform.

"—I'll free you."

"Tom!" said Lucy, clutching his arm.

"Shhh," hissed Tom. "It's all right—"

He was interrupted as the second Alien on the platform suddenly began to cry in a timid, despairing fashion.

"What's wrong with you?" asked Tom, turning on it.

"Oh, sir," sobbed the smaller Alien. "It would've been such an honor for a simple Pjenik like me. No real Assassin would lower himself to slay a Pjenik under the Pjonik class. Of course I know your honor's still only an apprentice and it's only to be a practice assassination, but—"

"Wait a minute," said Tom.

The Pjenik wiped its eyes with its white beard and sniffed.

"You mean," said Tom, "I'm supposed to practice assassinating on you?"

"Of course," snapped Drakvil, coming up with a metal plate tucked under one arm.

"—Begin with live targets right away," he went on. "The only way. I've got no patience with Master

Assassins that start their apprentices out on simulacra. No meat. No feel to it."

He unhooked one of the gadgets from his harness.

"Here," he said, "you can borrow my loset."

He shoved it into Tom's hand.

"Be careful with it. Meanwhile, I will psychoanalyze you and rid you of this wilfish affliction."

"You don't understand, I'm afraid, Sir Assassin," said Tom, in smooth, diplomatic tones. "I'm just ashore for a few hours from the Mordaunti ship at the space-port—"

Drakvil shook his head.

"Tut-tut, delusions as well. Not surprising, I suppose. My lad, the Mordaunti ship took off just five minutes ago; and, as you see, you are still here."

"Took off? But it had to have its drive control chamber realigned!"

"Come, come," said Drakvil. "To realign a drive control chamber takes several days. The ship needs to be completely torn down—that's one reason we Assassins never use ships. To work, my boy. There's your Pjenik, and you have the loset in hand."

He glanced at the metal plate he held.

"Meanwhile—let me see. I have some questions here. When you were an immature life form did you ever secretly like your primary immediate female ancestor?"

Tom was exchanging glances with Lucy. He whispered in English, "Play along—" and handed the loset back to the staring Master Assassin, bowing.

"Ordinarily," he said, "I'd be happy to assassinate this little fellow here—" he put his hand on the shoulder of the Pjenik.

"*Oh!*" cried the Pjenik in a sudden accent of joy. "It touched me! Its honor touched me!" It fell at Tom's feet and began kissing the toes of Tom's shoes.

"Oh, thank you, your nobleship—your kindnessness, little uncle."

Drakvil had gone completely white again. Now he began to return to his normal color and boomed with laughter.

"All right, you young rascal!" he said. "Caught me fairly that time. Takes some nerve to risk distracting a Master Assassin long enough to touch a piece of his property and adopt it. Well, you got away with it. Now, all that talk about the Mordaunti spaceship. Eyewash, right? That wilf of yours doesn't completely control you, after all! You deliberately got off here to put yourself in a position where I could see you and take you on as an apprentice, didn't you?"

"Er, yes," said Tom.

"Yes?" cried Lucy.

"Play along, we're stranded here without that ship . . ." muttered Tom between his teeth, still in English, smiling brightly at Drakvil.

"Well, come along then," said Drakvil, remounting the platform. "Bring your newly adopted nephew-slave along with you. Does the wilf have to come, too?"

"Just try to go without me!" said Lucy.

"Blasted faithful wilfs!" muttered Drakvil, as Tom stepped up on the platform and helped Lucy up behind him. "Sap the backbone out of a Being. Wouldn't have one myself for . . . hang on, here we go, across the galaxy to Pjo."

"Pjo?" echoed Tom. But already the city around them had vanished. The platform was now sitting in the midst of a featureless waste of sand, with what looked like a temple far off from the horizon.

"Well," Tom said, blinking a little in the light from a brilliant white dot that was evidently the local sun, "that's some transportation."

"The only way to go," said Drakvil with satisfaction. "Why travel by slow phase-shifting when this is available?

Of course there's always that statistical chance of coming out in the center of some sun or other. But death is an Assassin's constant companion, anyway. Let's get down to business."

He pointed to the distant, templelike building.

"Scene of your first assignment. First I'd better brief you." He reached down and touched something on the platform at his feet. A golden light flickered suddenly around Tom, who went down like a Pjenik shot by a loset, in a crumpled heap.

"Tom!" cried Lucy, frantically kneeling by him. He sat up groggily and shook his head.

"Who? What? Where—oh, hello, wilf."

"*Wilf!*" shouted Lucy. "Tom, don't you know me?"

"Of course I know you, wilf—I mean, honey. Help me up."

Lucy helped him to his feet. Tom shook his head a few more times.

"Bit of a shock, acquiring all that information at once. I'm all right, wi—Lucy. Oh, is that my harness?"

He reached out and took the cluster of weapons Drakvil was holding up to him. He put it on, checking its gadgets.

"Let's see," he said. "Spengs. Losets. Oh, and a gornul. Latest model, I see."

"Naturally," said Drakvil. "The workman is worthy of his tools."

"Thanks." Tom looked off at the building. "Subject in there?"

"Tom!" said Lucy. "What're you going to do?"

Tom ignored her and went on talking to Drakvil.

"Large establishment, I take it?"

"A Spranjik of the gark class," said Drakvil.

"Probably has a gnruth of jilks for guard?"

"Two gnruths, all porbornik-jilks."

"That's enough of this!" snarled Lucy. "Tom! You

answer me! What're you going to do? What are gnruths?"

"Bodyguard units of fifty jilks apiece," said Tom, absently, staring at the building.

"Tom, you aren't thinking of trying to assassinate someone who's got a hundred bodyguards?"

"You'll notice," said Drakvil to Tom, "the establishment is laid out for alnrits, both inside and out."

Tom laughed scornfully. "Alnrits!"

"Tom! Damn it, what're alnrits? Will you pay some attention to me?"

"They're disintegrators," said Tom, without looking around. "Don't bother me now, wilf."

Lucy shouted. "I am *not*, NOT a wilf!"

"Well, I'm off," said Tom. He reached down to do something to the platform, and disappeared.

"Bring him back!" said Lucy, fiercely to Drakvil.

But Tom reappeared again almost immediately, shoving one of the larger gadgets back into its holster on the weapons harness.

"Well, that was easy enough," he said. Lucy glared at him.

"Tom, you didn't—"

"Not yet," said Tom, cheerfully. "I just went in for a reconnoiter. On accelerated time."

"Report what you did, Apprentice," Drakvil said.

"Well, I approached the gate and spenged one of the jilks on outer guard there. When the rest turned to see what had happened, I slipped inside. As I expected, I found myself in a möbius maze of corridors. I calculated my way through, spenged the three jilks I found at the inner entrance, and took cover when the alarm sounded and a platoon came up at the double with porbornik guns at the ready."

"Did they suspect an Assassin was inside the gark?" asked Drakvil.

"No sir," answered Tom. "I overheard them guessing

that it was a dispossessed simulacrum—a rogue one. I ducked down a side street of the jilk quarters and found my way blocked by a full-armed tank. Well, of course a monstrosity like that could never be knocked out by a mere speng. I knew that."

"What did you do?" Lucy was staring at him.

"Oh, I just stood still in the center of the street, the way any ordinary dispossessed, mindless, rogue simulacrum might. And when it was close enough, I gave the tank a pong from my class two loset."

Drakvil beamed.

"Very good. And then?"

"I took over the tank and drove it through the inner defenses as if I was the tank crew coming back off duty. Inside I abandoned the tank and slipped into the ruler's personal family section of the gark. I set up a resolving point inside so that the platform could be brought in, and came back to get the three of you."

The pjenik squeaked with pleasure.

"Me, too? Oh, little uncle!"

"Yes," said Tom, giving Lucy a strange, meaningful glance that baffled her completely, "particularly you too."

"You wanted me to see you in action. Very good. The mark of a good Apprentice Assassin," said Drakvil. He reached down and touched the platform. They were all suddenly in a curtained alcove, dim-lit from above.

"Now what?" demanded Drakvil.

"You can watch through the curtain," said Tom. "Now I'm going to disguise myself and take on the nartled appearance of an illegal gossip-seller."

He reached down and touched the platform.

Lucy stifled an instinctive exclamation.

"It's still me," creaked the clawed and warty creature now standing before them. "Watch through the curtain."

Chapter 11

Tom slipped off the platform, parted the curtains and slid through into the corridor without. Lucy hurried to the parting, closely followed by Drakvil and the pjenik, and peered through. They saw a lofty ceiling hall with a guard of armed jilks, their eye-stalks stiffly at attention. A jilk officer was pilking* thoughtfully up and down beside them—his knees level with the base of his antennae.

Tom, in his gossip-speller's guise, sidled up to the officer, who growled something in a language Lucy could not understand.

"Blasted translingualspeaker!" muttered Drakvil, fiddling with something on his harness. "Ought to adjust automatically for everyone's ears—there!"

"—Juicy items," Lucy now heard Tom's whining as if in perfectly understandable English, "rare tidbits from strange worlds—"

The officer backed away distastefully and snapped, "Filthy creature! Keep your nartled claws to yourself."

"But Commander! I must go inside the door. A

Pilk: (verb) to proceed on any two of six legs, changing pairs of legs in sequence, according to a repeated rhythm, or pattern—associated with meditation or deep thought among certain insectoid Races: *Sector Reference, Volume 316. An.*

certain female of the ranking family—Your Freshness understands—"

"Your pass!" snapped the officer, extending a three-clawed hand.

"But she gave me no pass," Tom whimpered. "She simply said to come to this entrance—" He sidled closer. "Your Freshness would not want me to compromise the good name of one of the inner gark by mentioning it in public? But if I could talk to you aside—"

"Stand back," said the officer. "Very well." He let Tom lead him away from the guard. To Lucy's horror they approached the alcove, stopping just outside the curtain.

"Now," said the officer in a low, eager voice. Lucy was startled to see his eye-stalks wavering drunkenly. He panted. "I know you're lying. The female Orbash is the only one who could have called you, and she is elsewhere. So tell me! What have you got to sell?"

Tom whispered, "I knew Your Freshness was an addict, the moment I saw the angle of your eyestalks! It'll cost you."

"I am *not* an addict," panted the officer. "I like a little gossip like the next being, but I can take it or leave it alone. But price is no object. Quick, what've you got for sale?"

"Bend down, listen—" said Tom. The jilk officer doubled himself up. Tom threw a sudden hook to the officer's thorax. The officer, struck by Tom's fist just over his central nervous system, collapsed immediately, paralyzed for a good ten hours. He had fallen without a sound, and Tom shoved him through the curtain at Lucy's feet, meanwhile turning his appearance into a duplicate of the officer's. He marched across to the guard, which happily had been lined up facing in the opposite direction. Lucy, Drakvil and the pjenik watched.

"Attention!" Tom snapped from behind the armed

jilks. "Right face! Forward march." The soldiers marched off down the corridor.

"Magnificent discipline these porbornik-jilks have," remarked Drakvil, watching them out of sight as Tom, marching behind them, came level with the alcove and slipped back into it. "However, it sometimes works to their disadvantage."

"I assumed as much," said Tom regaining his natural appearance, much to Lucy's relief. "Now, shall we enter the gark-ruler's inner sanctum?"

He led the rest of them to the undefended door and opened it. They stepped through a series of filmy hanging curtains to find themselves in a pleasant, sunlit room where a fountain played. A pjenik in purple robes turned to look at them. Tom's adopted nephew-slave immediately prostrated himself before his duplicate.

"Rise, inferior," said the one in the purple robe. He helped Tom's pjenik to arise, and the two stood nose to nose, their white beards almost touching, their gentle eyes fastened in friendly fashion on each other. "To what do I owe the honor of this visit?"

"Rejoice, thrice-noble, sir," said Tom's pjenik. "You are about to be assassinated."

"Hardly a cause for rejoicing, inferior," the other protested mildly.

"It isn't, noble sir?"

"Not for a Pjonik pjenik, inferior. Possibly you're confusing my position with your own."

Tom's pjenik immediately prostrated himself again. "No, I didn't mean that."

He helped Tom's pjenik up once more. "I just mean we who are born to the purple don't consider being murdered quite such an honor as you lower classes."

"Really?"

"In fact," said the Pjonik pjenik, turning to Tom,

Lucy and Drakvil, "may I ask why I am being assassinated?"

"Why?" exploded Drakvil. "You ask *why*?"

"A natural question, isn't it?" asked Tom innocently.

"Why, I never heard of such a thing!" fumed Drakvil. "A subject asking why. What galactic nerve! If I hadn't promised you to my assistant here and an Assassin's word wasn't as good as his bond—" His fingers played angrily with the hilt of a wickedly curved knife attached to his harness.

"I suppose you don't know why, either, young apprentice?" said the pjenik sadly to Tom. "Well, I suppose I'll die not knowing. Farewell, inferior." The large eyes of Tom's pjenik began to fill with sympathetic tears.

"Go ahead," fussed Drakvil. "I can't. You must."

"No," said Tom.

"No?" said Drakvil, Lucy and the Pjonik pjenik all at once.

"No," said Tom, calmly. "I cannot, because of my wilf."

"I knew it!" bellowed Drakvil, turning chalk-white and staying that color. "That wilf! I knew it!" He turned to Lucy, who quickly got on the other side of Tom.

Tom faced him and said, "Once I would have gornuled this subject on the spot, without a moment's hesitation. In fact, with keen enjoyment. But my wilf has had its effect on me. This is—er—a far, far better thing I do than I have ever done before. The quality of mercy is not strained and no man is an island unto himself. If I should gornul this subject, I should be diminished, even as an island diminishes part of the main. Therefore never send to know for whom the bell tolls, because it's already tolled for me."

"Mad!" said Drakvil. "Stark staring, raving mad. Poor, poor boy." His color came back. His tone became more gentle. "Before I gornul you myself, Apprentice, and put you out of your misery—tell me. Why did you go this far before refusing to act?"

"It was the least I could do for the Master to whom I'd been apprenticed," said Tom. "I suspected your honor had been impugned. I had to actually get face to face with the subject and you at the same time to make sure. Now I know beyond any doubt."

"Honor?" said Drakvil, suddenly stiffening. "The honor of a Master Assassin impugned? Who would dare?"

"Who indeed," said Tom, nudging Lucy, "but an *amateur* Assassin?"

"Amateur?" Drakvil went chalk-white once more.

"Yes," said Tom. "I wouldn't have had the least suspicion of him, if it hadn't been for my wilf." He nudged Lucy again. "It noticed the difference in the way I was acting. Didn't you, wilf?"

"Yes, I did," said Lucy.

"It wanted to know what was disturbing me."

"Yes, I did."

"It warned me faithfully that this amateur was out to dispose of me."

"Er—" said Lucy, "yes, I did."

"Its warnings did not register on me properly until you slapped me with that briefing ray just before I went into the gark. In that briefing was the information needed to complete the picture. This amateur arranged for me to be left behind in Bug'raf, just as he hired you through the Assassin's Guild to try and train me as an Assassin's Apprentice. And he thoughtfully provided this innocent Pjonik pjenik as a subject for me to practice on, at less than the regular rates."

"Hmm," Drakvil said thoughtfully, his color returning. "What you say checks with my own knowledge, apprentice. But nothing of it affects my honor."

"I will explain."

"Go ahead," said Drakvil, taking a long, sinister-looking gadget from his harness. "I have to reset my gornul anyway. Take a couple more moments if you like."

"Thank you," said Tom. "I suppose you understand that what this amateur hoped and planned was that you would gornul me."

"How could he be so sure of that?"

"Because," said Tom, taking a deep breath, "he was prepared to violate your honor by forcing you to take on an apprentice that he knew would never pass the test. You see, he knew I had a wilf."

Drakvil's chubby, powerful fingers suddenly stopped moving on the gornul. He looked up and his dark eyes fastened on Tom's.

"He knew my wilf would stick by me," Tom said.

"Yes, I would," said Lucy.

"And that, faithful as it is to its principles and to me—"

"Yes, I am."

"—It would, wilflike, throw itself before my gornul when I attempted to assassinate the subject, thus creating a scandal that would reflect on you as my Master, and cause you to destroy me on the spot."

"Y—" began Lucy; and stopped dead, staring at Tom with eyes almost as big as a pjenik's.

Drakvil had beaten his previous paleness of shade. He was now so white he was nearly transparent.

"You see," said Tom to him, "he didn't care about the Pjonik here, whom he had no reason to hire assassinated. He didn't care about the expense he might be put to in buying a practice pjenik for me. He didn't care about the scandal which would blacken your name in the Assassins' Guild. All he was interested in was using you to get rid of me."

Drakvil was now not only nearly transparent, he was swelling like a balloon.

"Pardon me, little uncle," said Tom's pjenik meekly, "but why didn't he just hire the noble Assassin to destroy you in the first place?"

"Well, you see," said Tom in a kindly voice, "he couldn't. For the same reason I couldn't really adopt you. I'm an Ambassador-at-Large from a race that has not yet officially qualified for membership in this sector; but with Ambassador status I'm still legally protected against unlimited assassinations—although actually, being assassinated even once will permanently immobilize a Human. Most important, my Race hasn't ever subscribed to the Assassin Conventions. In fact— I'm on my way to Cayahno right now to discuss the Conventions and other things with forty-two of the forty-three other representatives of the leading, dominate Races."

Drakvil had finally found his voice. "Where is he?" he wheezed. "Where is he?"

"The Mordaunti Ambassador who, pretending to be the captain of a ship, marooned my wilf and me and hired you?" answered Tom smoothly. "I imagine he's on Cayahno by now. Very probably—" Tom glanced at his wristwatch "—he's already sitting down with the forty-one other representatives—in the Sector Council Building's Board Room."

"Platform!" said Drakvil, touching a spot on his harness. The platform appeared. "On!" he ordered. Tom jumped onto it and pulled Lucy up after him. Tom's pjenik started to scramble aboard also, then stopped, confused.

"Stay here, inferior," said the Pjonik pjenik. "I'll adopt you."

"Oh, little father!" said the pjenik, falling down before him. Drakvil touched the platform. The room winked out around them and they winked in again in a long, hall-like chamber, with a semicircle of seats around an oval table, filled with a rainbow diversity of different Beings. The Mordaunti Ambassador was standing in the open space before these seats, addressing the rest of the representatives.

"—Our responsibility to the former Jaktal members and those races formerly under their dominion—" he was saying, in some odd language; the words of which, however, a central translingualspeaker was now beaming into Tom and Lucy's ears in flawless English. He broke off abruptly as he saw the platform with its occupants.

"Now!" boomed Drakvil. Tom caught the Assassin's hand as he was closing it on his gornul.

"Just a minute," said Tom. "He's mine."

"Yours?" Drakvil turned on Tom.

"Though only an Apprentice, I believe I have rights under the Guild," said Tom.

"Yes," Drakvil admitted thickly.

"Then I believe I have the right of first offense from this being, and so may challenge him to a duel before you yourself take action?"

Drakvil glowered.

"I'm going to have to do some work on that briefing machine," he muttered. But he let go of the gornul. "Go ahead, then. I'll watch."

The Mordaunti had buckled slightly at the knees on seeing Drakvil. On hearing this he straightened up again and his hands spread inward toward his own weapon harness. He smiled at Tom.

"Though only an Apprentice," said Tom casually in an aside to Drakvil, but audibly enough so that his voice echoed through the chamber, "would you say I might prevail in a duel with this being?"

Drakvil snorted.

"Only!" he said. "*Only* an Apprentice! You've been briefed, haven't you? Naturally only another Guild member could hope to stand a chance with you, Apprentice or not."

The Mordaunti's knees began to give again. He tried to smile but his satanic grimace was a little loose at the corners.

"I just wondered," said Tom. "I wouldn't want the impression to get about the galaxy that I was trying to hide from the honorable Mordaunti Ambassador."

He got down off the platform and strolled thoughtfully, chin in hand, around the table; and sat down in a vacant chair he had spotted in the lowest tier of seats. Lucy was close behind him. The chair was a little large for him, being built to hold Jaktals, but he seated himself in it.

"Let me see," he said, "I will have to arrange for my wilf to be restrained, so that it cannot prevent—"

"Hold!" cried the Mordaunti Ambassador.

Tom looked up, surprised.

"No one could be more eager for a duel with a Being from Earth than I," said the Mordaunti. His knees were quite straight again. "But there is a higher duty: the obligations that fall upon one who is a Member of this Council."

"What?" said Tom. "I don't understand. You *have* to fight me."

"Alas," said the Mordaunti. "Forgive me."

"Forgive you? I insist you fight me. I insist—"

"Sadly, I must refuse. Sir, you have inadvertently seated yourself in the Jaktal chair, as a Member of this meeting. An Unconfirmed Member, of course, but still bound by the Council Membership rules."

"What?" cried Tom, looking about him. "What'd I do? You mean, just by sitting down here for a moment, I—"

"You invested yourself with a higher order of diplomatic responsibilities—even though you cannot yet be considered a legal Member of the council," said the Mordaunti. " 'Sector Interior Representatives and Council Members may not duel with each other.' That is a basic law of inter-Racial and interstellar politics. Otherwise, our meetings would become disasters."

"But I just sat down for a minute!"

"I'm sorry. The rule is strict."

"Damn it!" said Tom.

"We all sympathize."

"Why am I so absent-minded?"

"We all understand, I'm sure. It could happen to any newcomer. Unfortunately, ignorance of the rule is no excuse."

"My courage," said Tom, "will be called into question. The courage of the whole Human race will probably be called into question."

"Not at all," said the Mordaunti, smoothly. "I, myself, will be honored to introduce a resolution of confidence in your courage and that of every member of your Race."

"I oppose!" roared a large, tusked, walrus-like alien halfway down the table. Or rather, this particular Alien roared and the translingualspeaker changed his words into the various languages spoken by all there, including English for Tom and Lucy. "Today's subjects for discussion have already been accepted. Introducing a new item at this time is unconscionable!"

"I assent!" boomed the translingualspeaker as a series of squeaks came from a member so tiny that Tom and Lucy had to strain their eyes to locate it; until a sort of magnifying process suddenly went into effect, and they saw that it was something like a jaunty little seahorse from one of Earth's oceans, floating in mid-air above the seat of its chair. "All of me assents!"

A babble of squeaks, growls, roars, clickings—and a number of other sounds—overwhelmed the translingualphone, which this time made no attempt to translate for the benefit of Tom and Lucy. Then suddenly there was silence.

In that silence a member that looked like a Douglas

fir—in fact like an elegant Christmas tree that had not yet been decorated—grew another five feet to add to the ten-foot height it was already displaying in its chair, and slowly but steadily began to wave various of its branches.

The silence continued as it went on waving. After a while, Lucy put her lips close to Tom's ear.

"Do you know what's going on?" she whispered.

"I gather, from the information of my briefing," Tom whispered back in her ear, "that the tree-Member is making some kind of speech. But either it's in a language I wasn't given by the briefing; or for some reason it's completely untranslatable into speech—or the translingualphone would be passing on to us the message it's giving. I can't even imagine why it can't be translated. But the others are all paying attention to it—or him—or her, whichever. But I'm pretty sure we're expected to be quiet until the speech is over, along with everybody else."

Indeed, no one else was speaking, no one was moving. Even Drakvil was silent and motionless. Finally, after some while, the branches stopped waving and the tree—or whatever it was—reduced its height back to its original dimensions. Around the table, it could be seen that some of the humanoids had tears in their eyes.

"I thoroughly agree," said the one Oprinkian at the table, standing up. He spoke in English, looking directly at Tom and Lucy. Presumably the translingualspeaker was interpreting what he said to the others at the table. He turned and bowed to the tree-like member, who bowed majestically back, and the Oprinkian turned back to face Tom and Lucy again.

"Like our Member from Wavry," he said, "I honor the gallantry of our Accidental Member from the newly enlightened planet Earth. I agree also, that it would be unthinkable to interrupt today's schedule of topics to discuss the matter. As sponsor for the Race to which our Accidental Member belongs, I will be happy to act as host to him and his companion in Ambassadorship overnight; and I second, as suggested, the suggestion by the Member from Wavry that the unprecedented matter of this Accidental Membership be the first item for discussion at tomorrow's meeting."

There was a babble of Alien voices, and then chairs were floating backward, and the meeting was clearly breaking up. The Oprinkian left his own chair and came down to Tom and Lucy where they stood with Drakvil.

"Well, Tom and Lucy," he said, obligingly, "are you agreeable to accepting my hospitality until the next meeting?"

Tom and Lucy happily voiced their agreement. The Oprinkian turned to Drakvil.

"I will not venture to invite you, Master Assassin," he said, "knowing the rules of your order forbid you to trust the shelter of anyone's roof but that of a fellow Assassin. I take it then that the three of us will be parting from you?"

"Quite right!" said Drakvil. He frowned at Tom. "Behave yourself, Apprentice!"

He stepped back onto his platform and he and it vanished.

"Tell me, really," said Lucy that night, as they were preparing to retire on an Oprinkian bed that was like a golden cloud twelve feet around, "did that briefing really make you so dangerous? In just a second, like that?"

Tom climbed into the bed. Lucy was still in front of a four-way, three-dimensional image-mirror, tying the ribbons at the top of the filmy blue nightgown she had ordered from the room's robo-designer. Tom bounced experimentally on the bed. It bounced beautifully.

"Now there's a bed!" he said. "No, of course it didn't. I know all I need to know, but it'd take years of exercise and practice to make my muscles respond as they would need to for a direct confrontation in something like a duel. Drakvil, of course, wasn't going to admit I wasn't able, though. His honor as an Assassin was at stake. That's why I think he was secretly pleased I didn't have to duel the Mordaunti, after all— are you going to finish fiddling with that and come to bed?"

"In a minute," said Lucy. "I want you to tell me something first."

She was still looking into the mirror; and Tom knew she could see him clearly reflected there.

"What?"

"I want to know exactly what a wilf is. And you tell me the truth."

"Oh."

"Yes, oh."

"Well," said Tom, slowly, "they do look something like women. At least an alien might think they did. But they're really a totally different race—monosexual. It's just that they go around becoming deeply attached to beings of other races. Once they make friends, their faithfulness is proverbial, not merely in this Sector, but throughout the galaxy."

"But why?"

"Why?"

"Why," said Lucy, "do they become attached? What do they want to make friends for? What's in it for them?" She looked narrowly at Tom. "They look so much like us and they go around attaching themselves. I want to know why!"

"Oh," said Tom, "I see. Well, it's not what you might think at all."

"It isn't?"

"No," said Tom. "Different Race, and all that. It's just that wilfs have this very strong moral sense. They have extremely high principles and their greatest joy is in converting some other being to these same principles. Naturally, there's not much opportunity for them to improve other wilfs, these being as good as they can get already. So they try to get close to Beings of other races, in a strictly intellectual way. That's all."

"Oh," said Lucy, "that's all right, then."

She put out the lights and bounced into bed.

"I've got plenty of low principles," she said. "You like me that way, don't you? You'd better say yes."

"Yes," said Tom.

Chapter 12

"Can you explain something for us?" Tom asked. He and Lucy were having breakfast with the Oprinkian Council Member, whose name was Mr. Valhinda. To be correct, Tom and Lucy were having breakfast, and Mr. Valhinda was simply keeping them company, since Oprinkians dealt with nourishment in a slightly different fashion.

"Yes?" said Mr. Valhinda.

"We didn't hear a translation of the—er—tree-like Member who spoke so eloquently at the end of yesterday's meeting," said Tom. "Could you give us an idea briefly of what he said?"

Mr. Valhinda smiled.

"Actually," he said, "the honorable Member from Wavry did not actually say anything. You do not have the word in your language for what he did—perhaps the closest one you have is 'dance.' And what he dances are not words but information—therefore the T.L.-Speaker could not translate it understandably to you. If you should ever become a Council Member for your Race, you will learn to comprehend what he does in this respect."

"You were all deeply moved," said Lucy.

"It is the remarkable majesty and grace with which he addresses us," said Mr. Valhinda. "His 'dancing' expresses itself in emotional shades and terms. We are always deeply moved by these."

"But what did he *tell* you?" Lucy said.

"Briefly," said Mr. Valhinda, "he spoke about your gallantry and courage in taking the Jaktal's seat and predicted that, primitive as you were—you will forgive me for saying that, I am sure, Tom and Lucy—great things might be expected of your Race. In fact, he suggested that the Council take under advisement the idea of putting you in a position to possibly demonstrate the full extent of your qualities."

"That was nice of him," said Lucy. "But what about this business of Tom being an Accidental Council Member?"

"Oh," said Mr. Valhinda, with a wave of his black-furred hand, "that can be taken care of as a matter of routine. Time-consuming, but merely routine. You understand, what is concerned there is not your Accidental seating in the Jaktal chair, but the implications of what that might mean for the future of your Race, and for the Sector. Our immediate concern is whether or not to allow an Ambassador-at-Large from a primitive, and only conditionally accepted, Race—who has already managed to become an Apprentice Galactic Assassin, as well as 'accidentally' seating himself at the Council table of the Sector's Senior Representative Members—to travel around freely in our Sector. And if so allowed, how to be governed and directed in his and her movements."

"Oh," said Tom. Lucy looked serious.

"Yes," said Mr. Valhinda. "The Member from Xxxytl—somewhat resembling a small marine being called, I believe, a 'seahorse' on your native world— suggested there might be a possibility of using you under Council direction, in situations that would reveal your capacity in several areas—one of them being the critical one of diplomacy. Relationships between interstellar races are always touchy; and Beings who can deal with problems that arise in connection with this are highly appreciated."

"You think we're a couple of those?" asked Lucy.

"The Member from Xxxytl suggested that possibly you are," said Mr. Valhinda, "together."

"He did?" said Lucy.

"Yes, indeed," said Mr. Valhinda. "Come to think of it, however, that brings me to two subjects you mentioned last night before we parted to take our rest. As regards your co-worlder, Rex. The Mordaunti Council Member deeply apologizes, but by an error, he was taken back to the Member's homeworld of Mordaunt. He's now being sent here to rejoin you. Meanwhile, it seems he's been making friends everywhere and telling them all about you."

"Telling?" said Tom.

"How can he—" said Lucy, almost in the same instant.

"Oh, telepathy, of course," said Mr. Valhinda, with a wave of his hand. "All civilized and many barbarian Races have the capacity. The universal language. Limited, of course. Still, you must really pick up the knack of it as soon as you have a spare moment."

"But you said 'all about us,'" persisted Lucy.

"Yes, indeed," said Mr. Valhinda, "he can talk about one or the other of you, or his house and territory at great length, if either of your names is mentioned. But I mentioned this just in case you've been concerned about him."

"Oh, Rex will do all right," said Lucy. "But how about that Mordaunti apology—'error'! I'll just bet!"

"I'm afraid the Member from Mordaunt is not yet as civilized as some of the Council thought. As your Race may eventually be, the Mordaunti were only probationally allowed to occupy a seat acquired by conquest. It will probably fail confirmation to the Council, now, because of this barbaric attempt to keep you from Cayahno. But they are already returning Rex as swiftly as they can, with apologies."

"That's better," said Tom. "But you mentioned two subjects we brought up last night—?"

"Oh yes," said Valhinda. "I believe, you, Tom, suggested to me that I might authorize Lucy to receive the same briefing that you did, on Sector information and other Alien languages. I said I would speak more to you about it this morning."

"Is there any problem with it?" asked Tom.

"I'm afraid there is," said Mr. Valhinda. "An insurmountable problem. Unfortunately the fact is that rules governing such briefing are made, not within the Sector, but within Central Galactic Government, itself. I'm sure an exception could be made and Lucy given permission—but the red tape involved would cause us to face about a two-hundred-year delay in getting it from Galactic Center."

"Oh," said Lucy.

"I understand your dismay," said Mr. Valhinda. "But you see how impossible it is for the Council to authorize any such thing. It is even more impossible for me, as a member of your sponsoring race, to authorize it; since according to the rules of primitive contacts, you are a pair. Since one of you has been briefed, that's considered all that is necessary for both of you to act. A possibly fallacious assumption in this particular instance; but there it is—and I have a responsibility to my own Race not to endanger them by any illegal move in the process of sponsoring another, newer Race."

He stopped, and his eyes met Tom's meaningfully. It was an act as obvious as a wink. Tom stared back, puzzled.

"Tom," Lucy said, nudging him. "I understand. Don't you?"

Tom looked at her, frowning. Then, suddenly his frown cleared.

"Why, yes," he said to Mr. Valhinda, "I understand perfectly. But perhaps you'll tell me what the penalty would be if I did share my knowledge illegally with Lucy?"

"Well," said Mr. Valhinda, gazing out a nearby window, "in that case . . . since you're primitives, and not really even under Sector authority yet, it would only be a black mark against you—but the same Galactic red tape would apply. By the time the black mark was ready to be put there, the justification for your doing it—if it turned out to be justified—would already have been accepted. The two would simply cancel each other out. Oh, Galactic Government might decide to make something of an example of you individually, Tom. But there would be no repercussions as such against your Race as a whole—which is the important part."

"I've changed my mind," said Lucy, "I don't want to know."

"Of course," said Mr. Valhinda, "if the two of you, working together, end up reflecting great value and honor on your Race and the Sector, you would individually, both of you be applauded rather than condemned."

He exchanged a further meaningful glance with Tom and Lucy—just as a platform, like the one Drak-vil had carried Tom and Lucy on, floated into the room and approached the Oprinkian.

"Forgive my presumption," the platform said in a polite, middle-range voice, "the rest of the Sector Council has fully informed itself now on the background of the two Humans. It is ready to officially begin the day's meeting and discuss the matter. They would appreciate your presence, Mr. Valhinda, bringing the two Humans with you."

"Ah, yes," said Mr. Valhinda. "I think we should be going."

Tom and Lucy left the breakfast table with their host and mounted the platform. Tom hastily adjusted the buckle of his Assassin's weapons harness as he climbed aboard. A second later they were in the Council room and all the other Members seemed to be there, except for two vacant chairs, one being the Jaktal seat Tom had sat down in the day before.

Mr. Valhinda got down from the platform and started for his own chair, then stopped when he realized Tom and Lucy had not moved. He turned back.

"The Jaktal chair is yours, temporarily, of course," he said reassuringly to them. "I believe it's roomy enough for the two of you."

Then he turned back and went on toward his own chair. Tom and Lucy went down to the Jaktal chair, and its large seat did accommodate them both comfortably, sitting side by side. They looked around the table.

All eyes seemed to be fixed on them. But then the Member from Wavry grew five feet in its chair again, and began to wave its branches around. Everybody's gaze turned to observe the movements. The Member from Wavry continued, clearly making another statement, if not another speech.

"I wish we could know what it's saying!" whispered Lucy in Tom's ear.

"So do I," whispered Tom back.

But just at that moment, the Member from Wavry ceased waving its branches, shortened itself by some five feet and stood still.

"I heartily concur!" chittered the little seahorse-like Alien from Xxxytl; and Lucy, having been illegally taught some Xxxytl, and bits of other languages, by Tom the night before, understood him. The magnifying glass effect was on; and she, like Tom, could see him clearly, floating upright above the seat of his chair, with his tiny fins fanning back and forth energetically to emphasize what he said. "The suggestion is an excellent one!"

Belatedly, the translingualphone, now back in action, translated the words faithfully and unnecessarily into loud, clear English.

"I oppose!" boomed the tusked, walrus-like alien, glaring at the Member from Xxxytl from the opposite side of the table. "The idea of entrusting a Galactic Sector empire of some size to the primitive actions of a young, uneducated, near-barbarian Race, is against all that this Council and Galactic civilization stands for. We are putting a number of other, as yet unseated but promising, near-barbaric Races at risk. It is like giving a new-born being the powers that should only be wielded by an educated adult of that Race, even if that Race was qualified."

"That objection is entirely beside the point!" chirped the seahorse-like Xxxytl Member. "We have here an unparalleled opportunity, not merely to educate a promising young Race in the process of supervision of other Races, but by exposing them to the problems of such supervision, to educate this Council on ways of developing a new pattern for bringing younger Races along with greater speed than we have ever been able to do before! I most strongly concur— and I repeat that again—I most strongly concur!"

"Would the honorable Member from Xxxytl," roared the walrus-like alien, raising his head and flashing his tusks dangerously, "be willing to go on record with this Council as having an admitted Racial partiality for these two-in-one Humans?"

"Would the honorable Member from Duhn—" chittered the seahorse, bouncing up and down in mid-air, "—be prepared to issue an apology for what he has just said and which implies an unacceptable slight against myself and the whole Xxxytl Race?"

"I might also point out," Mr. Valhinda's voice gently inserted itself between the voicings of the two other Members, "with regard to the Member from Duhn, who spoke of two-in-one Humans—that the Human Race is simply bisexual, not two-in-one. That is not the same thing as individuals of that Race having two separate bodies apiece, as some Races have; nor the ability our fellow Member from Xxxytl is accustomed to having, in his own Race."

A flash of insight suddenly lit up Tom's mind. Recalling the enormous, whale-like Alien of his briefing, he wondered briefly if it was, somehow, the other half of the tiny seahorse shaped member. If not, what was the ability of the Xxxytl that had been referred to?

"Bisexual?" inquired a large snake-like Alien, coiled in a chair and with a tapestried skin in the colors of red, green, white and blue. "No parthenogenesis at all?"

"None," said Mr. Valhinda.

"Poor things," murmured the snake-like Member to itself.

"Bisexual, bisexual . . . imagine that! However," the walrus-like Member from Duhn lifted his head proudly once more, "no Member of the Race of Duhn has apologized for anything in our known history."

"May I suggest," said Mr. Valhinda, "that if, instead of apologizing, you simply withdraw your implication, the Member from Xxxytl might withdraw his demand for an apology?"

"Well . . ." said the Duhnian, looking doubtfully across the table at the seahorse.

"I will be glad to withdraw my demand for an apology," said the Xxxytl, "on assurance from the Member from Duhn that no slight was intended to my Race."

"I do so withdraw," said the walrus.

"And I withdraw my demand," said the Xxxytl.

"That matter being settled," went on Mr. Valhinda, "perhaps the Council could take a vote on the suggestion of the Member from Wavry, that the Member from Xxxytl a moment before so eloquently and wisely endorsed."

"Well said!" said what looked like an owl wearing spectacles with heavy tortoiseshell rims down near the far end of the table from Tom and Lucy. It was impossible to tell whether the spectacles were a natural part of his body or merely a device he was using. "I do so move."

"I second it," said the snake-like Alien, uncurling slightly.

A clamor of musical sounds, chiming on either one of two different chords, rang through the chamber all at once.

"The motion is carried by a two-thirds vote of the Council," announced the voice of the T.L.Phone. "The Humans are temporarily confirmed as Ambassador-at-Large for their Race and also—in the form of the coupled pair from Earth—temporarily and provisionally instated as Representatives to this Council for the empire of Races formerly controlled by the Jaktal Race; this to include the Jaktal Race as it presently exists—"

Lucy's hand squeezed Tom's hand out of sight below the table. He squeezed back. The translingualphone was being noisy again.

"—The Ambassador-at-Large from Earth is to make contact with other Races and empires within this Sector, but with none above their own comprehension level, without direction. They will be guided in this by a representative of their sponsoring Race, who is presently also a Member of this Council. It is suggested that that direction begin immediately; and

therefore the Humans are excused as of the present
moment, to be accompanied by the Oprinkian Member, who will direct them to their first world-of-call.
We will now turn to other matters for consideration
by the Council."

Mr Valhinda was already standing up and stepping
away from his chair. Tom and Lucy left their own and
followed him out of the Council chamber.

"No," said Tom, "try it again, Lucy. *'Gratkl!'* "

"*Gratkl*," said Lucy.

"No, no," said Tom, "you've got to come down hard
on the *k* and emphasize the end of the word—and
snap it all out! Try again."

"*GratKl!!*" snapped Lucy.

"Fine," said Tom.

"Does it really mean *'if you ever offend me one of
us must die'*?" said Lucy. She tried it again. "*Gratkl!*"

"Absolutely," said Tom. "You're doing it beautifully
now and that's just the way it should be. No, it's
roughly the same as saying simply 'hi, how are you' in
our language."

"You mean they don't mean it?"

"Oh, they mean it all right," said Tom. "It's just
the way the Skikana are. Very, very touchy and brave.
Coming down on that *k* in a word is very important—
it shows you mean it."

"Well, I'm glad you're glad," said Lucy. "But I hope
I don't have to say it. Are we almost down yet?"

Tom looked out the window of the spaceship at the
ground coming up at them.

"Almost there," he said, "and I think we're all
ready."

He looked around them at the lounge of the Imperial suite in which they had made the voyage to this
world of Mul'rahr. Four Hugwo lance-gunners stood
scattered about the lounge, like statues at rigid

attention. They looked like nothing so much as over-sized clams, equipped with armored legs and arms, their tall lance-guns upright in their grasps.

Luckily, thought Tom, the Hugwos did not understand English—in which he and Lucy had been talking—and while they could understand Skikana, that one word would have had little meaning for them without its context.

"I keep reminding you," Tom said, "how serious this is. As my Consort, you've got to be just as aggressive as I am. Otherwise the Skikana won't respect us."

He ran his fingers of his right hand through his close-cropped brown hair.

"We've been put in a position of over-extending our resources by being named as head of the existing Jaktal Empire—" He broke off. A fifth Hugwo, the corporal in charge of the Honor Guard of Lance-gunners, had just clanked in with a message in code which he handed to Tom. "—Thank you, Corporal."

"Sir!" shouted the Hugwo. He clanked backwards three paces, saluted with a precision for which these mercenary soldiers were famous, and became rigid. Both he and Tom had spoken in the lingua-franca of the civilized worlds of the Galactic Federation, which Lucy now understood. Tom scanned the message rapidly, translating as he read. He had had the recent codes briefed into him by Mr. Valhinda before leaving Cayahno.

"Oh, no!" he said. "This was all we needed!"

"What is it?" asked Lucy.

"Almost the worst possible thing that could happen," said Tom. "They've just opened up a branch of the Sector stock exchange on Earth. Domango was against connecting to the master stock board for this Sector on Cayahno so quickly. He felt we ought to learn how its elements worked—and he was right. But it seems there were powerful economic interests that couldn't wait for a chance to invest off-Earth. Well, the interests got their way; and now as a result a consortium of them have invested Earth resources heavily in the future development of the Wockii, the sub-dominate Race here on Mul'rahr. I wonder if that's why Mr. Valhinda sent us here?"

"I wouldn't be surprised," said Lucy. "There're always people like that. I take it that investment could be the wrong thing to do?"

"The Oprinkians consider it extremely risky," said Tom. He snapped a pocket loset from his Assassin's weapons harness and hastily disintegrated the message blank. "Earth could be plunged into debt for thousands of years if the Wockii futures are a dud."

"I gathered," said Lucy, staring at the spot where the ashes of the message would have been, if there had been any ashes at all, "something like that. But what makes them doubt the Wockii Race's future worth?"

"They were afraid of what's just happened. With the Sector stock market open, our over-eager and interstellarly ignorant investors plunged heavily on what looked like attractive investments. The Wockii futures looked attractive because they were so cheap. But Racial Futures are the most risky investments in the galaxy, according to my briefing—just imagine anyone who had their own worth solidly invested in Jaktal Futures, for example, up to a few weeks ago."

"I suppose some being did—they must have," said Lucy thoughtfully.

"Oh, yes," said Tom. "They would have thought investment in the Jaktal Empire was as safe as anything in the galaxy. Of course, what our investors on Earth just did was exactly what the Sector Investment Sharks had been waiting for. They immediately bought up the Jaktal futures shares that had been sold, and called for immediate repayment by our own Race."

"Why us?" said Lucy. "We shouldn't be responsible for the Jaktal debt, should we?"

"Remember," said Tom, "the Council provisionally confirmed us as possessors of the Jaktal spatial Empire."

"Well, in that case," said Lucy, "we ought to be able to use the Jaktal resources to pay these sharks off."

"Far from it," said Tom; "in a case like this we're like trustees without authority. A provisionally-awarded Empire is most strictly protected against use of its assets by those temporarily awarded control. That's why the Sharks have filed for repayment in Earth Human futures."

"We should tell them they'll have to wait until we're in control of Jaktal resources."

"We have," said Tom. "That's not the problem. The problem was an immediate effect in the Wockii Futures on the Interstellar Futurities Exchange. A bad wobble."

"Wobble?" cried Lucy. "What's that in ordinary language?"

"In ordinary language," Tom said, grimly, "the bottom dropped out of the market. On Cayahno now you can't give away a share of Wockii Futures; and when that happens, the Sector Council takes charge and enforces a schedule of payments from the debtor Race, beginning immediately. Already, on Earth, valuables such as useful minerals and other reserves are being readied for shipment to Sector markets, to begin payments to the Sharks that sold us the Wockii Futures. Eventually Earth will be stripped to the bone; and there'll still be interstellar credits owing."

"But why payments when the buyers bought and paid for them in the first place? Having that payment should take care of—" Lucy broke off. "Wait a minute! Do you mean the Wockii Futures were like commodity futures trading on Earth? You buy on margin—put up fifty dollars to buy five thousand dollars worth of something—but you can end up owing five thousand dollars if the price of it goes to nothing in the market?"

"Right!" said Tom.

They were silent for a minute.

"Well, at least," said Lucy, "we weren't on Earth when it happened, so there's no way we can be involved in this personally, until we have to go home, so—"

"Wrong!" said Tom. "You and I are now provisionally seated on the Sector Council, remember? That means we can be blamed for accepting control of the Jaktal Empire in the first place."

"But that's not reasonable—"

"Of course not," said Tom. "But Mr. Valhinda thinks the Sharks themselves suggested to our Human buyers of the Wockii shares that they blame us; and they have."

"That's nonsense," said Lucy, "no sensible person would believe for a moment that—"

"Want to bet?" Tom said. He pressed a button on his Assassin's weapon harness. The button immediately began to feed out a thin rolled sheet of paper.

"Why, that's the front page of one of our own newspapers in English," said Lucy. "How does the button do that?"

"I don't know," said Tom, grimly. "But look at what's on the page."

"The headlines take up more than half of it," said Lucy, fascinated. "They say—"

She broke off suddenly, staring. The sheet of paper had emerged all the way and unrolled itself into her hand. She and Tom read:

Inexperienced Ambassador-At-Large Obligates Human Race To Untold Future Generations Of Poverty

Jaktal Debt More Than Earth Can Pay In Millennia

Wockii Futures Not Worth Paper They're Written On

*"Recall Tom Parent and kill
him slowly!" chants angry crowd.*

At approximately 9:15 PM, Eastern Standard Time yesterday, Tom Parent, ALIEN AFFAIRS appointed Ambassador-at-Large, accepted the Jaktal Empire . . .

"How could they?" cried Lucy, indignantly. "When it was the investors' fault, not yours—or mine?"

"I suspect we're being used as scapegoats by whoever was actually responsible," said Tom.

"But this is terrible!" said Lucy. "We could go home and find everybody hating us—or maybe they wouldn't let us come home at all!"

Tom had begun to pace back and forth on the floor.

"Both the sixth and seventh of my para-instincts activated by the Assassin's briefing are alerted by this whole business of the Wockii futures. My seventh, in particular, is very positive about it. It was all too easy, and now we're committed. The Sector stock Sharks have spread a rumor that the Wockii have recently shown evidence of being forever incapable of acceptance by the Sector Council. If it weren't for that, the Wockii Futures could be placed in escrow for repayment of the Jaktal debt—so freezing the Jaktal creditors' claims against Earth. This would freeze any payment until either the Wockii were proved incapable of acceptance—say, they were predators on another possibly acceptable Race—or some chicanery is somehow involved."

He stopped pacing and stood eye to eye with Lucy.

"You think there's been chicanery?" demanded Lucy.

"I have no proof. My ninth para-instinct has no doubt of it. Still, how can I prove it? And if I can't prove it, as Ambassador-at-Large I'll have to let things follow their natural course, which at best means condemning our Earth essentially to slavery for several millennia."

"Then we'll have to uncover the chicanery. That's all," said Lucy, firmly.

"Yes . . ."

Tom started pacing again, then paused to glance at a screen across the room, which showed a wide expanse of concrete landing pad and a battalion of what looked like six-feet-tall praying mantises, armed and standing strictly at attention. "We're almost down. There's the Skikana Honor Guard drawn up to greet us. From now on be careful what you say. Even a mountaintop ten miles away has ears. Only in our ambassadorial quarters or aboard ship here—"

The landing bell of the ship rang suddenly through all the rooms, followed by a distant thrumming that seemed to pierce the hull and vibrate in their bones, in a melodious but unhearable way.

"What's that?" cried Lucy.

"The Skikana battle harps," said Tom. "You'll see them when we go out. They vibrate so powerfully they can be heard right through the hull of the ship. "Come on now. We get off first. It's protocol. Corporal!"

"Sir!" shouted the Hugwo Corporal, springing to life.

He rapped out orders in Hugwo and the lance-gunners formed up behind Tom and Lucy. Together they all marched out of the suite, down the ship's main corridor, and headed toward the air-lock.

Chapter 13

Just before Tom and Lucy could actually step through the air-lock entrance, however, a beetle-like alien, reddish-brown in color, came rushing up the outside gangway with a white rope, the end of which it pulled through the air-lock and laid against a metal part of the air-lock door, to which it clung.

"A cord of honor and acceptance," murmured Tom to Lucy as they stepped forward to the lock. The beetle-alien was standing at attention, beside it.

"*Gratkl*," said Lucy graciously to him, as they came level.

The beetle-alien immediately fell to the floor of the lock and tried to curl itself up, as well as its carapace would allow it, whimpering.

"He's not a Skikana," said Tom, "just one of their lesser-race servants. He thought you meant that you were about to have him executed." He turned to the whimpering beetle. "*Brnl Duhl jokt*," he added in a reassuring voice.

The beetle jumped up, looking joyful. It saluted, and resumed its stiff stance at attention beside the rope it had just attached. Tom and Lucy went through the port and down the ramp.

The wild screaming of the Skikana harps suddenly grew so loud that Lucy halted. Tom halted with her.

"They'll quiet down when we reach the bottom of the gangway," he shouted into her ear. "Come on now. We have to lead the procession. Corporal!"

"Sir!" shouted the Hugwo corporal behind him. He rapped out orders in Hugwo and led a dozen of the lance-gunners in order down the ramp behind Tom and Lucy. They marched out onto the hard surface of the landing pad. The harps quieted somewhat.

Before them were what looked like thousands of Skikana, bearing sword-like and gun-like weapons, and lined up as if on parade in units with ranks ten feet deep and twenty-five Skikana wide.

"Be sure not to squint," hissed Tom at Lucy in English as they went. "I know the sun over this world's very bright. But there's almost nothing Skikanas mightn't interpret as an insult. They take offense at the slightest provocation."

With the Hugwos before and behind them, Tom and Lucy marched through the lane between the units directly ahead of them, Lucy trying valiantly not to squint in spite of the sunlight that made the whole scene waver through a film of tears. They halted. The Skikana battle harps were now in view, lined up behind the troops; great, seven-foot, triangular, metal-stringed affairs, each resting on a spike driven deep into the hard fabric of the pad itself.

". . . And may I also present my Co-Ambassador, the Consort Lucy, Colonel?" Lucy heard Tom shouting in Skikana. She cleared her vision in time to see a six-foot-plus, praying-mantis shape leaning stiffly over her. The harps stopped playing.

"H-honored to touch acquaintance with you, sir," she managed in the Skikana tongue herself.

"Madam!" snapped the Skikana Colonel with a frosty bow. "May you dine on your worst enemy by sundown!"

"Oh, thank you!" said Lucy. "May you dine on yours even sooner than that!"

To her surprise she saw Tom frown.

"Madam!" Stiffening, the Colonel clashed his jaws together almost spasmodically. Oddly, a little froth appeared between them. "I would not presume! We Skikana take no advantages and need none. To dine before the Consort of my guest! Skikana manners would not permit!"

"Oh, I didn't mean—" Lucy was beginning. But Tom, with diplomatic smoothness, was already stepping into the breach.

"Happily," he said, "I may inform the Colonel that my Consort has already broken her fast, this day."

"May I be the first to congratulate her, then!" said the Colonel, relaxing. He relaxed, in fact, quite noticeably; and his gaze became unfocused. Then he pulled himself together with a jerk and clashed his jaws again. "Follow me. I will escort you to your quarters."

He led them and their Hugwos to a waiting flying platform, which took off with him and them just as the battle harps struck up once more.

"Whoof!" said Lucy in English, rubbing her ears when they were at last safely alone in their Ambassadorial suite at the Skikana fort. "What was that they were supposed to be playing?"

"None Shall Interrupt Our Feast," replied Tom. "Hmm. Did you notice anything odd about the Colonel?"

"I couldn't tell," said Lucy, truthfully. "Everything he did and said seemed odd to me. What's that you're humming?"

"That song of theirs they just played," said Tom, thoughtfully. "The Skikana are so touchy they're likely to give themselves away with anything they do. Something is definitely rotten about that whole business of Wockii Futures."

"I'm beginning to agree with you," said Lucy, "but what can we do about it?"

"Play along, and hope for a clue," said Tom, solemnly. He frowned. "What puzzles me," he said, "are the Skikana themselves. They took protectorate rights over the Wockii originally; and that by definition means they had to give up any right to a direct interest in Wockii Futures. So they shouldn't care one way or another about the gyrations of Wockii Futures on the Sector's stock exchange—but I can't escape the feeling they're mixed up in it somehow."

"Maybe we can think of some way to get them to give themselves away," said Lucy. "Betray their connection to the stock matter, I mean."

"That's a good idea," said Tom, thoughtfully.

He stepped across the room to a communications screen, and pressed a key. A second later the face of the Skikana Colonel appeared.

"Sir Ambassador!" said the Colonel and champed his jaws. "In what way may I serve you?"

"You may supply me with an escort, my dear Colonel," said Tom. "I, with my Hugwos and the Consort Lucy, will start for Wockiiland, immediately."

The colonel stared out of the screen blankly at him for a moment.

"But, Sir Ambassador," the Skikana said, "it has been arranged for Wockii chiefs to come to the fort, here."

"No doubt. However," said Tom, with diplomatic steeliness in his tones, "I have concluded that it is of the utmost importance for me to contact—" he bent a severe glance upon the Colonel in the screen "—the only subdominate race of Mul'rahr immediately."

"Sir!" The Colonel's jaws champed. "A banquet has already been ordered!"

"We shall go to it, then, but leave immediately after

putting in an appearance. Good day," said Tom, and cut the connection.

Almost immediately, however, he activated the screen again, this time with a view outside the fort gate looking backward into the wooded hills of the wild native countryside, toward Wockiiland.

"Who are you looking for?" said Lucy, after a moment.

"Watch. Wait," said Tom, without turning his head. Lucy watched. After a moment or two, a platoon of Skikana soldiers, mounted on individual flying platforms, left the gate and skimmed with haste toward the hills.

"I see," said Lucy, "The Skikana are involved with the Wockii in some illegal way, I'll bet—even without having one of your para-instincts."

"I'm sure you're right," said Tom. "The pot is starting to boil. Clearly for some reason the Skikana want to warn the Wockii against my coming. Why? There must be something in Wockiiland they don't want me to see."

The doors to their quarters gave forth a mellow chime, interrupting him. A second later the Hugwo corporal returned from answering it, leading a Skikana Captain of regulars, lean and hard-bitten in his insectoidal way, but just at the moment with unfocused eyes.

"Bells . . ." murmured the Captain, dazedly.

"Sir!" shouted the Hugwo Corporal to Tom, and the Captain came to. "A visitor to speak with the Ambassador, sir!"

He saluted and stepped back. The Captain pulled himself together and bowed to Tom and Lucy.

"Sir," he said, "I am Captain Jahbat of the Eighth Skikana here at Fort Duhnderhef. Possibly you noticed the medals on my prothorax?"

"Indeed," said Tom, his eyes narrowing.

"They are poor things, no doubt, in the eyes of an Assassin," said Jahbat, bowing again, gracefully. "Nevertheless I must confess to a nodule of pride in the medal on the far right. You see it there?"

"Ah, yes," said Tom.

"I received it," went on Jahbat, "on winning the championship of the quick-draw-kill-and-devour, of the Skikana handgun competition at the last All-Skikana World's Games. As an Assassin, of course, you are familiar with the Skikana hand-gunning-and-devouring art?"

"Of course," said Tom.

"Then, for the pride of the Eighth Skikana here at the fort," said Jahbat, "may I ask you to accept this small offering?" He produced a tiny gold whistle from his weapons harness and blew it. A Skikana enlisted soldier marched in bearing a silver dish with a cover, which he placed on the small table at Tom's right.

Bowing, both Skikana withdrew.

"They didn't waste any time," said Tom, as the door closed behind the two. He gazed with slitted eyes at the dish. "Devilishly subtle, these Skikana."

"What did he give you?" inquired Lucy, lifting the cover of the dish. "Oh—"

"Don't touch it!" said Tom, quickly.

Lucy had revealed a beautiful competition model Skikana handgun. "If a human hand touches the weapon itself," Tom said, "a signal will go off on the Eighth Skikana bulletin board, and I'll have accepted the challenge."

"Challenge?" Lucy hastily put the cover back on the gun. "And he's a champion? They're deliberately trying to kill you?"

"Nothing so crude, unfortunately," said Tom. "What they must be planning is to discredit me. As an Assassin, they expect me to make short work of Jahbat in the duel. However, having killed him, according to

their code I must finish off the matter by ceremoni-
ously eating every bit of him. It's the finest tribute
to a fallen foe, according to the Skikana code duello.
They've undoubtedly checked up and found that
we humans haven't the incredible Skikana capacity
for food—even if Skikana were eatable by Human
standards."

He looked thoughtful.

"On the other hand, if I refused to eat him," he
went on, "they've undoubtedly planned a protest that
will get me removed as Ambassador. And no other
Human has my qualifications to see through what's
going on here."

"Don't kill him, then," said Lucy. "Just scratch him."

"I'm not sure I can," said Tom, solemnly. "You forget. I've had the briefing, but I lack the necessary
years of intensive physical training and experience that
makes a true Galactic Assassin. The Skikana don't
know it, but their champion can almost undoubtedly
take me. I'd be dead before I could clear my weapon
from its clip on my harness."

"Tom!" said Lucy. "There's only one way out of this.
You've got to find a way not to fight him! Simply
refuse—he's below your dignity! Or else—stand on
your rights as an Ambassador and say that you can't
duel while on duty."

"Unfortunately there's that matter of my being an
Assassin," said Tom. "An Assassin back away from a
challenge? Impossible. The Assassins' Guild themselves would eliminate me if I did such a thing."

"Well, there must be a way," said Lucy, angrily. "I
don't see why a polite, firm refusal wouldn't work."

"It flies in the face of all the evidence," said Tom,
sadly. "After all, whole armies have been known to
mutiny and refuse to advance when they heard that a
single Assassin barred their path—that information was
part of my briefing."

He sighed heavily.

"Well," he said, "maybe together we can think of something. Meanwhile, we'd better get down to that banquet."

Surrounded by their Hugwos, they left their suite and were guided by an officer posted outside their door, down a corridor and into a vast, hall-like room with a lofty, raftered roof and no windows except narrow slits up near the rafters at the top of the walls.

These windows were set ajar, however, to the warm, sunset air of Mul'rahr. Inside the hall great ceremonial torches eight feet tall flared and sent their flames dancing above the long tables at which erect Skikana officers sat. Wide circular platters, the color of polished maple wood, sat before each diner or empty chair; and enormous toadstools like logs of wood gave up a savory smell like roast beef, as they lay at length on the tables between rows of plates.

The Hugwo corporal conducted Tom and Lucy to seats at the left of the Skikana Colonel.

"You have met our brave Captain Jahbat?" inquired the Colonel, as soon as the two Humans were seated.

"I have indeed," replied Tom.

"Even among we Skikana his courage is proverbial," said the Colonel. "He . . ." His gaze wandered and his voice trailed off.

"Colonel!" prompted Lucy, kind-heartedly.

The Colonel started, forked a bite of toadstool into his mouth, gulped it down and came alert again. ". . . Ah, yes," he said, significantly looking at Tom, "it is courage not even to be despised by an . . . Assassin, shall we say?"

"Actually," put in Lucy swiftly, "as an Assassin, the Ambassador is required to disregard—"

Tom interrupted her.

"—Many things," he said, "but the courage of a Skikana like Captain Jahbat would not be one of them.

But work before pleasure, my dear Colonel. The Wockii concern me at the moment."

The Colonel inclined his head and signaled to a Skikana enlisted soldier, who stepped forward to carve slices from the nearest huge toadstool. He served the slices on the platters before Tom and Lucy. Lucy sniffed unobtrusively at hers. The aroma was delicious.

"Is it safe for us to eat?" she whispered in English to Tom.

"I'll check," whispered back Tom. The Colonel's attention was momentarily devoted to finishing his own slice and ordering another with typical Skikana voracity. Tom had produced a small handbook from his weapons harness and was thumbing through it.

"Let's see . . . 'Mul'rahr . . . toadstooloids of, large: Agarica Mul'rahrensis Gigantica, page one hundred and forty-three . . .' here it is . . . 'See Rhu, page one-thirty-eight' . . ." He flipped pages. " 'Rhu, a widespread root system often extending over miles underground, putting forth root and tuberose projections of many varieties and types' . . ."

Tom's voice trailed off.

"Hmm . . ." he muttered, "interesting . . ."

"But can we eat it?" demanded Lucy.

"Oh!" Tom started, almost after the fashion of the Colonel. "Yes, I think so . . . *eatable by the following Races: Adjarts, Allahns . . . Hssoids, Hytszs . . .*' Yes, here we are . . . 'Humans.' "

"Oh, good, said Lucy, "it smells so appetizing—"

A twang from high above interrupted her, followed by an approaching high-pitched drone that ended in a thud. A small black arrow quivered in the center of Lucy's slice of toadstooloid, pinning it to the wooden platter. Shocked silence filled the hall and all eyes turned upward to discover a three-foot high, faunlike figure covered with white woolly hair and looking like a lamb, standing upright on his hind legs. This figure stood perched on one of the rafters by an open window, now reslinging a small bow over its shoulder and drawing a twelve-inch sword.

"What—what is it?" gasped Lucy, unthinkingly, in English.

"A Flal," answered Tom swiftly in the same language, "supposed to be one of the barely semi-intelligent local life forms—"

The rest of his sentence was drowned out by a bellow.

"A Flal!" the Colonel was roaring, starting to his feet and tugging at the ceremonial sword that was the only weapon the Skikana officers had worn to the banquet. "Get it down from there! Get it down, I say!"

With a sudden remarkable leap, the Flal left the rafter high overhead and landed on the table before the Colonel. In a twinkling the Flal's midget sword was menacing the Colonel's prothorax and an imperious whistle burst from the Flal's lamblike lips.

"Cut it down! That's an order," thundered the Colonel to his officers. "Never mind me!"

But the officers hesitated.

Taking advantage of this hesitation, the Flal turned and directed a stream of angry, musical whistling at Tom, gesturing with its free hand at the nearest toadstooloid. Then the Skikana officers dashed forward and the Flal, releasing the Colonel, dodged away, ducking into the sea of three-foot long, flashing Skikana swords, twisting, swivel-hipping and dancing on black hooves, as his own tiny blade, glittering with a speed of reflex the Skikana could not match, fenced a way for him to the nearest torch stand.

A leap carried him to the top of the stand. From there, disdainful of the licking flame, another leap carried him to crenellations in the wall and from there to a rafter leading to an open window. At the window he turned about; and, pulling a miniature hunting horn from his belt, he paused to blow a blast like some small, elfin bronx cheer at those below. The Skikana soldiers howled in baffled fury, waving their weapons. Then the Flal had ducked through the window and was gone.

"Sir Ambassador! Consort Lucy!" said the Colonel, gnashing his jaws but sheathing his sword and getting himself back under control—he paused to gulp a half-slice of toadstooloid—"please be seated. Forgive this minor interruption. These local life-forms—mere semi-intelligent animals—not even a language, just whistle to show their emotional state—please put it out of your mind. My soldiers will see that the banquet is not interrupted again."

"That won't be necessary, Colonel," said Tom. "I promised only to put in an appearance at this banquet and I consider that promise fulfilled now. I, my Consort, and my Hugwos will make use of that escort I asked you for, to leave for Wockiiland immediately."

"Of—of course!" said the Colonel, getting himself under control. "If you wish it, sir Ambassador. The escort is provided. However—" He hesitated. "I cannot permit the Consort Lucy to risk a night journey through the Mul'rahrian wilds. You and the Hugwos, of course, but—"

"Sir!" Tom's voice snapped him off in mid-speech. "Are you presuming to tell me where to take my Consort?"

"I have my duty," said the Colonel, stiffly, "as local Commander, to protect civilians—"

"May I remind the Colonel?" Tom's words in Skikana cut like a knife. Lucy looked at him with approval. "That the Consort Lucy will have an Assassin to escort her?"

"Sir!" said the Colonel, stiffening in his turn. "Am I to infer a lack of trust in my soldiers and myself?"

"Certainly not," said Tom, without hesitation; and

Lucy beamed on him for his quick thinking. It was perfectly clear that if Tom had expressed a lack of trust in the Skikana, the Colonel would have had grounds for a protest to get Tom removed as Ambassador. "I trust you and your officers and men implicitly, Colonel. It is the Consort Lucy I don't trust."

Lucy stared.

"You don't—" the Colonel's naturally bulging eyes seemed to bulge farther, "—trust your Consort, Sir Ambassador?"

"Not out of my sight for a moment," said Tom, firmly. "A purely Human situation, Colonel. I'm sure you wouldn't be interested in the details. And now, the escort?"

"It'll be waiting for you at the west gate," said the Colonel, stiffly. "Captain Jahbat, escort them!" Gnashing his jaws in defeat, the Colonel stepped back and allowed them both to proceed past him, followed by their Hugwos.

Chapter 14

Fifteen minutes later, they were floating westward
on flying platforms over the rolling, semi-wooded land-
scape of Mul'rahr, under the enormous single moon
that made the night seem almost as bright as day. Tom
and Lucy were sharing a platform, with their faithful
Hugwos riding individual platforms before and behind
them. Beyond and behind the Hugwos were half a
dozen platform-mounted soldiers of the Skikana
escort. None of these seemed close enough to be in
ear-shot; but, just to be safe, Tom lowered his voice
and spoke to Lucy in English.

"Lucy—" he began.

"Don't speak to me," said Lucy, staring off in the
opposite direction at the shadowy woods. "We have
nothing to say to each other."

"Now, Lucy—" said Tom.

"If you please," said Lucy. "I said, there's nothing
for us to discuss. Nothing at all."

"Don't you understand?" pleaded Tom. "The Colonel wanted you as a hostage. I didn't dare leave you
in his hands. I had to come up with the first excuse
that came into my mind!"

"No doubt. It was very clever of you. Curious, is it
not, though, that the first thing that should come into
your mind was the idea that I am untrustworthy? No

doubt that was why you, the Oprinkians, and all the other Aliens, wanted me to go along with you. To be someone you could blame for whatever you wanted to do.

"I do not wish to make a point of this," went on Lucy in syllables resembling splinters of jagged ice. "It merely crossed my mind. In passing, so to speak."

"Lucy, you know I trust you! You know it!"

"How bright the moonlight is upon this world," said Lucy, splintering a little more ice.

They rode in silence for the following forty minutes or so, at the end of which Tom tried again.

"Lucy—" he began. He broke off suddenly as he caught sight of the Skikana officer in charge of their escort whipping his flying platform about and zipping back toward the one Tom and Lucy occupied. "Yes, Captain?" asked Tom, as the officer swung about and flew alongside.

It was Captain Jahbat, of course. The moonlight glittered in his black eyes in what Lucy, at least, could not help but feel was a very sinister fashion.

"Sir," said the Captain to Tom. "We approach the Wockii chiefs now. They have been signaled to meet your unexpected visit. We should meet them in the next few seconds."

"Excellent. Tell me, Captain," said Tom, thoughtfully, "just as a matter of interest, I find myself curious about the Flals. The one we saw in the hall seemed to demonstrate more in the way of ability and technology than would be expected of a Race that was considered incapable of eventually graduating to the level of Civilization. Could you perhaps enlighten me on that subject? Also, in passing, was it a case of your earlier Skikana scoutship platforms seeking out the Wockii chiefs after I had said I wanted to go to Wockiiland right away? Or did the Wockii come forth on their own initiative just now to meet us?"

"The Wockii came forth on their own, sir," said Jah-bat. "We consider it a tribute to our Skikana approach-ability, and honor. The Skikana honor is without stain. None may accuse us of being merciful in victory or resentful in defeat."

"To be sure," said Tom. "But about the Flals?"

"I am afraid I am no expert on potentialities for Civilization, sir," said Captain Jahbat. "But I under-stand that the Flals have other failings—beside their inability to be able to acquire and use a spoken lan-guage. I would say they are hardly worth your curios-ity, Sir Ambassador."

"I'll keep your recommendation in mind, Captain," said Tom. "However, aside from that—would you tell me if the Wockii are a particularly truthful race?"

"Hardly, my dear sir," Jahbat gave the low rasp of Skikana laughter. "We have a little saying at Fort Duhnderhef. *The only Wockii that don't lie are the dead Wockii, and even they lie about being dead!*" Jahbat rasped again. "You follow the joke, Sir Ambas-sador and Consort Lucy? See, the Wockii lie when they are alive, and when they're flat on the ground—"

"Very humorous, Captain," interrupted Tom. "Very humorous, indeed. But aren't those the Wockii chiefs I see up ahead approaching now?"

Jahbat turned and looked up beyond the head of the column.

"You are right, sir Ambassador," he said. And, mov-ing his platform about, he shot off ahead to meet the group that was approaching on foot through the forest in the moonlight.

In a moment the platforms had settled to earth and the two parties were face to face. The Wockii stood about nine feet high on average. They looked some-thing like enormous badgers with curved short tusks; and wore heavy, six-foot long cutlasses, but nothing else except ribbons tied about their tusks.

"Sir Ambassador," said Captain Jahbat, presenting these hulking figures to the platform on which Tom and Lucy were still standing, "—and Consort Lucy, may I introduce Hlugar, Chief of All Chiefs for the Wockii?"

Captain Jahbat had spoken in Wockii, which was another language, along with Skikana, that Lucy now understood.

"All hail, Hlugar!" said Tom, in Wockii.

"All hail, foreigner!" grunted Hlugar in a deep bass voice that seemed to shake the bones of the two humans. "Welcome to Wockiiland. My burrow is your burrow."

"And my burrow is your burrow. Let us go feast this happy occasion," said Tom. In a shrewd tone of voice he added, to Lucy's startlement, "What shall we feast on? Perhaps—some roasted Flals?"

Hlugar's bass bellow echoed among the trees in the moonlight of the Mul'rahrian night.

"Never!" he roared, dropping on all fours and beginning to dig frantically in the earth before him. "Never eat Flals! Never, you hear?" He thrust his tusked muzzle down into the hole he had dug, roaring muffledly—"*Never!*"

"Sir!" began Jahbat in an outburst of indignation. But before he could continue, sudden bedlam broke loose.

Shrill whistles sounded from the tree shadows on all sides of them. Small black arrows began to drone among them. The billowing roars of the Wockii mingled with the harsh battle commands of the Skikana.

There was a swirl of motion and little faunlike, hooved figures with gleaming swords were all about them. Before Tom and Lucy could move, some things like heavy cloths fell over their heads. They felt themselves picked up and carried off at a run.

It was useless to struggle. They were carried for

some distance and gradually Lucy felt her senses slipping away from her. The cloth, or whatever heavy material it was that was wrapped around her, seemed to give off a pleasant, faint perfume with a sedative effect. She roused herself to struggle against it, but it was too late. She drifted off into unconsciousness.

When she opened her eyes again, she was lying on a slope of a pleasant, grassy hillside, beside a large granite boulder that until now had been shading her eyes from the sun. Dawn had just broken and the bright star that gave life to Mul'rahr was rising in the blue sky at her right. A little distance off stood Tom, facing some armed Flals. Surprisingly, only a dozen feet or so away, the faithful Hugwos also stood at attention, lance-guns in hand.

". . . It's no use," she heard Tom saying in Wockii to the Flals. "I can understand the meaning-symbols you whistle, but I can't whistle them back at you. Anyway, you understand me when I speak in Wockii or Skikana."

Drowsily, Lucy remembered she should still be angry with him for some reason, but she felt so pleasant that she could not at the moment remember what that reason could be.

"Tom!" she cried, trying to sit up. Tom turned, saw her stirring and hurried over.

"I didn't know you were awake," he said, helping her to her feet. "You feel fine, don't you?"

"As a matter of fact, yes," said Lucy, surprised. "I do." She got to her feet. "But what—"

"What they wrapped us in was the veil, or undermembrane, of the Rhu toadstooloid, *Agarica Mul'rahrensis Gigantica*, the same toadstooloid they served us for dinner at the fort," said Tom. "It appears to have slight narcotic, as well as excellent analgesic and tranquilizing properties. But never mind that now. I'm finally beginning to get the general picture of the

situation here on Mul'rahr, and it's more desperate
than I thought. Ordinarily, as the Consort of an
Ambassador, you'd be safe trusting to the Skikana
sense of honor. But the Skikana, as I suspected when
the Colonel tried to hold you back as hostage, are no
longer to be trusted. They're engaged in an attempt
at actual genocide—but there's no time to go into that
now. Do you have your Consort's credentials with
you—the ones Mr. Valhinda got for you?"

"Of course," said Lucy, surprised, reaching down
into the small belt-purse of her superbly tailored green
and silver dinner gown. "Mr. Valhinda told us never
to go any place without them, remember. I keep them
right in—yes, here they are."

"Good!" said Tom, plucking the credentials from
her fingers. He whipped a stylus out of its holster on
his weapons harness and scribbled rapidly on the margin of the topmost paper. He folded the credentials
and thrust them back into Lucy's fingers. "Put those
carefully back where you had them—" he said.

Lucy nodded and hid them once more in the purse,
giving its lock a twirl with one finger, so that anyone
not knowing the secret would never be able to open
the purse.

"If you hear that anything's happened to me," Tom
went on, "I want you to contact the nearest representative of the Assassins' Guild—I've written there how
you should go about that—and then show them what
I've written. And—"

"Happen to you!" cried Lucy, her fingers closing
tightly on the purse. "What do you mean happen to
you? What do you mean, 'if I hear—'?"

"You've got to get back to the safety of the landing
field and the spaceship we came in on," said Tom.
"Now don't argue—"

"I have no intention of arguing!" burst out Lucy.

"And I have no intention of going! I'll leave here with you—or not at all!"

"But it's important one of us get away!" said Tom, urgently. "The Hugwos will see you safely to the ship—"

A sharp whistle from the group of Flals interrupted him. He looked over at the small hooved figures and groaned.

"Too late," he said. "I'll just have to hope that the Skikana have enough sense left to spare you when they attack. Come on then, we've got to get together with these Flals."

"Slow down!" said Lucy, sharply, as they moved back toward the Flals Tom had been standing with when Lucy woke up. "Explain a few things. Why should the Skikana attack?"

"Because," said Tom, "this spot here is the place the Skikana have been searching for ever since they first developed technology and rose from being little more than large, predatory insects—fierce insects, to be sure, but nothing more than insects. They have legends about this place, but the Flals have kept secret the actual spot during the Skikana's swift rise to what they considered civilization. The Wockii also lost their memory of the exact place—and the Flals refused to tell them. But the Skikana have just found out, because they coated the cover for the dueling weapon Jahbat sent me with telepathic tracer organisms—and you remember you lifted the cover?"

"But how do you know?" demanded Lucy.

"The Flals have told me the whole story," said Tom. "The present situation came about because—well, it's a longer story than we have time for right now," said Tom, urgently.

"Telepathic molecules—ugh!" said Lucy, wiping her fingertips on the boulder.

"Oh, they're all dead by this time," said Tom. "But

the Skikana now know where we are and are on their way to us in full strength."

"Why?" said Lucy, looking at her fingertips.

"Briefly," said Tom, "because the Skikana want to destroy what's here. Otherwise, the mistake that was made when this planet was first found and listed in the Sector catalogue would be discovered. The Flals, being naturally shy and retiring, hid from the Sector data-takers at the time the world was first looked at; and so the data-takers took the Skikana's word for it that they were the most advanced and intelligent life on Mul'rahr, and that the Wockiis were the closest thing to being another intelligent Race on the planet. The Flals have never had a chance to get that corrected. That's the reason they kidnaped us and brought us here to help them."

"Well, I'm certainly in favor of helping them," said Lucy. She thought about licking her fingertips clean and, with a shudder, decided against it. *They're dead, anyway*, she reminded herself. "I can understand why now," she went on, "but I was certain from the beginning, anyway, that they were in the right; and I didn't need some sort of para-instinct to tell me that. I just knew."

Tom stopped short. They were still a little way from the Flals, and Lucy stopped when he did and stared at him.

"What's so surprising about that?" Lucy asked.

"You're a genius!" said Tom. "Of course, what you were listening to *was* one of your para-instincts."

"I was?" said Lucy. "This doesn't make sense. If I have para-instincts, why didn't I know it?"

"Oh, all Civilized beings above a certain level of intelligence and awareness have them," said Tom. "Their Civilization just teaches them to ignore the p-signals."

"That doesn't make sense," said Lucy.

"It's true, though," said Tom. "For example, it's been known for years that we Humans pick up all sorts of signals from other people and creatures. But we've been in the habit of disregarding these, because we assumed everything important fell within the logical area of thought. Our nose and ears tell us lots of things we ignore. It takes something like the smell of something burning, to make us suddenly afraid there's a fire in the house. But most of the smaller, more subtle signals, we ignore. However, they go on registering, anyway; and if we'd pay more attention to them we'd pick up all kinds of information. Our conclusion may be wrong—there may be no house-fire; but very often we ignore them and miss an understanding we wouldn't reach otherwise. Have you ever taken an unreasoning like or dislike to somebody else?"

"Lots of times," said Lucy.

"Well, there you are," said Tom. "In those cases you were listening to your para-instincts but not realizing why you felt that way. In this case, you came to the right conclusion. But it was just a feeling—you couldn't produce a logical reason in words to back it up. But then, you didn't need to."

"If this is a para-instinct," said Lucy, "which number is it?"

"Oh," said Tom. "Para-instincts aren't numbered according to type. They're simply numbered according to how you discover them. This is the first you discovered. Therefore, it's your first para-instinct."

"Ah," said Lucy. With an effort she came back to the present emergency. "But couldn't we help the Flals more by getting in touch with Mr. Valhinda? We could get on our platforms with our Hugwos and go back to the spaceship. The Skikana wouldn't dare touch us; and from the ship we could get in touch with Mr. Valhinda."

"You could," said Tom. "I wanted you to, but you wouldn't."

"I said I wouldn't leave without you!" snapped Lucy. "Why can't you leave? Then I'd go with you."

"For me," said Tom, solemnly, "there's no choice. The galaxy knows no Assassin could ever be kidnaped unless he permitted it. You can't kidnap an Assassin. Kill one, yes, if you have sufficient fearless battle-hardened troops and mobile armored vehicles. The only conclusion that would be drawn is that I allowed myself to be kidnaped by the Flals out of cowardice, in an attempt to avoid facing up to Jahbat's challenge—unless I can get to the bottom of things here and clear myself by showing what I was really trying to do."

"But—" Lucy broke off helplessly. Tom turned and started again toward the small group of Flals and Lucy went along with him. Those small individuals were now looking up at Tom and Lucy inquiringly. Their little pink noses, furry faces and kindly brown eyes were lit up by the golden rays of the rising sun.

"I'm not completely sure I'm understanding their speech, at that," said Tom. "I'm using my para-instincts now, too, and playing by ear as I go. These Flals have a high nobility-of-character index. My para-instincts assure me of that. But since their language, and they really do have one, is musico-emotional at base, I can't understand the fine points of the explanations they've been trying to give me. It's as if they see the universe around them in terms of varying degrees of right or wrong and define those degrees in musical terms to make up their language."

"Yes," said Lucy, looking at them with a softening glance and remembering the single Flal in the banquet hall fighting off all the Skikana officers. "And they're such brave little Beings, too."

"That's true, they are. And," said Tom, "because of

their natures, able to read the characters of others at a glance. They were able to sense, as a result, right from the start that we and the Hugwos could be trusted. Just as they sensed from the earliest years that the Skikana were cruel and rapacious; and they've always known, of course, that the Wockii are brutal and greedy."

"But if they want you to help them, but can't tell you—" Lucy was beginning, when a whistle from the closest Flal interrupted her. Tom turned to the Flal and whistled the first few bars of Mendelssohn's *Wedding March*. The Flal turned to Lucy and bowed politely.

"Why!" said Lucy, delighted. "You can, too, talk to them!"

"Only after a fashion," answered Tom. "I was trying to tell him that you're my wife. But that's an oversimplification. In this case the concept of 'wife' almost undoubtedly missed him completely, in spite of the fact that the Flals, like us, are bisexual. What he probably got were just some of the emotional overtones of our relationship."

"But I should think a language could be worked out from that as a base," said Lucy, thinking for a moment as the linguistic expert she was.

"No doubt. In time. But time is just what we don't have—" A silvery Flal horn sounded off among the giant toadstooloids and the trees at the base of the slope on which they stood. A second later, another sounded from the far side of the hill.

"There come the Wockii and Skikana," said Tom. "Just as I'd hoped."

"You hoped? I thought—"

"Yes," said Tom, "but I think I've evolved a plan that might solve things here. Only, I particularly need those Skikana battle harps." He turned to the Flals and made pounding motions in the air with his fist. "Try the drum again," he said in Wockii.

The group parted; and just beyond them Lucy saw what seemed to be a drum mounted on a stake driven down into the earth. Two Flals began to beat the drum vigorously.

It did not sound so loud in the air; but Lucy could feel the vibration of it through the ground at her feet. A sudden new chorus of whistles broke out below, down on the slope. They all turned to see the first line of armed Skikana infantry, marching into view from a further clump of trees and heading toward the foot of the slope. Mixed in among them were heavy Wockii figures carrying their mighty cutlasses in hairy fists. The Flals drew their swords.

A strange sound vibrated all about the scene.

"Tom! Did you hear that?" cried Lucy. "That noise—almost like a yawn!"

But Tom's attention was directed down the hill toward the Skikana battle harpsmen, who were emerging from the trees in front of the troops and driving the supporting spikes of their harps into the earth, so that the harps stood upright ready to play.

The first Skikana to come into view, halted and stood at attention. Their Colonel emerged next, with Captain Jahbat marching correctly at his left and half a pace to his rear. Together and alone, they marched up the hill toward Tom, Lucy and the Flal leaders. Halfway up the slope the Colonel said something to Jahbat, who stopped and held his position there midway between the forces of the Flal and the Skikana.

The Colonel came on up the slope by himself and stopped before Tom. "Sir and Madame!" he said stiffly.

He stood for a second, champing his jaws a little uncertainly as if he was having trouble remembering what he was going to say. Then he went on, "I must ask you to use your influence with these Flals to cause them to surrender themselves. We must dig up this area to discover goods reported stolen from our fort. Please counsel them not to think of resistance, please. Their case is hopeless—what was that?"

"Another yawn," said Lucy.

"Nonsense!" snapped the Colonel, sharply. Recovering himself, he made a courtly bow of apology in Lucy's direction and got his voice under control. "—As I was saying, resistance would be useless. Their position on this slope is hopeless."

"Permit me," said Tom, "to disagree with you, sir. My Consort and myself are inclined to back the Flals in their stance on this. Flals, as your Skikana have cause to know, are not unworthy fighters in spite of their small size. All the galaxy knows the reputation of the Hugwo lance-gunners. And, last but not least, I am myself an Assassin."

"True," said the Colonel, champing his jaws convulsively once more. "However, I must inform you that your recent actions in allowing yourself to be kidnaped by these Flals, here, have cast some grave doubts in our minds on your status as a true Assassin."

"How dare you!" said Lucy.

The Colonel's head wobbled a little as he turned to look at her.

"May I add," he said, "that no such suspicion, however, exists in our minds about the Consort Lucy—"

"I am not amused!" said Lucy, raising her head proudly.

"You have insulted my Consort!" said Tom, grimly.

"But I—but there was no intention—" stammered the Colonel, his eye-stalks wavering.

"Perhaps not," went on Tom in a steely voice. "The Consort Lucy was her usual agreeable self, when the two of us were at the fort with you—"

"Yes. Yes, indeed."

"However," went on Tom, relentlessly, "you have discovered that there is more to her than her politeness. The Consort Lucy comes of fighting stock—to wit, she is a born Thorsdatter."

"I had no idea—" the Colonel began but Tom cut him off short.

"Too late now for apologies, Colonel," he said, "the damage has been done. Back to the immediate matter here: your presence in this place and your wish to dig up this area. No doubt I am mistaken in my conjecture that the supply of unharvested toadstooloid you know of is rapidly approaching the vanishing point?"

The Colonel staggered visibly, but pulled himself erect once more.

"There's plenty of toadstooloid!" he snapped.

"Plenty," said Tom in steely tones, "for the native Flal and Wockii populations. After all, the ecology would balance that way. But not enough for these and a rapidly increasing populace of Skikana soldiery, when each Skikana is capable of eating his own weight or more of food at a sitting. And moreover, once the effect of the toadstooloid upon the Skikana eaters becomes known—"

"Stop!" shouted the Colonel. "Assassin or not, I warn you. There are some secrets not meant to be uncovered."

"The secret," went on Tom, unflinchingly, "has already been uncovered. It began when one or more of the Sector stock market Sharks learned of the true situation here; and realized the Wockii futures here were worthless. This would inevitably call for an investigation by the Sector Stock Board, itself; and that forced you into a situation where you had to seek out the true dominant intelligence of Mul'rahr and destroy it. Deny that if you can!"

Chapter 15

"There's nothing to deny!" snapped the Colonel, his antennae going rigid. "We Skikana are the dominant intelligence of Mul'rahr! The Flals are not intelligent! And no normal civilized race would consider the crime of genocide, even if—"

"The Flals are fully intelligent," said Tom, relentlessly. "You found out the Wockii had lied to you about that shortly after the original Sector survey was here to look over Mul'rahr; and it was shortly after that you discovered you Skikana had an appetite for the toadstooloid—which before this you had dismissed as merely food for animals."

"Lies!" roared the Colonel. "If that were true, we'd have made an agreement with the Flals at once, rather than risk prosecution as a Race knowingly permitting the subjugation of a potentially civilized other Race. Why didn't we?"

"For the same reason," said Tom, "that you Skikana could contemplate what would otherwise have been abhorrent even to you. You were not normal any longer. You—"

"Stop!" champed the Colonel.

"No," said Tom, "it's too late to hide the truth. *Agarica Mul'rahrensis Gigantica*, or the local eatable giant toadstooloid on which you, like the Wockii and the

181

Flals, have been feeding, is not dissimilar to the *Agaricus muscarius*, or 'fly agaric,' one of the poisonous mushrooms of our Human world."

Lucy glared at him. "And you were going to let me eat some!"

"It's harmless to humans," he said to her hastily, and turned back to the Colonel.

"*Mul'rahrensis*," he said, "produces a derivative of the alkaloid muscarine; which, however, acts not so much as a poison, but as a narcotic, a tranquilizer and a euphoric on this world. Taken in small amounts of toadstooloid a Flal—or even wockii—is capable of consuming at one time, the toadstooloid is merely a mild and harmlessly intoxicating food, containing all the necessary valuable vitamins required by the native Races, here on Mul'rahr—"

"Stop!" said the Colonel weakly, his voice cracking in a very un-Skikanalike way.

"But," continued Tom, "taken in the enormous quantities in which the smallest Skikana soldier will consume at a sitting, the toadstooloid becomes a powerful, habit-forming drug. A drug that the addict will go to any lengths to obtain; and which no intelligent, civilized being would allow another intelligent being to consume—"

"Very well," said the Colonel. He had pulled himself together, and there was now a regretful note in his voice. "You wouldn't let me stop you. We have honored you, Sir Ambassador-Assassin, and honored the Consort Lucy. But now you've sealed your own fate."

He turned and bowed to Lucy.

"I regret, Consort Lucy," he said, "that you need to be included with the rest. No Human, Hugwo, or Flal must leave this spot alive." He looked back sadly at Tom. "Didn't you realize that soldiers like my troops would stop at nothing once our secret was out? Death means nothing to us, compared to being cut off from our toadstooloid supply. With it, we Skikana expect to move to unforeseen heights. One day we will rule the galaxy. In the face of that certainty, the existence of you, the Flals, the Hugwos—yes, and even the Wock-iis—means nothing. You are doomed once I give the word for the battle harps to sound the attack."

"I think the toadstooloid has given you a false picture of the situation," said Tom. "Sound the harps, then, and find out."

The Colonel stared at him.

"Sir!" he said. "You *wish* me to sound the battle harps for the attack upon you?"

"Yes," said Tom.

"Yes!" echoed Lucy, almost in the same breath bravely, but was unable to avoid darting a momentary questioning glance at Tom.

Tom intercepted it.

"It's all right, Lucy," said Tom. "I know what I'm doing. Go ahead!" he said to the Colonel. "What are you waiting for? Sound the harps. *I defy you!*"

"Defy me?" In a sudden, typical, towering Skikana rage, the Colonel spun about and shouted down the hill to Captain Jahbat. "Sound the Harps! Prepare to advance!"

Below on the slope, they all saw the Captain salute and turn. His voice floated faintly back to them as he shouted down further to the battle harpsmen of the Skikana.

"Sound the Prepare to Advance!" they heard him call. *"Shortly We Shall Eat You, Now!"*

The battle harps broke suddenly into their air-rending, ground-shaking melody. The Colonel spun back and shouted thinly above their unbelievable harmonies.

"You've asked for it!" he cried. "No quarter! No prisoners and no—"

His voice caught in his prothorax. The ground had suddenly heaved up alongside him and the cap of a toadstooloid six feet across poked itself above ground. Abruptly it split apart into two enormous lips; and the aperture between them inhaled with a gust that almost sucked them all off their feet.

"What's going on up here?" boomed forth a voice from the lips in accentless Wockii; and with such volume that it overrode even the harp music. Downslope, the amazed and aghast harpsmen fell into jangling discordances and from there into silence. In the quiet that followed, a smaller toadstooloid poked itself above ground, grew upwards suddenly to about ten feet in height of stalk, and bent its cap toward the Colonel. The surface of cap drew back to reveal half a dozen large eyes. "Who are you?"

"'Colonel, commanding ... Eighth Skikana ...'" mumbled that officer, obviously badly shaken, but trying valiantly to pull himself up in military fashion. The toadstooloid with the eyes swiveled toward Tom and Lucy, twisted toward the Hugwos, turned toward the Flals—and at last looked down toward the distant ranks of the Wockii and the Skikana.

"I am the Prar'Rhu—or Proto-rhu of the Rhu root system here on Mul'rahr, as you strangers would doubtless put it," announced the toadstooloid lips. The eyes swiveled to take in everyone else present.

"Children, children!" it boomed. "Can't I even take a little nine-thousand-year nap without all of you getting into a fight with each other? What is it this time?"

One of the Flals stepped forward and began to whistle rapidly, staring at the Wockii and the Colonel. The eyed toadstooloid, which had been watching the Flal, swiveled again toward the distant Wockii.

"For shame!" boomed the enormous lips. The Wockii all immediately fell on their faces. Tom stepped forward to the toadstooloid with the eyes.

"Excuse me," he said, "possibly I might be useful in explaining the situation. I am Ambassador-at-Large and Assassin Tom Parent, and here beside me is my Consort, Lucy Parent. We are here with the blessing of the Sector Council, composed of the most advanced races in this Sector of the galaxy. Those insectoid beings you see below the slope there are the Skikana—"

"I know the Skikana," boomed the toadstooloid with the lips, "they were wandering tribesmen, when I decided to take my nap. They appear to have developed rapidly since then."

Down below the slope, the ranked Skikana moved uneasily.

"Indeed they have," said Tom, "in numbers as well as technology—so much so that when the Sector Council ordered a survey of Mul'rahr, only a few hundred years ago, the Skikana presented themselves as the dominant life form on this world, the Wockii as the next sub-dominant, and allowed the Sector survey to make the error of classifying Flals as semi-intelligent at best, with no promise of ever developing a civilization."

"Tut-tut!" boomed the lips. "I see that I shall have to take care of some things around here, before resuming my nap."

"Resuming your nap may not be necessary," said Tom. "May I ask you a question—a simple question?"

"Any question at all," said the lipped toadstooloid, graciously.

"It's just this," said Tom. "Might I inquire of you what the relation happens to be ... of mass to energy?"

"Not at all. A simple question!" boomed the toadstooloid. "As anyone who has devoted even a few millennia of thought to the question must realize at once, E equals em cee squared. Or, energy equals mass times the constant, squared—in the present and immediate universe only, of course. I assume you were only asking about the relationship as it exists in the present and immediate universe?"

"I was," said Tom.

"Very wise," boomed the Prar'Rhu. "Because that relationship becomes somewhat more complicated when we consider an infinite series of parallel universes in an enfolded hyperspace. Are you planning to make use of the relationship in any immediate, practical, nuclear sense, may I ask? Because, if so, I could perhaps warn you of certain dangers—"

"No, I was not," said Tom. "I asked the question only as a preliminary to introducing you to the fact of a whole galaxy of different, intelligent and educated races, some of them capable of conversing with you on your own Civilized level."

"A whole—" The lips stopped, trembling slightly with emotion. "You say, intelligent, educated races capable of conversing . . ." The Prar'Rhu was clearly unable to continue. Its half-dozen eyes on the taller toadstooloid blinked rapidly.

"I mean just that," said Tom sympathetically. "I base my knowledge on a briefing that was given me. Your hundreds of thousands of years of loneliness are over. No longer will you need to take ten-thousand-year naps to escape unbearable and sanity-threatening boredom. No more will you be forced to exist only in the society of your intellectual inferiors. At last you will be able to communicate with minds the equal in capacity and accumulated wisdom with your own—"

"*Never!*" screamed the Skikana Colonel, frothing at the jaws. He turned around and shouted down the slope at Jahbat. "Never mind the Prepare to Advance! Never mind the Advance! Sound the Charge! *Now!*"

Jahbat wheeled about to repeat the order.

"You shall not!" thundered the toadstooloid lips. Barely had the thunder of that voice died away on the surrounding slopes and hills when hundreds of thousands of little purple puffballs began to sprout around the feet of the Skikana soldiery, and an enticing, spicy fragrance filled the air.

With wild cries, the Skikana soldiers threw aside their harps and weapons and fell upon the purple puffballs, cramming them into their jaws and passing quickly into a foolishly grinning stupor.

"No!" cried the Colonel, staggering, torn between his military pride and the enticing odor of the puffballs that had sprouted at his feet. "Get up . . . Charge! Get up, I say!" He was almost weeping. "Get up and fi . . ." The scent of the puffballs overcame him. He collapsed on the ground and tore into those within arm's reach like a starving man.

"But what's going to happen to the Skikana soldiers now?" asked Lucy, later, as she and Tom strolled from the edge of the concrete landing pad out toward their spaceship. The Skikana soldiery, including the officers and the Colonel, had escorted them back to the fort, marching as if hypnotized by the orders of the Prar'Rhu. "They're addicted to the toadstooloid, and—"

"No more," said Tom. "When I was in the fort just now to take our official leave of the Colonel, I found the fort kitchens had, of course, whipped up a large meal of toadstooloid, as was customary for the returning troops. However, to a soldier, the Skikana turned their heads away weakly and couldn't stand the sight of the food. They ate battle rations instead."

"Aha!" said Lucy. "The Prar'Rhu put something more in those puffballs than just what was necessary to stop the Skikana from fighting and get us escorted back to the fort." She peered ahead. In the brilliant sunlight, the shadow at the base of the spaceship was almost too dark to see into; but she thought she saw several Skikana figures there, waiting by the air-lock ramp.

"Yes. The Colonel realized that," said Tom. "That's why he asked to see me alone just now before we left. He offered to make a clean breast of the facts here for Interstellar publication, if I would help explain to the Sector Council that the original addiction wasn't the fault of the Skikana—which it wasn't. Actually, it was an accident having to do with the Skikana capacity for food—what's the matter?"

"Tom!" Lucy clutched at his arm. "Isn't that Captain Jahbat and a couple of other Skikana officers waiting for us at the ship?"

"What? Oh, yes," said Tom. "I was expecting him." He called ahead in Skikana: "Good afternoon, Captain!"

"Good afternoon, Sir Ambassador!" replied Jahbat, briskly, as Tom and Lucy came up into the shadow at the foot of the ship. "I believe that before you leave you and I have some little matter to discuss."

Lucy's heart sank. Abruptly, she remembered the competition model Skikana handgun which had been brought to Tom in the fort, earlier.

"Ah, yes," Tom was saying easily. "Do you have it with you?"

"Right here, sir!" said Jahbat. Another Skikana officer stepped forward with the dish containing the handgun. The handgun's twin, Lucy saw, was clipped to Jahbat's harness, waiting.

"Tom!" she cried urgently in English. "Don't touch it!"

"Certainly, my dear," said Tom in Skikana, smoothly. "It will be a pleasure to encounter the prospect of being hand-gunned and devoured by such an eminent opponent as Captain Jahbat." In English he added hastily, "Stop worrying, Lucy! He must be an excellent shot, or he wouldn't have won that medal!"

Tom took the handgun with his left hand, since Lucy was still holding his right arm.

"Are you crazy?" snapped Lucy in English. "Do you think I want you killed and devoured? Even by an excellent shot? Tom, come back!"

But Tom had already pulled himself away from her and was moving off with Jahbat and the Skikana to place themselves for the duel.

"Tom!" said Lucy, following. "Stop this! You just as good as said yourself he was bound to be a better shot than you! What's the matter? Have you gone completely out of your senses?"

"Not at all," called Tom back in English. He had now taken up his position facing Jahbat and was waiting for the signal to fire. "Don't get between us now, Lucy. It doesn't matter if he can outdraw me if he misses me, does it? Stay there. I'll be right back."

"But you said—" These words were interrupted as a presiding officer gave the command to fire. Jahbat's reflexes were too fast for Lucy's eyes to follow. One moment he was standing there. The next, his handgun was in his grasp and a pale lance of fire was driving toward Tom.

It passed some inches above Tom's head. Lucy stared. Tom had not even drawn his own handgun.

"Tom! Shoot!" cried Lucy.

"Certainly not!" he called back in English, annoyedly. "Please, Lucy, be quiet. You're disrupting the order of the occasion with all this talk."

Jahbat had not stirred. With the typical unshakable pride and courage of the Skikana, he was standing waiting.

"Sir!" he called to Tom. "I believe you have a return shot coming."

"That is quite correct, Captain," Lucy heard Tom reply through her whirling confusion. "However, I do not believe I will take it at this moment."

It was an almost physiological impossibility for a Skikana to show fear. However, it seemed to Lucy that

Captain Jahbat paled somewhat. Evidently there were limits even to Skikana courage, and waiting eternally for a possible return shot, which he would simply have to stand still and receive without fighting back, was testing even the brave Captain's nerve.

"No, sir?" Jahbat answered now. "May I ask when you do intend to?"

"I'm not sure," replied Tom, idly. "Possibly the next time I come back to Mul'rahr. Possibly not even in our respective lifetimes. In fact, the more I think of it and busy as I am, the more I think I'll probably never be able to get around to it. I apologize for that."

"Not at all," said Jahbat with extreme courtesy, bowing. He raised his handgun and saluted Tom. The other officers did likewise. "It has been an honor to know you, Sir Ambassador and Assassin."

"Well, that's finished," said Tom, coming back to Lucy. "Let's get aboard so the ship can take off."

He patted a pocket attached to his weapons harness as he walked up the ramp. Lucy walked in ominous silence at his side.

"Ah, there you are, sir," he said to the ship's first officer, waiting at the air-lock. "My compliments to the ship's Captain, and will he take off as soon as possible?"

"You men can go to your own quarters," he said to the Hugwos who had followed them aboard. "The Consort Lucy and I will be settling down for the return trip." He watched them file out of the Imperial Lounge and shut the door behind them.

"Loyal beings," he remarked to Lucy. "But it's simply not good policy to let anyone but you see where I hide the written admission by the Colonel of the facts behind the situation here."

"I suppose not," said Lucy between her teeth.

"You realize how well we've come out of all this?" he asked, turning back to Lucy. "Not only do I have the Colonel's signed admission, but I was able to get an—unofficial, of course—option from the leading Flal to buy the Flal futures. They'll probably more than reimburse our race for the worthlessness of the Wockii futures. And you remember how the Prar'Rhu promised us his eternal friendship, which can't help but be valuable to our Race in the future—since that Being is a biochemical synthesist with skill beyond imagination—" He broke off, staring at her.

"Lucy, what's wrong?"

"*You!*" cried Lucy, fighting down the temptation to kick him or hit him with something. "What do you mean, getting in a duel, when I called and pleaded with you not to do it? What do you mean trying to get yourself killed? What if Jahbat hadn't missed?"

"But he had to!" protested Tom. He backed off a couple of steps just to be on the safe side. Lucy followed like a panther about to spring. "Lucy, you don't understand. The Skikana are proud of their honor being without stain. '—*Never merciful in victory, never resentful in defeat . . .*' Remember what Jahbat told us in the beginning? The chance to challenge had been offered. I couldn't leave the planet without dueling him. But good Skikana manners forbade that he should try to kill me after I had defeated them, here on Mul'rahr. It might have looked like sour grapes. He had very deliberately to avoid trying to kill me in the duel. That's why I refused to shoot back. It would have been no better than murder."

Lucy stopped approaching him. Tom also stopped, feeling a little safer.

"To say nothing of the fact," he added, hastily, "that I have now stymied all future challenges to a duel. I can say that I can fight no one until my present duel with Jahbat is completed."

"But that makes it even worse!" Lucy burst out. "You knew there was no danger, and you let me stand out there and worry. And you told the Colonel earlier I wasn't trustworthy! Oh, I could kill you myself! I could—"

"Wait!" yelped Tom, as she started to advance on him again. "Wait! You know I trust you—"

"You don't."

"Didn't you read what I wrote on your credentials just before the Skikana attacked?" said Tom. "How could I trust you any more than that? I left it all up to you if anything happened to me."

"What do you mean you wrote—?" Lucy ripped open her belt-purse, snatched out her credential papers and unfolded them. "If you've done something else—"

Her voice faded. She was staring at Tom's handwriting.

"To all Assassins' Guild Officers . . ." she read aloud, *"the individual presenting this is not a wilf, but my Consort Lucy, on whom falls the duty of completing a mission in which I have just been slain. I charge all Guild officials and members with the obligation to which I am entitled, to assist her in completing that mission in both our names, stating that I have the utmost trust and faith in her capabilities to do so. Thomas Parent, Apprentice and Guild Member . . ."*

"You see," said Tom, "all the time I did—"

Lucy flung herself upon him. Prepared for attack rather than affection, Tom lost his balance and went over backwards onto the deep rug that covered the deck in the Imperial Lounge. Lucy fell on top of him.

"It's very undignified," he managed to mutter, a few moments later, "for an Ambassador, to say nothing of an Assassin, to be on his back on the floor—"

"Oh, shut up!" said Lucy, kissing him.

Chapter 16

"What?" said Tom.

"Tom!" said Lucy, exasperatedly. "You heard him perfectly. You'd just finished telling Mr. Valhinda that not only was the situation on Mul'rahr straightened out; but the matter of the worthless Wockii Futures mistakenly bought by our Earth investors had been taken care of; and he said 'I'm afraid not.' You heard him perfectly."

"I didn't say 'What, question mark,'" said Tom. "I said 'What, exclamation point.'"

"Well, it certainly sounded like "What, question mark.'" said Lucy.

"Exclamation point!"

"Question mark!"

Mr. Valhinda coughed politely.

Tom and Lucy looked at him and then at each other.

"Well," said Lucy, "maybe it was an exclamation point, after all—that just sounded to me like a question mark."

"Come to think of it," Tom said, "I might have pronounced it just a bit like a question mark."

He and Lucy reached out toward each other and solemnly hooked little fingers together for a moment.

"Now, on other topics," said Mr. Valhinda; and Tom and Lucy gave him all their attention. The three of them were seated in a Conversation Room of Mr. Valhinda's Council Representative's quarters. It was a pleasant room with a thick rug of deep green; and remarkably Earth-like (reconstructed just for this talk with them, wondered Lucy?) with overstuffed, comfortable furniture, in shades of various other earth colors to match the carpet. Along one side of the room a rank of tall windows flanked them, admitting the light from a cheerfully pink sun that was a duplicate of the star over Mr. Valhinda's home planet.

Mr. Valhinda went on, "I believe you might as well know the facts now as later."

"What are the facts?" said Lucy, crisply, before Tom could say anything more.

"The facts are," said Mr. Valhinda, "first, our Council and the advanced races of this Sector welcomed the fellowship of the Prar'Ruhr joyously into our fellowship—though it must be admitted that such an experienced and capable mind undoubtedly will go far beyond us; and wind up finding intellectual companionship with the truly great minds closer to the center of our galaxy. For this, we are all grateful to you two for discovering such a supermind in our little, outlying galactic Sector. In saying this, of course, I speak for everyone on the Council. However, your success on Mul'rahr has, I'm afraid, merely further tangled and confused the issue as far as the home world of your Race is concerned. You remember I spoke to you about the red tape and the delay involved in dealing with matters?"

"I remember," said Tom, grimly.

"Well, just as I said then," went on Mr. Valhinda, "down in the bureaucratic center of galactic paperwork, your latest achievement with the denizens of Mul'rahr has been noted down, assigned an order in which it will be dealt with, and it will be chasing the numbers of your temporary control of the Jaktal Empire, which is in turn chasing the numbers of the stock dealings of the investor Sharks here on Cayahno; our best estimate now is that it will be closer to eight hundred of your years—"

"Eight hundred—" said Lucy.

"I'm afraid so," said Mr. Valhinda. "—Eight hundred years before the whole matter is ironed out, as the three items are all considered in relation to each other, and an understanding reached by those who must see that the regulations of the galaxy are respected by all Races allowed into galactic civilization."

"But a delay like that's not fair!" said Lucy.

"You're damn right!" said Tom.

"Of course," Mr. Valhinda spread his hands. "It is unfair. But with a whole galaxy to be observed and regulated, you must understand things like this can't be dealt with in a hurry unless there is some great, overriding reason."

"Like what?" asked Lucy and Tom, together. They stopped and stared at each other.

"All right, you talk," said Tom.

"No, you," said Lucy.

"All right," said Tom, "I will—what sort of reason, Mr. Valhinda?"

Mr. Valhinda waved a furry hand deprecatingly.

"Oh, something that would affect the whole galaxy," he said. "For example, suppose there was a danger of another galaxy colliding with ours, and you somehow managed to avert it. This would put consideration of your successful deed at the head of all things to be considered by the Galactic Council itself, on which this Sector of ours presently doesn't yet qualify to have its own Representative—we're lumped with another cluster of Sectors to elect a single Galactic Rep for all of us. But I wander off the point. Since whatever service you performed for the galaxy as a whole would need to be considered first, then any other items connected with you would also be dealt with at the same time. But otherwise, as I say, our estimate would be something like eight hundred years—as your Race counts them."

Tom sat silent, digesting this information.

Lucy gave him a look that plainly said, "All right, you wanted to talk. Go ahead."

"Er—isn't there anything you could suggest?" he said to Mr. Valhinda. "I mean, isn't there something we could try to do about this situation?"

"Short of some large heroic action that would benefit the whole galaxy," said Mr. Valhinda, "I have no idea. Perhaps you can come up with one."

There was a poignant moment of silence in the room.

"I can't," said Tom, glumly. "But I can't go on being Ambassador-at-Large as things stand, just as if there was no problem at all. On the other hand I hate to head back to Earth with them thinking about us the way they're doing."

"I would suggest that you don't head back to Earth at all right now," said Mr. Valhinda. "The Prar'Ruhr deduced the presence of our Sector Council here even from the few words you said to it about other intelligences it might enjoy talking to; and, telekinetically, it dispatched a message spore to us on the Council, giving us the gist of what had happened. Naturally, we told your home world immediately, thinking the news would please them."

"Oh, good!" said Lucy. "Were they pleased?"

"Far from it, I'm afraid," said Mr. Valhinda.

He tapped the surface of a table next to one arm of his chair, and its gleaming top produced a slot and expelled a sheet of paper. He passed it to Tom, who looked at it with Lucy.

It was the facsimile of a front page of the newspaper that had produced the sheet with other devastating headlines from a button on Tom's Assassin's harness, earlier. This one read:

Ambassador-At-Large And Consort Banqueted And Entertained While Sharks Move Forward With Plan To Impoverish Earth

Parents Play, And Are Applauded For Helping Minor Alien Race, While Human Future Sways In Balance

Worldwide plebiscite votes overwhelmingly that Tom and Lucy Parent should no longer be considered members of the human race

"Oh, Tom!" said Lucy. "Just what I was afraid of. We can never go home!"

"There now . . ." Tom put an arm around her.

"I'm not upset," she said harshly, sitting very stiffly inside his arm and refusing to blink. "I am perfectly all right!"

"Of course," said Tom. But he kept his arm where it was.

"There must be something we can do!" Lucy glared at Mr. Valhinda.

"Well, you can try doing another good deed with one of our Sector Races, who also have trouble with the Sharks," said Mr. Valhinda. "Possibly if you were successful, you might be able to force the Sharks to withdraw their claim to the Jaktal debt. With that out of the line-up, there would be no more danger of a Sector court foreclosing upon the Earth's futures to pay off the Jaktal debt—which is what your Race seems chiefly worried about."

"But you've got no specific suggestions on how we could start?" asked Tom. "Outside of my briefing, I don't have any idea of how we could find a world where we could be useful."

"I'm afraid I don't," said Mr. Valhinda.

Nonetheless, his eyes met Tom's and Tom found a feeling growing in him that Mr. Valhinda was actually hinting at an action that they might take; but was determined not to commit himself by directly suggesting it.

"Perhaps then," Tom said, casually, "you could tell us something about the Sharks themselves. I assume the word *Shark* is used to refer to Beings from all sorts of different worlds in the Sector, all of whom act in similar ways within the Sector Stock Market— wherever that is—"

"Actually, it's here on Cayahno," said Mr. Valhinda. "And you're quite right to think they come from a number of different civilized worlds. However, there is the curious fact that they're all, physically, very similar Beings. They all come from worlds with extensive oceans on them. A very common form of life through- out our galaxy on such worlds. I believe you even have primitive ocean creatures on your own world which would resemble them physically."

Lucy had gradually unstiffened. Tom took back his arm, which had itself grown rather stiff in its position; in spite of the fact their chairs were side by side.

"You mean," Lucy asked, "sharks like our sharks?"

"That's a good way of putting it," said Mr. Valhinda. "Yes, as Tom just suggested, the Sharks are marked by behavior; but in fact also by their general physical features. There are varieties even among your sharks, I understand. There is the one with a wide head . . . what is its name?"

"The hammerhead shark?" said Lucy.

"Yes, that's the being I was thinking of," said Mr. Valhinda. "Although most sharks more resemble the general shape of the majority of your shark families—

of which, I believe, an outstanding specimen is the great white shark."

"But sharks are water creatures," put in Lucy. "Is the Stock Exchange here on Cayahno equipped for them to live under water so they can do things there?"

"Oh yes," said Mr. Valhinda, "if necessary. But most of the accepted, civilized Sharks that you will find here are perfectly happy either in air or water. You may have remarked the Council Representative from Xxxytl, a counterpart of a small creature called a 'sea-horse' in your own oceans. The Race of the Xxxytl Representative were also underwater creatures, but learned to adapt quite happily to either atmosphere or water environments—though, it must be admitted that, like most of us they used technology at one time to enable them to do so."

"But why are Sharks from different worlds so much alike?" said Tom.

"You hardly need to ask that question," said Mr. Valhinda, "if you examine even the sharks of your own world. Consider what efficient predators they are, and how well adapted to their liquid environment. They have stayed physically pretty much the same for some millions of years on your world; and, although on other worlds they may have evolved by different routes, their physical shape, simply because of its efficiency, has tended to be repeated."

"So," said Lucy, thoughtfully, "the Sharks *are* sharks. And if evolution makes them look alike, it also makes them *act* alike."

"You could put it that way," said Mr. Valhinda.

Tom's feeling that Mr. Valhinda was hinting at a certain direction for them to take, suddenly made a possible connection in his mind.

"And do you know of any world," he asked, "that's having trouble right now with the Sharks, besides our own world?"

"Why, yes," said Mr. Valhinda, "now that you men-tion it, the home world of the Xxxytl Race has recently been having a lot of trouble with their local Sharks. We have discovered that the essentially Barbarian Sharks of that world are closely in touch with the Sharks of the Stock Exchange; and the Xxxytl have been suffering from the local ones more than ever, just lately."

Mr. Valhinda coughed.

"Understand me," he said. "I do not mean to imply that the Xxxytl Shark trouble has made them in any way partial to your Race and *its* present Shark problem."

"Of course, that never crossed my mind," said Tom. "But all this is very interesting. You say they're having some extra trouble with them right now?"

"Since you ask—as a matter of fact, yes," said Mr. Valhinda. "As your briefing undoubtedly informed you, it is a matter of principle that the Sector Council never interferes with internal Racial problems on specific worlds. Otherwise it couldn't survive. So, we've been forced officially to ignore this problem between the Sharks of Xxxytl and the Xxxytl Race, itself—which has been the only one on that world to qualify for Sector citizenship; though the Xxxytl are, above all, humane, scholarly and useful."

"But small," put in Lucy.

"True," said Mr. Valhinda. "However, don't under-estimate them. On the other hand, their very civilized attitudes put them at a disadvantage to the Sharks; since the Xxxytl never attack the Sharks themselves, only defend themselves, if attacked. But the Sharks attack at any time they want; and sometimes catch a city of the Xxxytl unprepared, causing great damage and loss of life."

"I don't know how we could help them," said Tom, thoughtfully, "but perhaps Lucy and I could go to

Xxxytl and look at the situation—that is, if the Xxxytl people wouldn't mind our doing that?"

"They're a very hospitable Race, and wise enough to know that an Alien mind may see something that they have overlooked as a possibility in defending themselves. I suggest you go by all means. If you like, I will contact my fellow Representative on the Council, and arrange with him for the Xxxytl's in their chief city of Nxxx to welcome you."

Tom looked at Lucy.

"Yes, why don't we?" Lucy said. "I liked that little Xxxytl Representative."

"So did I," said Tom. They both looked back at Mr. Valhinda.

"Yes," said Lucy, "please arrange for us to go there and be welcomed in Nxxx."

Welcomed they were. Some days later, when their spaceship dropped them off at about two thousand feet above the surface of Xxxytl, they were met by a flying platform, which rose to meet their spaceship as it hovered on atmospheric drive above a rolling countryside, green with meadows and clumps of what looked like trees.

Tom and Lucy stood in the open air-lock just inside the invisible weather shield, peering downward.

"There's no one on it!" said Lucy.

"Yes there is," said Tom. "Adjust your eyes for telescopic with terminal microscopic."

Both of them had been sent by Mr. Valhinda to see a Doctor of Physical Alterations on Cayahno just before they left. He had taught them a few simple exercises to adjust their eyes physically to have either telescopic or microscopic vision—or even a combination of the two, which was what Tom was suggesting to Lucy right now.

Lucy did adjust her eyes accordingly. It was like

seeing the platform through a telescope, then concentrating on a small area of it with a magnifying glass.

"Oh, yes," said Lucy. "I see him now. A little seahorse-like Being, just like the Representative on the Council."

"I suppose it's like any people you don't know very well—they all look alike until you've known them for a while," said Tom. "Like the shepherd that can tell each one of his sheep at a glance; but they all look exactly the same to somebody who's seeing them for the first time."

The platform came up to the air-lock and the Xxxytl on it waved his fins, or whatever they were, vigorously at them. Like his fellow Race-member on the Council, he was hovering in air, above the platform's surface.

"So good to see you," he squeaked in English—which they were only able to hear because they were wearing translingualphones in their ears; and these also amplified or diminished the sound of what was being said to them, so that it all came in on a comfortable level.

"Welcome to Xxxytl," the little being went on. "Please step on to the platform. Thank you. I am Hmmm."

Tom and Lucy stepped on the platform, which immediately dropped down from the spaceship and headed away from the declining sun of this world; which was slightly larger than the sun of Earth, and a more pale yellow in color, but altogether not that different.

"Pleased to know you," said Lucy. "I'm Consort Lucy Parent, and this is Ambassador and Apprentice Galactic Assassin Tom Parent. I take it you were expecting us, then?"

"Oh, most certainly!" said Hmmm. "Word came from Cayahno a good third of a day ago. I was fortunate enough to be picked as your greeter-and-guide; and was ready to leave to meet you as soon as the spaceship messaged us it was in the atmosphere. You are familiar with the Xxxytl Race?"

"I wouldn't say familiar," said Tom, cautiously. "But we've sat in the Sector Council with your Representative there, and we were both very impressed by him."

"Yes, he is a splendid Xxxt," said Hmmm. "I understand your Race is bisexual. As it happens I'm being male today, myself. Does this suit you? Would you prefer me to be female?"

"Whichever you want," said Lucy, graciously.

"Oh, but it's no trouble to be whatever you would like me to be," said Hmmm. "It's merely a matter of mood, you know. There was just something about today that made me feel maleish. *And then I think of many things, like rushings-out and rescuings . . .'* That is from a poem by your A. A. Milne, a poem about a young male Human. I am a fan of your Human Civilization—that was why I was chosen to be your greeter-and-guide."

"And I suppose that's why you speak English so well," said Tom.

"Do I really?" said Hmmm, sending his fins into a literal flurry of activity. "How kind of you to say so! I know it's not exactly true. The translingualphones can handle the language of almost any civilized Race, of course, but it is so nice to be able to speak to Beings in their own tongue."

"Yes, it is," said Tom. "I'm afraid the Consort Lucy and I must apologize for not being able to speak Xxxytl equally well. For example, I'm even now a little bit unsure about your name. You said it was something like Hum?"

"Hmmm," said Hmmm. "A small difference."

"Hmmm," said Tom, trying it out. Lucy also pronounced the word.

"But you say it excellently!" said Hmmm. "It is a shame, is it not, that our physical structures prohibit us from actually sounding like members of the Race we want to speak to in their own language. Nonetheless, if you mentioned my name to another Xxxytl who knew me, he would know immediately who you were talking about."

"Well, good," said Tom, heartily. "I'm glad we come that close."

"You will not be offended if I say," added Hmmm, "that the Consort Lucy does, in fact, pronounce it a little bit better than you do, Mr. Ambassador. Possibly the higher tones of her voice allow her to approach more closely the lilt with which the latter part of the syllable needs to be said in order to give it a polite intonation."

"Maybe I should use a translingualphone," said Tom.

"Oh, no, no, no," said Hmmm. "There's absolutely no need at all. There—if you'll look ahead now, you will be able to see the tops of the towering buildings in the center of our greatest city. The city of Nxxx."

"Nxxx?" said Tom and Lucy, simultaneously.

"I'm sorry," said Hmmm. "I was endeavoring to imitate your human pronunciation of it. Actually the name of the city is Nxxx. I hope I haven't confused you."

"Not at all," said Lucy. "In fact you're quite right. But if you don't mind Tom and I would like to try to call it Nxxx, if you can understand us when we do."

Hmmm's fins went into agitation again.

"That would be very, very agreeable—in fact, polite in the extreme," he said. "We should be landing on one of the buildings very shortly now."

And indeed, they had been approaching the city rapidly. They were still about fifteen hundred feet up, and Tom and Lucy could see all of it at a glance. It covered an area of approximately ten square miles by Earthly measure; and was built back a very short distance from the shore of a blue-green ocean that stretched away to the horizon.

Oceanward of the city—which was built on somewhat higher ground—there was a strip of greenery, and then a dark, clay-colored shore, sloping down to the waves of some very Earth-like surf, that came in to exhaust themselves on the clayey beach.

The city, in fact, was very like a miniature of a Human city, its tallest buildings making a clump in the center of the built-up area, with streets that seemed hardly a few inches in width between the scaled-down skyscrapers at the city's center point.

But what was most different about the city, however, was the fact that it looked like an enormous toy assembled from thousands upon thousands of tiny building blocks carved from different jewels, glinting with all conceivable colors in the afternoon light of the pale sun. The buildings lost something of their toy-like aspect and the streets showed a more respectable width as their platform descended; and when it finally landed on a roof-top landing space of one of the tallest buildings, Tom and Lucy found that the area they were in was a good forty yards square.

"I would invite you down inside one of our structures," said Hmmm, "but there is a slight problem of—er—"

"We completely understand," said Tom. "We're entirely too large and clumsy to come inside any of your buildings. But there's no disappointment to this for us at all. We assumed that'd be the case."

"How thoughtful of you," said Hmmm. "In any case, our own Table of Regents, who legislate not only for this city but for the whole world, has proposed that they meet you on the rooftop of a building not far from here, which is designed as a feeding place for us, and has been equipped with furniture and foods to suit Human taste."

"But that's delightful!" said Lucy. "Thank you so much."

"Yes indeed," said Tom. "I'm surprised you didn't take us there directly."

"Oh, Xxxytl manners would not permit," said Hmmm. "I wished to make the suggestion of the meeting to you on neutral ground, so to speak. But if the idea meets with your approval we will go right now."

"Let's," said Lucy.

They had not gotten off the platform, and now it simply rose into the air, zipped off among the rooftops and landed on an open space that was the top of a building even larger than the one they had originally come down on. A number of Xxxytl were hovering like butterflies around the area where Hmmm set the platform down, their fins pleasantly agitated. Tom, Lucy and Hmmm got down from the platform; and the Xxxytl already there crowded in close to meet them.

Chapter 17

It was like being greeted by a polite flock of humming-birds. Hmmm plunged into a welter of introductions—the Host of the Table of Regents—the First Regent—the Second Regent—the Suggestor of Social Mobilization—the Chief Empathic Counselor—

Tom gave up trying to keep them straight, and was fairly sure that Lucy had also given up. The various Xxxytl, as they were introduced, spoke to them politely in their own language, which the humans now at least understood. Tom had coached Lucy in it, on the way here. It was an easy language, worn simple by thousands of years of use, at least as far as ordinary conversation was concerned. For example, the single word *"Xxxytl"* worked for any and all references to the Race, its home world, its individuals, or anything pertaining to them, or it.

Tom and Lucy both answered in English, which tiny translingualphones worn by the Xxxytl present translated back into Xxxytl.

". . . And finally, may I have the honor of bringing forth to make you welcome," said Hmmm in English, "our current Poet Laureate. She has been looking forward to meeting you both."

The crowd of Xxxytl moved back on either side, creating a lane, as if for royalty. Down this lane

fanned a small, bowed Xxxytl, snow white in color
and moving slowly. Partway to Tom and Lucy, she
suddenly slipped and lost a little height. A couple of
Xxxytl darted forward as if to help her up; but she
testily waved them off with her fins. She continued on
until she could confront Tom and Lucy from a distance of about half a foot.

"Welcome to our ancient and honorable world!"
Her chitter cracked a little, as if with age, but she held
her position firmly enough, looking proudly into the
eyes of Tom and Lucy with her own left eye, her
head tilted a little to one side to get a good view of
them both.

"Indeed, Madam Poet," said Lucy, graciously, "you
do us great honor by meeting us."

Madam Poet brushed the compliment aside with a
brusque movement of one of her fins.

"Not at all, youngsters," she said, "I understand
you're here somewhat in the interests of your own
Race, but also out of some concern for our own problems with our local Sharks. It's both my duty and joy
to be of any assistance to you I can. We'll talk. But
first, it's only good manners we should all eat
together. I'll stay by your side here—let the banquet
commence!"

There was a sudden flurry of the Xxxytl around
them. As if from nowhere, there appeared what looked
like little cube-shaped, topless tanks, each with a large
colorless tube coming upward from it. The other Xxxytl
flitted around sipping from the top of these tubes.
Thick cushions about two feet square also appeared
for Tom and Lucy to sit on, and a couple of large
tanks were brought to them through the air, six Xxxytl
carrying each one.

These were set down before Lucy and Tom, with
their tubes arching up toward their lips. Tom sipped
cautiously at his tube and a whitish brown liquid

flowed up through it. His eyebrows lifted in pleasant surprise. It tasted exactly like a root beer float. He looked over at Lucy, and Lucy was looking happily surprised as well. Her drink, whatever it was, was a light green in color.

Tom looked at Madam Poet, who had landed on a smaller cushion and was sitting there just at his right with her tail half-curved under her.

"You are not banqueting yourself, Madam Poet?" he asked.

"I never feed at this time of day," she said. "However, don't let my not eating spoil your meal; and meanwhile I'll be glad to answer any questions you might have about our Sharks."

"Why don't you just tell me generally what they're like, as far as the Sharks that trouble you are concerned?" said Tom.

"Very well," said Madam Poet. "Our Sharks are considerably evolved over any that I understand you have on your home world. Ours have developed a fairly high level of intelligence; but they're still too barbaric in attitude to qualify for admission to Sector Civilization; and naturally, they have the basic instinctive reflexes and behaviors that are found in Sharkish Races everywhere. As you know all Sharks are ruled by instinct."

"Instinct?" Lucy said. "But isn't that what drives everyone when they're animal level or below?"

"I'm not quite sure what you mean by animal level," said Madam Poet. "The most civilized Races still possess instinct. But only the lesser Races are totally driven by it. The brains of Sharks on many worlds have never progressed beyond instinct for millions of years—their physical form was too efficient for them to feel the need to grow intellectually. But when they do grow intellectually, the worst part of their instinct seems to stay with them. So that even if they get to the point where they're accepted on a fully civilized level—as you already may know, they've never been successful in getting one of their Race accredited as a Representative to the Sector Council; simply because, as I say, their instincts stay with them, though in more subtle ways."

"What instincts are these?" asked Lucy.

"I'm sure you know them from your own Sharks," said Madam Poet. "From your primitive forms. All Sharks still have them. But the main one is their feeding frenzy—you'll be familiar with that?"

"Yes," said Tom, who had seen a shocking film of one such feeding frenzy of Earthly tiger sharks on a particular occasion. "This is where they seem to go wild and bite at anything. Even the uneatable parts, like the boat from which they're being observed. Our scientists have concluded they can smell—or taste, whichever's the right word—blood in the water from a great distance."

"Yes," said Madam Poet, "no matter how civilized and intelligent a Shark has become, if one of them sees something it wants, it wants all of it, whether that makes sense or not. They will even turn on their own kind in such a situation. As I say, it's instinct, and no amount of education or argument seems able to change it."

"Since you're on land," said Lucy, "and they've got all the oceans to themselves, why should they bother you?"

"As a matter of fact," said Madam Poet, "recently— in the last ten thousand years or so—their evolution has speeded up and they've become amphibious. They breathe air quite easily and can come up on land to get at us."

"But why do they want to get at you at all?" asked Lucy. "After all there must be all the food they want in the sea. Why should they bother you?"

"We think," said Madam Poet, "it's because they

hope to supplant us on this the home planet of our
Race. If they could kill us off or supplant us, it would
strengthen their claim to be the dominant intelligence
on Xxxytl."

"Have you had an attack lately?" asked Tom.

"Not for about a year here," said Madam Poet.
"This being our largest city, we have the largest number of loyal Xxxytl to help fight them off. But there's
always the fear that they'll come in strength." She hesitated. "And, to be completely honest with you, we
think that perhaps some even more intelligent Sharks
on other worlds may be masterminding their plans of
attack. If so, word that you were coming here may
have gotten out, and that could precipitate an attack
at any time now."

"You really think so?" said Lucy.

"Oh, it's only a possibility." Madam Poet waved it
away with a fin. "Let us talk of more pleasant things.
How do you like our fair city?"

"I think it's beautiful," said Lucy. "I've never seen
or even imagined anything like it."

"You please me intensely by saying so; and you will
please all others when I tell them you said that—which
I'll do," said Madam Poet. "Indeed, we're the only city
where all the central buildings are completely made
of jewels—that being something that we Xxxytl rever-
ence and love. As primitives, we considered them holy.
Others of our cities may have a central area that may
be constructed out of jeweled parts and building
blocks; but they are considered much more humble."

"I can see why," murmured Lucy.

"Yes," said Madam Poet. "It's the jeweled part of
our cities that the attacking Sharks particularly covet
and try to take in their attacks. They not only destroy,
they carry off the materials of our jewel buildings, so
that we will have to find other individual jewels, and
go through the intricate process of forming them into

shapes to fit together for our architecture. We are famous for that, throughout this Sector; and even, I understand, to a certain extent throughout our galaxy."

"But how do they manage to take away the jewels?" said Lucy. "I mean, the jeweled parts of your buildings once they have been smashed or destroyed?"

"In typical Shark fashion," said Madam Poet, "they eat them. There is no nourishment in jewels, of course, but a Shark can swallow just about anything and by swallowing them and going back to the sea, where they possibly disgorge them again and cover them up with mud or stones, they hope to diminish the amount of jewels available to us for building. At least, that is the only reason we can imagine why they would want to take away our ruined buildings, once they have beaten them down, crushed, and destroyed them."

"How cruel can they be?" said Lucy. "That sort of a thing is—" she struggled for a word "—despicable!"

"I agree with you," said Madam Poet.

"You Xxxytl have a Representative on the Sector Council," said Tom. "Can't you bring the matter up with them, somehow?"

"No," said Madam Poet. "I believe you already know the answer to that. The Council as a matter of principle does not interfere between Races native to the same planet."

"Well, is there some way you can talk to them yourselves?" asked Tom.

"Oh, yes, they have a language," said Madam Poet, "and many of us can speak it. We have tried to talk to them in their own tongue and reason with them; but there is too big a gap between us. We Xxxytl are an old, wise, non-violent Race nowadays; and they are complete barbarians still. We tell them that they are killing off the soul of our Race by robbing us of our jewel-buildings. Our arguments don't register on them at all, however. We can talk Sharkish and they can talk

Xxxytl, so the words may be mutually known, but the understanding of them is completely different."

Tom and Lucy looked at each other, then they looked back at Madam Poet.

"Perhaps," said Tom, "we, as emerging barbarians ourselves, may be able to come up with something useful."

"It would be nice to think so," said Madam Poet. She sighed.

"However," she went on, "we have wandered back to the unhappy subject of these predators, in spite of ourselves. But for now the buildings still stand. I know it is impossible for someone as large as yourselves to see them from inside, but perhaps I might describe to you how they are built."

"Please," said Lucy, "I'd like to know."

"Well," said Madam Poet, "we look for gems both in rock formations on land, and in the sea."

"In the sea?" said Tom. "Isn't that dangerous? What about the Sharks?"

"There is a certain amount of danger involved, of course," said Madam Poet. "But a single Xxxytl, prospecting along the sea bottom, is usually too small and doesn't give off the kind of signals that would attract the attention of a large cruising Shark. If, however, the Xxxytl is discovered and has to flee, the only safety for the prospector lies in reaching the surface of the water, since then they can take to the air; which the Sharks have not yet learned to do. At any rate, when jewels are found, they are mined; then of course they've got to be cut and shaped—"

She broke off suddenly. Chimes were sounding all over the jeweled city and most of the Xxxytl at the banquet had already taken to the air, heading for other locations. Hmmm was already on his way toward Tom and Lucy, and right behind him were a couple of other Xxxytl who were aiming at Madame Poet.

"Even while we talk about it!" said Madam Poet. "That's a Shark attack warning now. You'll have to get on your platform and be carried safely inland. I, too, must leave the city, with the little ones and those unable to help defend it—"

The two Xxxytl right behind Hmmm had passed him up and were now on either side of Madam Poet. With their fins they gently assisted her into the air.

"I'll hope to talk to you later," she called back to Tom and Lucy as she was hustled away. "There are other matters—"

But she was already out of hearing and in fact out of sight, lost among the other Xxxytl who were now zipping about, back and forth.

"Please," chittered Hmmm to Tom and Lucy, "get on the platform. We'll go safely over the hills back there. The Sharks never come very far inland."

"Not on your life!" said Tom. "I want to see this. But you can take the Consort Lucy—"

"Absolutely not!" said Lucy. "The two of us work together, remember, Tom? I'm seeing this, too."

"Lucy," Tom started to protest, then checked himself. She was right, of course. He reminded himself that he had all his Assassin weapons; and at least the briefing on how to use them. He gave Lucy a hand in climbing up onto the platform.

"Take us to where we can get a good view of the Sharks as they come ashore," he said.

"If that is what you wish," said Hmmm, unhappily. Then he brightened. "Of course, you'll be completely safe as long as we're in the air. The Sharks are restricted to the depths of the sea and the surface of the land—at least so far."

He lifted the platform into the air and sent it swooping up the coast from the city, so that they saw at once the whole expanse of ocean shore and the sea beyond it, plus the city itself; and having reached that position, he hovered the platform there.

"What kind of weapons will they have?" Tom asked.

"So far," Hmmm said, "they have had no weapons but themselves. Their size makes them very powerful. Simply by flailing their tails about they can knock down skyscrapers, for example."

"Knock down skyscrapers?" said Lucy. "How large are they?"

Hmmm had to think for a minute.

"I think, in your Earthly terms," he said at last, "you would say they are about twenty feet long and weigh something like a ton—or two tons? Measured on land, that is, out of the water."

"That's big," said Lucy, staring back at the tall, slender, jeweled structures that Hmmm had been referring to as skyscrapers.

"And what sort of weapons," persisted Tom, "do you Xxxytl have to defend yourselves against them?"

"Unfortunately," said Hmmm, "we are an old Race who long ago abandoned violence, and our only weapons nowadays are—" he hesitated, and then came up triumphantly with a equivalent to what he wanted in English "—tranquilizer guns. By that I mean weapons that shoot a pre-targeted missile that would put even one of the Sharks to sleep.—Is that the right name? Tranquilizer guns?"

"Exactly right," said Tom.

"Ah, good. It is not an important weapon by any means. But our problem is that the Sharks attack in such tremendous numbers. Even with every Xxxytl available to fight, they often overwhelm us and reach the part of the city they want to knock down. We keep on tranquilizing them, of course; but more keep coming, and some are able to feed while others get knocked out. The bodies of those who've been tranquilized help to hide those who are destroying the buildings and swallowing their jeweled parts. That part is like their feeding frenzy. They bite anything, even each other, then. When they've swallowed all the materials of our buildings, they go back to the sea and leave us with nothing but the space where our city once stood; and of course, thousands of tranquilized Sharks."

"What do you do with the tranquilized Sharks?" asked Lucy.

"We load them gently onto platforms," said Hmmm. "It is possible to link platforms like this together with others the same size until we have very large carrying surfaces and load the tranquilized Sharks very gently on to them, take the raiders out over the sea and return them to its deep waters, where they will come back to their senses in about twenty-four hours and be as good as ever."

Tom and Lucy both stared at him.

"Don't you ever think . . ." Lucy hesitated, "about . . . killing them?"

"Oh, my no!" said Hmmm. "Our Xxxytl point of view is that only a Race with strong traces of barbarism still within them could consider killing another being. Better we die ourselves, than indulge in such uncivilized behavior!"

The warning chimes from the city suddenly ceased, and a sad but noble sort of music took its place. Hmmm immediately inverted himself, so that he floated head-down in mid-air just above the surface of the platform, his fins barely moving.

"You need not follow my example," he said hastily to Tom and Lucy. "But we Xxxytl always stand at attention when our racial anthem is played. It is being played now, of course, because many of us may not survive this day."

The anthem ended and Hmmm turned back upright. A single, higher chime note rang out from the city.

"The Sharks are now within instrument range," he said. "Would you care to view them?"

"Very much," said Tom.

An upright circle, like a green hoop, formed over the seaward side of the platform; and, looking into it, Tom and Lucy saw—not the land and seascape beyond it, but an underwater view of close ranks of great Sharks, swimming steadily and in remarkable military order. They were dark gray in color, otherwise they looked very much like sharks from Earth with which Tom and Lucy were familiar from pictures. There was only one large difference between them and the sharks known on Earth.

"They're fatter than our sharks," said Tom.

"Is that so?" said Hmmm. "I didn't know that. How much fatter are they?"

Tom hesitated, trying to think of how to describe them. Lucy filled in the conversational gap.

"They're about twice as fat as any sharks I've seen pictures of," said Lucy. "It's rather surprising. Sharks are usually such streamlined things. The thickness in the middle part of the body of those you have here tends to make them look a little clumsy."

"They are anything but clumsy, either in the ocean or on land," said Hmmm. "But it is interesting to know there is that difference between them and the members of the parallel Race that are indigenous to your world."

"How long before they get here?" asked Tom.

"They should begin to come ashore in about fifteen of your minutes," said Hmmm. "That's just an estimate, a guess on my part. But I would say about fifteen minutes."

Tom looked over at the city; but could see no other Xxxytl in the air at all.

"Where are your people?" he asked.

"They will be down at street level," said Hmmm.

"It'd be safer to shoot at the Sharks from high up in the buildings; but the tranquilizer missiles are most effective when fired into a Shark's open mouth. A Shark hit that way ceases to move in seconds. Hit any place else in its body, a Shark could go on thrashing around for ten of your minutes or more, knocking down buildings and still destroying property, before the tranquilizing effect stopped it."

"Why haven't you simply put a heavier dose into your tranquilizer missiles, so it'll work faster and can be used anywhere on the Shark's body? It must be somewhat dangerous to get close enough to a Shark to fire into his open mouth."

"We could've, of course," said Hmmm. "But while the heavier dose might work quickly if it struck the Shark elsewhere than in its most vulnerable area, the heavy dose would go on working and the Shark might get overdosed and die. We wouldn't want that to happen."

"No," said Tom. "I see." But he didn't.

They fell silent, watching the Sharks through the green ring.

"You must understand," said Hmmm, breaking the silence after a little while, "what our jeweled buildings mean to our Xxxytl Race. They are the way in which we express our oneness with our world and the universe. If we are to end up eventually losing all our jeweled structures, something will be lost by us, Racially. The heart will go out of our Race, perhaps. There's been a sadness in most Xxxytl because of these Shark attacks, for the last few generations. If you were able to read and enjoy Madam Poet's work in our language, you would find a strain of sadness in it that looks toward a twilight, perhaps the end of our day of existence. We think that the Sharks who are attacking us know this—that they have been told this by more intellectually developed Sharks such as you find active on the Stock Exchange. It is only a theory, of course; but it is a theory that saddens us a little."

Tom and Lucy could think of nothing to say. Then Lucy tried to bring the conversation back to a lighter note.

"Tell me," she said, "when we first met you you gave us the impression you could change sexes at will, just depending upon how you felt. Why is Madam Poet called *Madam* Poet? Is it because she just decided to be female all the time?"

"Oh, that," said Hmmm. "All those in any generation of our people who are acknowledged to have risen to historic status tend to follow an ancient practice of—I believe your human word would be 'freezing' themselves in one sex or the other for the rest of their lives. They can choose the sex they want, of course. Madam Poet felt that she would prefer to be female. She could, of course, quite freely have decided to be male, instead. In that case she would have been addressed—pardon me, I mean *he* would be addressed as 'Sir Poet.' "

A sudden uproar of high-pitched chiming came from the city.

"I was wrong!" cried Hmmm. "The Sharks were closer than I thought. They'll be coming out of the water up onto the beach any moment now!"

Tom and Lucy turned their gaze from the ring through which they had been looking at the Sharks swimming underwater—and where they seemed to be still swimming underwater—and looked with fascination at the crescent of mud-colored beach-slope. They looked. They waited. But they saw nothing but the waves coming up, uninterrupted by any form, breaking upon the beach and being followed by the waves just behind. There was nothing else in sight.

"Any moment now," repeated Hmmm.

Chapter 18

Tom's mind was spinning like the drive shaft of an engine being driven at its top number of possible revolutions per minute.

Could it be that Mr. Valhinda had nudged them into coming here to Xxxytl in hopes he and Lucy could do something about protecting the Xxxytl from these Shark raids?

It could.

Gloom flooded Tom like a wave of cold, blue-green ocean water. It was true he had the weapons and had been given the briefing of an Apprentice Assassin; but those Sharks looked very large and numerous and there was only one of him. His mind scrambled, tying together everything he had heard about Sharks; and trying to formulate a plan of action.

"What was that?" said Lucy suddenly, turning on him. "Were you trying to say something in French?"

"Well, yes," said Tom, guiltily aware of his bad French pronunciation. "What's that quote from Georges Jacques Danton, back in the time of the French Revolution? *Il faut de* . . . something."

"You mean *'Il nous faut de l'audace, encore de l'audace, toujours de l'audace!'*" said Lucy, crisply. " 'We must dare, dare again and always go on daring.' Tom—what are you thinking of doing that's daring?"

"I don't know yet," said Tom, "that's the trouble."

"Look in the ring!" said Hmmm, sharply, interrupting them.

Tom and Lucy looked. They saw the Sharks now, with the white ceiling of the breaking surf just above them, looking strangely fatter than ever. In fact they seemed to be growing in their middle body area. It was hard to tell for sure because the view they had was almost head-on to the sea predators; and gave them little more than a frontal view of them. But the movement of the sea creatures had changed. It was no longer the smooth progress of someone swimming but more jerky and regular; and at the same time Tom and Lucy became conscious of something else.

There was a vibration coming from the shore area below them—a rhythmic vibration. It was like a drum beat without the sound of a drum.

"They are in shallow water and beginning to march now," said Hmmm. "In a moment you will see them coming out of the waves; we've already started to feel and hear them."

"Feel and hear—?" began Tom. And then hear them they did. The vibration they felt was in time with a deep thumping sound; as if hundreds of pile-drivers were at work at once beneath the surface of the waves—and just then the first of the Sharks started to emerge.

As they came from the sea, Tom and Lucy saw that the Sharks had slimmed down remarkably. Even more interesting was the reason for this. As they emerged from the water, narrower of body, they could be seen to have grown four stumpy legs—like elephant legs, only much shorter and very much thicker.

These were still growing, in that they became longer as the sea-Beings got slimmer and more dangerous looking, mounting the beach. As the Sharks came to a halt, their legs were lifting each of them about as high off the clay surface in proportion to their size as a crocodile might lift itself with its legs at full extension. The sound of those still marching from the water down along the shore behind them shook the air.

Thud—thud—thud (pause) *Thud. Thud, thud—* (pause)—*Thud!* . . . Even as high up as their platform was, it felt to Tom and Lucy as if the impact of their heavy feet shivered the platform itself.

The first six Sharks out of the water had come one after another, forming a line up the slope of the beach. Once they were all out, they turned as one to face in the direction of the city; then stood where they were, marking time like soldiers, the sounds of their heavy feet mixing with the foot-strikes of other Sharks emerging behind them.

Gradually a long line of Sharks six abreast began to take shape along the shore, all marking time, all now facing the jeweled city; which almost seemed to tremble from the vibration, in spite of the distance between them.

The Sharks continued to come. Tom and Lucy stared as their ranks extended further and further down the beach; until even at a glance it was plainly not merely hundreds of Sharks emerging from the sea, but thousands of them.

"Why do they do all this stamping?" Lucy asked Hmmm. "Is it instinctive, or are they doing it deliberately for some reason?"

"It is probably a combination of amphibious instinct and deliberate intention," answered Hmmm, shouting now to be heard over the noise from the beach below as the heavy feet kept up their rhythm. "We have land animals with hooves who stamp their feet as a warning, or when they're in a rage. Maybe it's that. But we think the Sharks hope to frighten us into abandoning the city, so they can march in and take our jewels without trouble. They always try it. We never go. But they keep doing it just the same."

"It's frightening," said Lucy.

It was indeed, thought Tom. Intimidating. It was the sort of drum-beat sound that seemed to signal an unstoppable power—a power that could walk through mountains, smash through any barriers, invincible.

He turned and spoke to Lucy.

"What did you say?" Lucy shouted in his ear. "I can't hear you over the noise!"

"I said," Tom shouted back into her ear, "I need more information. I'm going to get Hmmm to take us down to meet that front rank of Sharks."

"Tom—" began Lucy. But he had already turned away to shout at Hmmm. Before she could get Tom turned back to hear her, the platform had begun to swoop down to the shore; a moment later it was landing just in front of the first rank of Sharks.

They had come down less than forty feet from that first rank; and, in spite of the distance and the sea creatures' short legs, it seemed to Lucy that the first six of the sea-monsters loomed over the platform and its riders, their enormous mouths shut, their dark, unblinking eyes staring at these land dwellers who dared approach them. Down here, right next to them, the vibration and sound of their stamping seemed to fill the world. Speech was impossible.

The Shark at the farthest right of the front rank made a sudden change in the rhythm of his thumping—to a *thump*—(pause)—*thump thump thump*—(pause)—*thump THUMP!* Then he stood still.

The five Sharks next to him also stood still. The change in rhythm and the cessation of the pounding moved back through the long serpent of Shark ranks for a number of minutes. At last, a silence that was almost more ominous than the noise had taken its place.

Tom stepped down from the platform and walked several steps toward the first Shark. The one who, by his example, had stopped all the rest from marking time.

Lucy, unwarned, was still only half a step behind Tom as he left the platform but right beside him by the time he stood facing this one particular Shark.

"What are you?" demanded the Shark in Xxxytl, with a flash of great murderous teeth, in several rows behind each other in both upper and lower jaws.

Unlike most of the sea creatures that Tom had known of before, from the dolphins of Earth to the several sea-living Aliens shown Tom in his original Sector briefing by Alien device, the Shark did not speak in a high squeaky voice; but in about the range of a human tenor. Still, the utterances came out harshly and aggressively—even sneeringly.

"For one thing," replied Tom also in Xxxytl, "you ought to be able to see from my weapons harness that I'm a Galactic Assassin. Beside me is my Consort, Lucy. Or are you Sharks of this world so barbaric that you don't know what a Galactic Assassin is—and can do?"

"We know," said the Shark. "But also we know you are not a full Assassin. You are only learning to be an Assassin."

"And who told you that?" asked Tom.

"None of your business!" said the Shark, closing his jaws with a ringing snap. "We have our ways of knowing."

"*L'audace . . .*" thought Tom.

"As I was well aware," he said. "But your admitting it now was all I needed to take action."

"Admit? What do you mean?" said the Shark in a new tone of voice. "I didn't admit anything."

"You didn't need to," said Tom. "But to answer you—the fact you think I'm a learning Assassin makes no difference to this situation here and now. I have my weapons and I know how to use them. In the wink of an eye I can move my hand and all of you would be gone."

"Our eyes do not wink," said the Shark. "And we have no interest in you. Only in the city that waits for us. Out of our way, or be trampled into dust."

"Don't try it," said Tom.

"Tom!" said Lucy warningly.

"It's all right, Lucy," said Tom, never moving his eyes from the eyes of the Shark in front of him. "You and your fellow Sharks are here to destroy the city you talk about, and carry away in your bellies most of what it is built of, back into your own territory. Deny that, if you can!"

"I do not have to deny it, Thing!" said the Shark. "That is what we are here for; and it is what we intend to do—and neither you nor anything else in the universe can stop us."

"You're already stopped," said Tom. "By what you said just now, you further admitted you've come here to commit theft. A Galactic Assassin is also a reserve Member of the much-feared-by-criminal-classes Interstellar Sector Police, in any Sector where the Assassin happens to be at the time. He can be activated as such by the Sector's own police, themselves; or the Assassin can decide to activate himself. I do so now decide to activate myself. Don't move. You're all under arrest!"

The Shark stared at him, gape-mouthed.

"We're what?" he said.

"Under arrest," said Tom. "I just arrested all of you in the name of the Galaxy."

"Are you insane?" said the Shark. "Do you think you can stop us with words?"

"If you are sufficiently civilized and knowledgeable, yes," answered Tom, crisply, "however, if you are not—"

He pulled his loset from his harness and swung it before him, aiming it at the earth between him and the Shark. At the end of its swing it had disintegrated a trench some thirty feet long, eight feet wide, and a dozen feet deep between him and the front line of Sharks. The sides and bottom of the trench glistened as if it had been covered with molten glass, for all the material there had been subjected to such terrific heat from the loset that it had melted and formed a lining which was keeping the level of seawater in the clay from coming up inside the opening.

He had also pulled a small bulbous device from his harness with his other hand; and now he sprayed something from this along the bottom of the trench. Immediately, fierce flames flared up in it, reaching out, licking toward the sea creatures. In spite of themselves, the front rank of Sharks recoiled, bumping into the rank behind, which then bumped into the one behind it; and a ripple of movement went backwards through their company.

"Yay!" came the tiny cheer of Hmmm, on the platform.

"This is just by way of example," said Tom to the Sharks, talking over the flaming trench. "If you think you could march over me into the city, just come forward. I'm still standing here, waiting."

"Yay!" said Lucy also, before her better sense could stop her.

"Well?" Tom asked the Shark.

"We are unstoppable," the Shark answered, recovering from his first start backward. "If necessary we will fill the trench up and quench the fire with our own bodies. And I will be one of the first to do so!"

He took a step toward the trench.

Tom leveled his loset.

"As fast as you can come, you will be disintegrated," he said. "In fact, if I should put my loset on full setting—" his thumb moved ominously on the side of the loset "—I could wipe all of you from this shore in an instant!"

"Tom!" said Lucy in his ear in English. "Can you really do that?"

"No," muttered Tom back.

"Oh," said Lucy.

"All right, then, go ahead!" said the Shark, triumphantly. "Tranquilize all of us. We'll just be back here two days from now and you'll have to do it all over again. You can't stand on this seashore forever!"

"My weapon doesn't tranquilize," said Tom. "It disintegrates! You saw what happened to the clay I just disintegrated to make this trench. If I point it at you and press the firing button, you'll all be blasted into nothingness forever, the same way it was!"

A buzzing of Shark voices began just behind the front ranks and moved backward through the column.

"They must be talking Sharkish," said Lucy in a low voice to Hmmm, who had come up to join them. "What are they saying?"

"They're all asking what Tom said and then telling the Sharks behind them," answered Hmmm.

"You won't get away with this!" The Shark was saying to Tom. He and the other Sharks close to him clashed their jaws so that it sounded like innumerable car doors slamming. Then it was silent again. "You may call yourself Reserve Sector Police," the Shark went on, "but interstellar law has no authority over internal matters on a single world! You couldn't arrest us if you wanted to."

"I'm arresting you for interstellar theft!" said Tom. "And that clearly falls within the province of the Sector Police."

The Shark opened his mouth as if to say something, then closed it again. He did this several times.

"Be reasonable," the great sea carnivore said at last.

His voice was as harsh as ever, but now he was plainly trying to speak more agreeably. "There isn't a Shark here who's ever left the surface of this world."

The statement was undeniable. *L'audace* . . . Tom reminded himself once more. A happy inspiration came to his mind of a movie scene of a British barrister in an English court of law, pinning a cowering villain in the prisoner's box relentlessly, with statement after statement, to the point where the guilty man had to admit his villainy. The barrister had used simple statements, prefaced by a certain short, but effective phrase. Tom had always liked that phrase; but he had never had a chance to use it until now.

"I put it to you," said Tom, grimly to the Shark. "You have been disgorging the jeweled buildings you swallowed, and your fellow Sharks from Cayahno have been coming and buying them from you."

"It's a lie!" cried the Shark. "Why would they do that?"

"I put it to you," said Tom, relentlessly, "that where there are works of art, there will always be collectors of that art; and in a galaxy this size some of those collectors will be enormously rich, rich enough to sell a whole world to pay for a single Xxxytl building, which they would rebuild themselves, once they had all the parts—because such buildings were their hobby!"

"It's lies! All lies!" shouted the Shark.

"Further," went on Tom, hooking his hands in the upper straps of his harness, as if they were the lapels of a barrister's robe—"I put it to you that your fellow Sharks on Cayahno have been taking enormous advantage of you. They have been paying you next to nothing for these things; and selling them for enormous prices—up to the worth of a whole world—to collectors who can afford to pay that price."

"No, no!" cried the Shark, with a touch of panic in its voice for the first time.

"Yes, yes," said Tom. "I also put it to you that you know your fellow Sharks; and therefore know that they would do such a thing, because it's exactly what you would do if you were in their place. You, too, would cheat Beings who did not know the priceless worth of what they were selling; and were completely unaware of the tremendous amounts this could be sold for, interstellarly. Finally, I put it to you that they will leave you to take all the blame, as being the ones who stole the building fragments in the first place; and they will sit in their palatial homes on Cayahno and laugh at the thought of you as a simple, barbaric Race being stupid enough to find itself on trial for its existence!"

There was a moment of utter silence from all the Sharks in front of Tom. Then the one Shark that had been doing all the talking burst into an explosion of words.

"Those dirty—" the Shark broke off. "We never did trust them! I beg you, Sir Assassin, understand our situation. As you say, we are poor, simple, barbaric Sharks, who know nothing about the great universe outside our own world. Dupes, no more, of evil members of our own Alien-born, but similar Race, who have contrived to get higher Sector status. Surely someone like you can understand how we might be led astray and talked into something of which we are now deeply ashamed."

There was an angry chitter from the air between the heads of Tom and Lucy.

"Simple barbarians, hah!" Hmmm shouted. "You knew what you were doing! You're no better than your more Civilized, but dastardly, Race-alikes who hang around the Stock Market, and other such low places, on Cayahno!"

"A Xxxytl!" said the Shark, savagely, focusing down on the tiny figure of Hmmm. "So you did not come alone—" He quickly changed his voice back to attempting the same more pleasant tone he had just been using with Tom. "Please understand, Xxxytl. We Sharks have a rather aggressive nature—it's true. We admit it. But we would never have ruined your beautiful buildings if we had realized it was only to pleasure some fat galactic collectors!"

"I don't believe you!" chittered Hmmm. "Besides, we want our buildings back."

"I'm afraid," Tom interrupted, "that getting them back may be a problem, Hmmm. Galactic-wide detective work may eventually track them down; but it will probably take some hundreds of years. However, these Sharks here can be tried; and if found guilty—which I'm sure they will be—part of their sentence can be to hunt new jewels for you from the ocean floor— For a few weeks, that is," he added, thoughtfully. "Before all these here are executed."

"Wait a minute—" The tone of the Shark's voice suddenly changed and became triumphant. "Got you! The Xxxytl would never execute anyone!"

"What makes you think the Xxxytl will be the ones making the decision?" said Tom. "I explained—this has now become an Interstellar crime because of your trafficking with this Sector's illegal jewel-sellers. Interstellar laws, as you probably know, are devastating— but fair. The decision will be by Interstellar Court, which as everyone knows cannot be swayed from doing justice."

"Oh, no!" chittered Hmmm behind Tom, as neatly as if they had rehearsed the moment. "Poor Sharks! If we Xxxytl plead for them and ask they be given mercy, won't that save them?"

Tom had not meant to take Hmmm in, as well, with his *I put it to you . . .*" speeches. But since he could hardly admit that now with all these Sharks listening, he might as well make the most of the situation while he had the chance.

"Well . . ." he said, slowly. "The court might instead agree to sow your oceans with invisible spy-eyes to record any illegal activity by any Shark. And you Xxxytl possibly would want to notify Sector police of any more attempts to steal your jewels . . ."

"Oh, we could do that, easily!" said Hmmm.

"Well, that might help," said Tom. He looked severely at the Shark he had been talking to. "But you Sharks would naturally have to give up every jewel you now hold. And never attack any Xxxytl city or individual again."

"Yes, yes!" said the Shark. He half turned toward the Sharks behind him and lifted his voice to an astonishing volume to make it carry as far back as it could. "We'll be glad to do all that, won't we, Sharks?"

All the other Sharks within the sound of the leading one's voice, roared agreement; the roar spread back down through the ranks away and away along the shore, as those back there heard the ones in front of them roaring. The ones toward the back did not know, of course, what they were roaring approval for; but with typical Shark instinct, they were not going to be left out of whatever was going on.

"Very well, then," said Tom. "Back to the sea with you Sharks; and return as quickly as you can with the jewels you haven't yet sold to your Cayahno friends. Pile them up here—and we'll know if you hold back a single one. But bring them all and I'll release every one of you temporarily in the custody of the Xxxytl Race."

The Sharks did not wait to hear any more. In a moment each group of six had turned and charged back into the surf. In less than a minute there was nothing to be seen but open sea and the empty shoreline.

Tom turned back and got on the platform.

"Take us back to the city," he said to Hmmm.

"Wait a minute!" said Lucy. "—At least, until I'm aboard!"

She finished scrambling up onto the platform herself. Hmmm lifted it off into the air and sent it swooping up toward the city. Lucy dusted her hands and looked at Tom who was staring off into the distance. It was a little thing, his not offering to help her back up onto the platform; but it was irritating, particularly after he'd been acting almost as if she hadn't been there, all through his dialogue with the lead Shark. Of course he knew things about the Interstellar Police and things like that that she didn't know, but it still annoyed her. If he hadn't done such a marvelous job just now with the Sharks—

As she looked, he suddenly collapsed in a heap on the platform.

"Tom!" cried Lucy, diving for him.

Chapter 19

Tom opened his eyes. He was lying on some soft surface. High above him he could see an arched, jeweled ceiling of many colors.

"What is this?" he said.

"Oh, Tom!" said a woman, hugging and kissing him. "Tom, are you all right? You're awake again!"

"Is my name Tom?" he said. "Who are you?"

"I'm Lucy, Tom!" cried the woman, and Tom, looking at her, saw that she was right. She was Lucy. He was Tom. Everything came back with a rush.

"I made it all up . . ." croaked Tom.

"Come, come," a Xxxytl voice chittered in English, "I happen to know that most of what you told the Sharks is exactly correct. Interstellar law, though, is not that severe."

"Correct?" rasped Tom, blinking about him unsuccessfully to see who had just spoken.

"There, now," said Lucy. "It doesn't matter. Don't try to talk. You were magnificent. Just lie back and rest."

"No, really, I'm all right—just a momentary creative overload. But where am I?" he asked.

"You're in one of our stadiums," the Xxxytl voice went on. Tom looked toward the other side of the bed, or whatever it was, on which he was lying. Focusing in that direction, he saw a small seahorse-like character bobbing up and down in mid-air.

"Hmmm?" he asked.

"You recognize me, too!" said the seahorse, fanning up a pair of miniature whirlwinds with his fins. "Yes, it's me. And you're here in the quarters that we had set up for you. We had to use one of our stadiums because you're so big."

"But Tom," said Lucy, "are you really all right?"

"I'm sure I am," he said. He tried sitting up and swung his legs over the edge of the surface he was on. He had no trouble doing it. "Yes, I'm all right," he said.

"You scared us all to death!" said Lucy. "What made you collapse like that?"

"Did I collapse?" Tom looked around him. "Where are the Sharks? What happened to them?"

"Don't you remember?" demanded Lucy.

Bits and pieces of memory began to come back to Tom, but they did not make a coherent shape. "I think I'm beginning to," he said, "but help me out. What happened?"

"Why, you stopped them and sent them back to the sea, never to attack the Xxxytl buildings again," said Lucy. "Don't you remember any of that?"

"I'm afraid not," said Tom. "It's beginning to come back, but it'll take a little time. You see, it was a desperate situation."

"Yes, indeed!" chittered Hmmm.

"We know that," said Lucy. "But what I don't know is what happened to you, or what you've done to yourself. You were magnificent, dealing with the Sharks. But now you say you don't remember any of it?"

"I remember bits and pieces, as I said," said Tom. "But they don't quite hook up. You said I sent the Sharks back to the sea and everything is all right now?"

"Why yes," said Lucy. "You scared them half to

death and they're never going to attack anything Xxxytl ever again."

"Well, I'm glad for that," said Tom. He felt his own forehead. It was cool. "No, I don't think I did myself any harm—nothing permanent, anyway. But the situation called for everything I had so naturally, I went into Assassin's Emergency Concentration State One. It's like the mental tunnel vision you talk about. It focused my attention completely upon the problem of the moment; and with the whole of my mind concentrating like that, I was able to bring together all sorts of available information. It gave me a tremendous advantage over my normal state of mind."

"I should think so!" said Lucy. "All that business about your being a Reserve member of the Interstellar Police, and invisible spy eyes to watch the Sharks so that they don't do anything illegal. But the most marvelous bit was your showing them you knew about the fact that they were selling the jeweled parts of the buildings they took back into the sea to Shark Interstellar Traders, who sold them illegally to Galactic Collectors."

"Did I tell them that?" asked Tom.

"Don't you remember these things now that I've mentioned them?" Lucy asked.

"No," said Tom. "I thought I made it all up. When you're in Concentration One, evidently, anything is possible. I remember something about the Interstellar Police, and Assassins being Reserve members of it," said Tom. "But that's all."

"You surely didn't make up the business about the illegal Interstellar Traders?"

"Oh, no," said Tom. "That was simply my hyperactive mind putting together all sorts of little bits of knowledge. One bit was something Madam Poet said about a possible connection between the Sharks of Xxxytl and the Shark traders on Cayahno. That tied in with the Shark who talked to me saying he knew I was just a learning Assassin. He couldn't have known that, unless he'd learned it from someone from off this world. That confirmed the fact that they were in contact with other Sector Sharks; and the mention of collectors was just an inescapable deduction from the total set of circumstances."

"Very good," said Lucy.

"I suppose so," said Tom, "but what was that about spy-eyes—oh, I remember now. That's the problem!"

"Why?" asked Lucy.

"Because neither in the briefing I got back home on Earth, nor in my Assassin's briefing, is there any mention of uncounted numbers of spy-eyes that could keep track of every Shark in the ocean of a world this size. I must have actually made that part up—in Concentration One nothing would matter to me but getting results. Maybe I flat out lied to the Sharks."

"What of it?" said Lucy. "The results would have been the same in the long run. You already had them scared enough to back off. Anyway, how's anyone to know? The Sharks can't tell anyone but the other Sharks they've been trading with. And if the trader Sharks say there's no such thing as spy-eyes, the Sharks here will think they're just trying to talk them into risking their lives to get the trader Sharks more jewel pieces to make fortunes on. I won't tell anyone."

They both looked at Hmmm.

"What?" said Hmmm. "Were you saying something? I'm sorry, I wasn't listening."

"You didn't hear anything." Lucy looked hard at him.

"Hear? Oh, I hear very well," said Hmmm, "but I don't know why it is, somehow when the subject is Sharks or anything to do with them I just tune out and forget about it right away."

Lucy looked back at Tom.

"See?" she said.

"I suppose so," said Tom. "But my conscience—"

"Don't be ridiculous!" said Lucy. "Haven't our astronomy people even back on Earth already figured out before we even knew anything about the other intelligent aliens, that there are billions of billions of stars in our galaxy?"

"Well, yes," said Tom.

"—And," went on Lucy, "that some billions, or something like that, of them have to have at least one Earth-like planet circling around them? And of those billions of Earth-like worlds, some thousands of millions, anyway, have to have life on them; and at least some millions of those must have life that's developed a technology even better than ours?"

"I suppose," said Tom.

"So can you really tell me there's nobody in the galaxy that would have the technology to produce spy-eyes like the ones you talked about?"

"No," said Tom. "There could be not one but lots of intelligent races capable of producing spy-eyes that could check on every individual Shark in the oceans, here on Xxxytl. But—"

"So how does anyone know that the Sector Police in this Sector don't know about those spy-eyes, and use them?"

"I guess you're right," said Tom. "I think I'd better tell Mr. Valhinda, anyway, when we get back to Cayahno."

"I think he'll laugh," said Lucy. "But what's this about going back to Cayahno?"

"I'll have to tell him, so he can tell the Sector Council about the Shark trade in jewels stolen from Xxxytl. While I'm there I can talk to him and maybe get him to give us a clearer idea of what we ought to be doing."

"Couldn't we just send him a message?" said Lucy. "After all, he had to send a message to Xxxytl to tell them we were coming, or else they wouldn't have known it; and none of them, including Hmmm here, would have been ready for us when we came."

"Yes," said Tom, "but I want to talk to him *privately*."

He emphasized the last word a little, looking at her meaningly.

"Oh. Well, I think it's a good idea, then," said Lucy.

"You're not leaving right away?" chittered Hmmm. "You'll stay for the celebration? This will be declared a world holiday and we'll all want to commemorate your tremendous victory over the Sharks and an end to the fear of destruction of our Xxxytl civilization, with all it stands for!"

"No," said Tom, "I'm sorry. But we travel the slow way—by spaceship, you remember. Lucy and I will be with you in spirit while you're celebrating."

"You are so good!" said Hmmm.

"So that's what happened," said Tom to Mr. Valhinda some ship-days later, when they had landed at last in Cayahno and were talking privately with him. "Lucy suggested I might have simply deduced the fact that the police in our Sector here have and use something like the spy-eyes I told the Sharks about—since I was in Concentration One. But I don't know—"

"Oh, it's entirely possible," said Mr. Valhinda. "If the Sector Police had such a tool, it would be top secret, of course, and they wouldn't be telling anyone about it. In any case, as Lucy said, the results are the important thing; and you did stop the Sharks from attacking Xxxytl cities. But you're also quite right. This Sector will as well have a responsibility for any illegal trading of collector's items, taking place from here to other Sectors of the galaxy. That would involve us in problems with other Sectors. This isn't something for an open Sector Council meeting. I'll talk to certain responsible people here first, including the Xxxytl representative and other Council Members. What's done about the trading by the Sharks needn't be any of your concern from now on."

"I'm glad to hear it," said Tom.

"—But?" said Lucy, looking narrowly at Mr. Valhinda.

"But?" said Tom, looking from her to Mr. Valhinda and back to her again. "But what?"

"What's the but-whatever Mr. Valhinda was about to go on and tell us—unless he's thought better of it," said Lucy, sternly, looking at the black-furred, wise, but discreet face of Mr. Valhinda.

"Lucy is quite right," said Mr. Valhinda. "I must tell you I'm being replaced as the Oprinkian Representative on the Sector Council; and I have an old friend of yours whom you'll be glad to see. He's been waiting in the lounge next to this private office of mine, so that he could surprise you. I'll call him in now."

His hand reached out toward the set of control buttons on his desk.

"Wait!" said Lucy. Her mind had been rushing at computer speed over the list of their old friends to think of one with whom she and Tom might wish to be closeted here on Cayahno under the present circumstances; and finding none that made any sense. "You don't mean—Mr. Rejilla?"

"Ah," said Mr. Valhinda. His hand dropped from the control buttons. "You see through my little attempt to surprise you. Yes, it is indeed Mr. Rejilla, who's replacing me. I see you remember him."

"Oh, we remember him very well," said Lucy. "It's just that I've got one quick question for you before he comes in. It would be embarrassing to ask it after he gets here."

"I see," said Mr. Valhinda. "By all means ask me then."

"It's just this," said Lucy. "You speak our language perfectly. But Mr. Rejilla . . ."

She hesitated, searching for the correct words.

"It's quite all right," said Mr. Valhinda, reassuringly. "—I should explain. I used all our up-to-date techniques and technology to acquire use of your tongue. But Mr. Rejilla is a scholar; and prides himself on learning languages only by direct study of available data on those who speak them. As a result, while his vocabulary is as good as mine; and he understands your grammar completely, he may occasionally express himself in a manner that seems a little strange to you."

"Ah!" said Lucy.

"Yes," went on Mr. Valhinda. "He's quite aware of the drawbacks of his method; but, being a sincere student of the Universe, he feels it's a more honest way of attempting to converse in an Alien language than by using artificial means to learn it. He's not the least disturbed about the fact that he doesn't produce the highly polished, if perhaps artificial, rendition you hear from me, I assure you. Since you've now guessed what I was going to do, shall I bring him in?"

"Please!" said Lucy.

He pressed the button that had been under his finger a moment before. A space in the wall on one side of his office vanished; and Mr. Rejilla walked through, smiling at them. The wall became whole again.

"Hay-lo, hay-lo," Mr. Rejilla said, approaching them. "A long time since I have seen you double."

"Hay-lo, Tom!" he repeated, and shook Tom's hand. He turned to Lucy and shook her hand. "Hay-lo, Lucy! I have a surprise for the twain of you."

It occurred to Lucy that these Oprinkians were far too much in love with surprises.

"How nice!" she said. "What can it be?"

"Your grandfather!" said Mr. Rejilla, happily.

Lucy's head spun for a second time. Of her three

surviving grandparents, none was in physical shape to make a visit to Cayahno, no matter how transported; and none would have any reason for wanting to come here, anyway. Then, too late, she realized what Mr. Rejilla meant.

A volley of wild, roaring barks echoed through the office and Rex, their Great Dane, came bounding in at top speed. He leaped upon Lucy with such a wild excess of joy that he knocked her over.

"Love Lucy!" roared Rex's canine thoughts in the telepathic center of Tom's and Lucy's minds. "Love Tom. Love, love, love . . ."

"Tom!" shouted Lucy, fending off Rex's loving attempt to lick every square inch of skin off her face.

But Tom already had a good grip on Rex's collar and was pulling the dog off her. A moment later he was in a battle himself to keep from being knocked down and washed with Rex's tongue. Finally, order was restored. Rex had, at last, obeyed the command *"down!"* and was lying panting at Tom's feet and smiling up at both of them.

"Rex down," he telepathed eagerly. "Good Rex? Tom and Lucy love Rex? Give doggy treat?"

"Good dog," said Lucy, petting him. "But we haven't any treats for you here. Sorry. Good Rex!"

"—A remarkable grandfather," Mr. Rejilla was commenting to Mr. Valhinda.

"So I see," answered Mr. Valhinda.

"Though companionable and agreeable in all respects," went on Mr. Rejilla to his fellow-Oprinkian, "he yet retains the instinctive savagery of his ancestors."

"Ah," said Mr. Valhinda. He turned to Tom and Lucy. "While Mr. Rejilla is to take my place in the Sector Council, that will not be for a short while yet. I must stay with certain matters in which I have been engaged with other Council Members until all of these are taken care of. That leaves Mr. Rejilla free to pursue other matters, in which he will be needing the assistance of the two of you. He will tell you all about this."

"Without fail," said Mr. Rejilla. "Shall we go—Tom, Lucy and grandfather? Perhaps the best place for us to talk would be your own residence here on Cayahno."

"Do we have a residence?" asked Tom.

"Yes, indeed," said Mr. Valhinda. "It was where you stayed last night, after landing here yesterday on Cayahno."

"Oh," said Tom.

"We will go immediately," decided Mr. Rejilla. So they did.

Without warning they were back at the place Tom and Lucy remembered from the night before, which appeared to be a small cottage surrounded by woods. In some inexplicable way, this was supposed to be part of the same building that held the meeting place of the Representatives of the Sector Council. Mr. Rejilla had hardly finished speaking before they were standing in the lounge that was its front room, looking out through transparent windows on three sides at an apparent forest, and what seemed to be a closely cropped lawn between the trees for as far as they could see.

"There is much to tell," said Mr. Rejilla. "Shall you sit?"

"Maybe we better," said Lucy to Tom; and they both sat down on a very ordinary looking Earth-style sofa. Mr. Rejilla seated himself somewhat angularly in an equally Earthly over-padded armchair facing them. Once in the chair, he seemed all thin arms and legs, his black-furred knees and elbows projecting in various directions.

"In much of what I have to tell you," he began, "you will find cause for startlement. In fact some revelations will undoubtedly knock your noses off. However, perhaps before I get into that, we should be joined by our one missing partner—with whom you are also familiar—if that is agreeable to him?"

There was a ghostly "yay!" out of thin air and a Xxxytl materialized before them.

"Hmmm?" demanded Lucy, staring at him.

"You recognized me!" said Hmmm. "How kind! My sudden appearance here doesn't disturb you too much?"

Hmmm had ended on a slightly anxious note.

"Not at all," said Tom. "We just weren't expecting you, that's all—were we, Lucy?"

"Not at all," said Lucy.

"Of course you were not," said Mr. Rejilla. "Such expectation would be unreasonable to you because of lack of data. Hmmm has graciously consented to join us in the dangerous search we are about to make that may lead us to an end that I will not even mention now, in hopes that I may never have to mention it."

"We're glad to see him anyway," said Lucy.

"In any case," Mr. Rejilla went on, "the quick perception of the Xxxytl is a by-word, not only in this Sector, but in other places throughout our galaxy. You will remember how the Xxxytl Council Member immediately leaped to the proper conclusions about the two of you, when you appeared before the Sector Council and Tom sat down in the Jaktal seat. That Member had also suggested to the Council earlier that one or the pair of you might sometime do just that; and of course he was right. This perception had been prompted by my own study of you, back on your world of Earth, when you were so good as to have me as a guest in your home; and also the way you, Tom, activated yourself, when made an Apprentice Assassin."

"You know about that?" asked Lucy.

"I must shamefully admit that I not only knew about it," said Mr. Rejilla, "it was my idea. The reasons are convolute and recondite. Nonetheless, perhaps I can explain something of them to you now—possibly with the help of Hmmm."

"It was all done with the best of intentions," said Hmmm, apologetically.

"True," said Mr. Rejilla, "yet necessity drove us. It all dates back, as I say, to the time I spent in your home on Earth, and particularly to that evening while you slept and I inadvertently made you conscious of grandfather's thoughts. Astonishment captured me when I discovered your various capacities—alarmingly powerful for ones of a Race barely admitted to the fringes of civilized society in this Sector."

"Well," said Lucy, "thank you."

"Er—yes," said Tom.

"You have nothing to thank me for," said Mr. Rejilla with a dismissing wave of a long black arm. "I only uncovered what was in the first place there. Yet it was enough to inspire me to wish discovery of more. I should explain that, though Oprinkian through and through, I am also a Past-Master of the Lodge of Assassins in this Sector."

"You?" said Tom, goggling at him, "I mean—I hadn't exactly expected . . ."

"Tut-tut," said Mr. Rejilla. "Expectation of your perceivingness was not to be looked for at a time when you did not even know Galactic Assassins existed. In fact, I only mention the fact now, to explain how I could arrange secretly for Assassin Drakvil, unknowing, to be hired by Mordaunti Representative to take you on as an Apprentice. I may say your behavior, when you were put to test by being sent into a gark-class establishment to assassinate the ruling Pjonik there, was such that I was delighted by your handling of the situation; and Drakvil, who did not know I was observing, was equally so—"

He broke off and turned to Lucy.

"—And your pretense of deep concern at Tom's necessary challenge of two gnruths of Porbornik-jilks was breath-taking. If I had not known that your own latent ferocity rating was comparable to Tom's, I, too—who was secretly watching at that moment—would have been taken in."

"Well—" said Lucy, "as a matter of fact, I wasn't exactly—but you did say just now my ferocity rating was *latent*—"

However, Mr. Rejilla was going on.

"—But it really was not too surprising," he was saying, turning to Tom, "considering that—if you will remember—Drakvil also had gotten a reading of point seven two from you on the ferocity scale. Then, when you, Tom, balanced that capacity with such diplomatic finesse, verbally eluding assassination of the Pjonik Pjenik, I felt justified in recommending you be given access to Sector Council Room, expecting you and Lucy would, indeed, be bold enough to take over the Jaktal seat, just as predicted. Add to that, your masterful way of dealing with the long-insufferable Sharks of Xxxytl, left no doubt in any mind—least of all my own—that together we could attack this greater problem."

"A terrible problem," chittered Hmmm.

"Indeed," said Mr. Rejilla, "our whole galaxy may tremble in the balance."

Chapter 20

Tom and Lucy looked at each other. Without having to say anything, they both knew they agreed perfectly that they would just as soon not be in the position of helping to try to save the galaxy.

"Perhaps, we—" Tom paused to clear his throat. "We shouldn't—"

"Shouldn't really be in this," said Lucy. "After all, we have our own duties and jobs back on Earth; and perhaps being an Ambassador-at-Large is really too large a job for us, too."

"Dear me," said Mr. Rejilla, "do not misunderstand, I beg. If the Sector Council decides that you should control the worlds and Races formerly held in subjugation by the Jaktals—including the Jaktals themselves— it will not be because you want to do such a thing, but because you are of the best Race to do it. As such it becomes a duty. A duty overwhelming. And if that is a duty overwhelming, how much more overwhelming is the duty to save all the Races of our galaxy?"

"From extermination," supplemented Hmmm.

"Extermination?" Tom and Lucy looked at each other again.

"I see the double of you are at one in your response to this," said Mr. Rejilla. "It should have occurred to me that of course you would not know what happens to everybody when the Race or Races of one galaxy decide to conquer another galaxy."

Tom and Lucy looked at each other again.

"Everybody?" asked Tom.

"Everybody," said Mr. Rejilla, solemnly. "You must be aware of the exponential rate at which your own Race multiplies generationally in numbers of individuals; and requires more area necessary for all to live a proper life. The figures may seem too large for belief to you right at the moment; but consider a galaxy like ours, with billions of worlds where intelligent Races live, in conjunction with a great many less than intelligent Races. Imagine them all multiplying at exponential rates. Eventually, while their galaxy may have a number of empty solar satellites which are usable worlds, only a certain number of these are comfortable, let alone ideal, for the happy existence all of those of all Races."

"I see what you mean," said Tom.

"Yes," answered Mr. Rejilla. "Eventually more space is a mustness. They recognize this fact. Their attention turns to a nearby galaxy where there are available unused worlds on which their Races could live and grow. They must have space. The space is there. Their response—not a true Civilized response, we must all admit, but still their response—is to take that nearby galaxy away from whatever native Races are already existent in that other galaxy."

"It doesn't seem to make sense that all life in the universe uses the same sort of planets that we and the Skikana and Xxxytl need," said Tom. "It's enough of a coincidence that a certain percentage of us—in this Sector anyway—seem to like what we'd call Earth-livable worlds, and so we've developed on them. But certainly that can't be the rule throughout the whole universe?"

"Of course," said Mr. Rejilla, "it is not. However,

the invading races will want to make sure that there
are no technologically-capable, or otherwise dangerous-
abilities Races, already possessing worlds in the same
areas they wish to colonize. The original inhabitants
may not seem a danger when first colonized; but—
safety first! To play safe, invaders will cleanse the planets of our galaxy of all life, before taking over the kind
of worlds they like to colonize themselves. It is only
universal common sense, after all—harsh as it seems."

"Harsh is hardly the word for it," murmured Lucy.

"True," chittered Hmmm, sadly. "But there it is.
They have to play safe. We have to play safe, by making sure they never even get started invading us."

"How do you know anyone's starting?" asked Lucy.
"You don't have spies in other galaxies, do you? And
even if you do—how do the spies know who to spy
on?"

"No, of course we don't," said Mr. Rejilla. "But an
infallible prelude to any such invasioning, is always an
attempt by invaders to send a test number of their
people into the galaxy they wish to invade, to see how
well they survive, or whether the life forms already
there are powerful and decisive enough to immediately
destroy any attempt, even that small."

"You see," said Hmmm, almost confidentially, "this
isn't a new problem. In the history of our galaxy—as
far as historic records go back—there've been a number of attempts by other galaxies to move in on us;
but each time we found a weakness in them. Something that showed us how we could stop them if they
tried to move in in force. If we don't find it this time,
then they will move in. We've lots of races who are
very brave and ready to fight—you met the Skikana;
and there's the Jaktals, for example, plus many others.
Even we Xxxytl . . . but even if we do manage to stop
them, once they've tried a full scale invasion, it'll be

at the cost of countless lives of intelligent and worth-while beings."

"Ummm," said Lucy, thoughtfully.

"If I understand you right," said Tom, "they've already sent a few of their Beings into our galaxy to see what we could do to them; and if we can't do anything to them then the rest of them will come. That's it in a nutshell, isn't it?"

"It is nutshelled to perfection," said Mr. Rejilla.

"Then you know where these sample Extra-galactic Aliens are, then?" said Tom.

"Oh, certainly," chittered Hmmm. "But we've been watching and waiting, hoping they'll do something to betray where their strength lies, or where their weakness could lie. Now, thanks to your deduction about the sale of our Xxxytl buildings to illegal galactic collectors—some of whom, I may tell you now, are Extra-Galactic—you've opened up a new opportunity to test these invaders. We believe they've been dealing with the illegal Shark traders for the jewels from our buildings. Representing another whole galaxy as they do, they can out-bid any single collector in our own galaxy with no trouble at all. Our foolish, wicked Cayahno sharks have possibly been selling to them. It's doubtful the Extra-Galactics could really want our buildings or jewels. They must use their trading only to gain information about us. If so, it's a matter of finding out what they've been trying to learn; and then seeing if we can't deduce from that a weakness in them, which we could take advantage of to drive them off!"

"But how can Tom and I help you in this?" said Lucy. "You've got a whole galaxy full of very intelligent, trained beings who could do a better job than we can."

"That is not necessarily thinkable," said Mr. Rejilla. "Each new Race admitted to civilization has qualifications no other Race holds. In the case of your Race, you have this highly pugnacious rating."

"What makes you so sure of that?" said Lucy. "In many ways, we're really quite Civilized—kind and decent and so forth. We may quarrel a little bit among ourselves, but—"

She stopped, for Mr. Rejilla had held up a long, dark-furred, placating hand.

"Our instruments are never wrong," he said. "You must take my word for it. Because of your various actions, and your superb records, since you and Tom left Earth last, there is no one else in our galaxy better fitted to do what we would like you to do, than you, yourselves."

"But if we didn't exist, you'd be finding someone else to do this, wouldn't you?" said Lucy.

Mr. Rejilla did not answer right away.

"Well, er . . ." said Hmmm.

"Just tell me one thing!" said Lucy. "Why us? Why Tom and me? Don't tell me we just happened to be the two most dangerous people on Earth."

"I will not," said Mr. Rejilla. "The honesty which is the backbone of all Oprinkian Civilization compels me to answer you correctly. As Individuals, you are not the two most ferocious people on Earth. But as a pair you are unmatchable among your Race. Our instruments missed nothing. Every two-Being pair on your world was compared to you once you had been found, and you came out far and away above the rest."

"We did?" said Tom.

"That is right," said Mr. Rejilla.

"But we're really very different," said Lucy. "I'm quite ferocious, or pugnacious, or whatever you want to call it. And Tom . . ."

Loyalty blocked the further words Lucy had been about to say.

"I'm more happy-go-lucky," said Tom. "Not that I

can't get wound up if something serious comes along. But it's as if I had only two speeds, on or off; and I'm on off most of the time."

"Both these things are absolutely right," declared Mr. Rejilla. "However, this difference between you is exactly the reason you are as you are—two most unlikely individuals to form the pair you do. Clearly you have both made great adjustments to achieve your relationship. This is only possible because you both have high empathy quotients—as witness Tom taking a deep interest in an anonymous spider—Lucy throwing diplomatic politeness to the winds by singing *Marseillaise* to rescue a Bulbur. The two of you have harnessed empathy to make unusual adjustment. The result is very interesting—I might say, almost unbelievable!"

"Unbelievable?" said both Tom and Lucy.

"Magnificent!" suggested Hmmm.

"The bonding resulting has tremendously increased your potency for offense and defense for the pair of you. If ordinary pairing of Humans is considered as adding potentials of two individuals, you two have multiplied. Foremost among these is the will to defend each other. So, when your race is threatened by these Extra-Galactics, each one of you feels the other threatened also, and reacts accordingly. Believe me, you were without doubt, our best choice."

Tom and Lucy looked at each other, wordlessly.

"Nonetheless," went on Mr. Rejilla, "I must also in fairness point out that your selection is not completely complimentary. As the last Race admitted to membership in Civilization, you are still close to the barbaric stage and therefore the fiercest presently recognized. In short, you combine minimum elements of Civil with maximum elements of Fierce. I need scarcely add you are the only two with enough exposure to our Galactic situation to fully understand the need for what you are now asked to do."

"Yes!" chittered Hmmm. "And already you've demonstrated a truly galactic sense of responsibility toward other Races of our galaxy, by what you did for us Xxxytl in the case of the Sharks."

"That also is very true," said Mr. Rejilla. "Responsibility is a cornerstone of Civilization."

Tom and Lucy looked at each other again.

"Maybe we should sleep on it," Tom said to Lucy.

"I'm afraid," said Mr. Rejilla, "such will not be possible. You have yet to learn the intricacies of interstellar timal action, not to mention intergalactic timal interaction. You must take my word for it that if you take a night to sleep on it, the invaders will have the equivalent of fifty more of your world's years to consider the situation here."

"Fifty years!" said Tom.

"Yes," said Mr. Rejilla, "though this only applies if you wait to accept the task we offer you. Once you do, the timal fraction for the Extra-Galactics becomes exactly the same as ours, because of interaction. You no doubt find that a paradox; but I must ask you to trust me. It is a timal fact."

"I don't see why—" Lucy broke off. "You mean if we even think about doing it, this time fraction changes?"

"Yes," said both Mr. Rejilla and Hmmm.

Tom and Lucy consulted each other with their eyes for a third time.

"Well . . ." said Tom.

"I suppose," said Lucy.

They both looked back at Mr. Rejilla.

"Yes," said Tom, heavily, "I guess we'll try it!"

"Yay!" said Hmmm.

"I am congratulating, with admiration," said Mr. Rejilla. "Shall we shake hands to celebrate?"

They shook hands solemnly to celebrate; and each took one of Hmmm's fins gently between the tips of two fingers and moved it slightly up and down after shaking hands with Mr. Rejilla.

"Well, then," said Tom. "How do we start?"

"We start," chittered Hmmm, "by interviewing the most notorious of the trader Sharks here on Cayahno; and getting what information he has out of him about his connections with the Extra-galactic aliens."

"And the timal fraction is now in effect," said Mr. Rejilla, "so, if all are agreed, we will go immediately."

And (this being Cayahno) immediately they did so.

The room around them was suddenly another room: walled, floored, and with a ceiling—all of blue marble and holding an atmosphere of damp, scented air. There were half a dozen hassocks scattered around the floor, on which visitors could sit, crouch, lie, coil, or whatever they wished to do while they waited; and beyond these a businesslike desk, behind which a purple, worm-like Being about four feet tall was seated on something or other out of sight and wearing a fanciful sea-green hat, but nothing else.

"I am Mr. Rejilla, the incoming Oprinkian Sector Representative on the Sector Council," that individual said to the worm, affably. "With me, is a Representative from Xxxytl and the doubled Ambassadors-at-Large from the Human Race. It is important we see Mr. Slasjik at once."

"Will your Eminences be seated?" whined the worm. "I will tell—" it broke off, then went on almost immediately "—Mr. Slasjik has just informed me he already knows you are here; and he will be honored to see you immediately. Shall I effect the change of rooms?"

"If you would be so kind," said Mr. Rejilla.

Instantly, they were somewhere else again, with walls, floor and ceiling and atmosphere very much like the one they had just left. There were also hassocks here; and, on a large sort of chair-bed, a dark, gray shark-like being about fifteen feet long reclined at an angle of forty-five degrees.

There was a slit in the back of the piece of furniture that upheld him to accommodate his back fin. Otherwise, he had stubby arms and legs; but his pointed snout, under-slung jaw, and in that jaw the several rows of vicious teeth he displayed as he smiled at them, were as shark-like as anyone could expect.

"You are welcome," he said; and added, turning to a small red-shelled, crab-like being who was busily polishing his tail-fin, "you may scurry away now, Niglik!"

The crab-like being gave a wordless squeak, scuttled across the floor with amazing speed and disappeared through a wall, although there was no visible opening in it. Meanwhile, Mr. Rejilla had switched from the Cayahno official language to English to explain something to Tom and Lucy in an undertone.

"Mr. Slasjik," he murmured to Tom and Lucy, "is a leader among the Gnassh—as the collective races of Sharks are generally referred to here on Cayahno."

The conversation switched back into the official Cayahno language again, which was one of the ones that Tom had been taught in his original briefing, and which he had since taught to Lucy, utilizing some of the Alien techniques he had learned in the briefing.

"In what way can I be of use to you?" said Mr. Slasjik. "Anything that an unimportant trader can do for you would be my pleasure."

"Come, come," said Mr. Rejilla. "We know your interstellar worth—and your capabilities. Let us not pretend to underestimate each other. It is of importance to me, and to my colleague here from Xxxytl— and to a great extent that of the Sector Council itself— that Tom and Lucy, here, accomplish the tasks they have now set out to do. And kindly spare us the pretense you don't know what that is; we know the underhanded capabilities of you Gnassh. In furtherance of their accomplishment, we could use information; and, with your well-known connections, we have guessed that you could tell us what they need to know."

"I will be only too glad to so help," said Mr. Slasjik. "Meanwhile, may I offer you some fresh, warm blood?"

His guests politely declined.

"In that case, if you don't mind," said Mr. Slasjik, "I believe I'll have a noggin, myself. I always get a little thirsty while talking."

He extended one of his stubby arms and abruptly there was a tankard in it, like a large pilsner glass about three feet long, and holding perhaps a gallon and a half of red liquid. Lucy closed her eyes briefly, then opened them again.

"What would you like to know, then?" asked Mr. Slasjik, courteously.

"As you undoubtedly know," said Mr. Rejilla, "there are Extra-Galactics currently here on Cayahno."

"Dear me," said Mr. Slasjik, "you don't say so. I hope someone has warned the rascals off, so they'll be gone shortly."

"I would guess that you know better than that," said Mr. Rejilla. "I believe you are not only aware of their presence, but that they seem resistant to any kind of physical force known to the Civilized races of our galaxy. Let us not fence verbally, Mr. Slasjik. You are informed, and we merely wish a piece of that information."

"It's true, I did hear something about some Extra-Galactics," said Slasjik, waving his glass dismissively, "but I took it for mere rumor, and paid no attention to it."

"I put it to you, Mr. Slasjik," said Mr. Rejilla—and Tom looked at him with new respect. Could Mr. Rejilla, he asked himself, while learning about the Human Race in proper scholarly fashion, have also studied British movies with courtroom scenes in them? "—That your knowledge is far greater than that. I suggest you not only knew first-hand of the presence of these beings from an Alien Galaxy, but have personally been in contact with them."

"Dear, dear, dear," said Mr. Slasjik, smiling as winningly as he could with his full mouthful of teeth, "but you must not jump to conclusions, Mr. Rejilla—"

"These are not conclusions," said Mr. Rejilla, "they are essential certainties in the minds of myself and my companion here from Xxxytl. We know you not only know these invaders, but have done business with them."

"Mr. Rejilla!" said the Shark, in a tone of distress. "I hardly know how to deal with such an accusation. It seems almost ridiculous for me to deny what you suggest. But, if deny it I must, then I will. I do categorically assure you I—"

He broke off suddenly, for Mr. Rejilla was slowly raising a long, black, furry forefinger.

"You force me," said Mr. Rejilla, in a tone of voice that Tom and Lucy had never heard him employ before, "to make use of the one power of dominance that we Oprinkians have not discarded in the progress of our development into a stage of Upper Civilization. I therefore require you—"

"No! No!" cried Mr. Slasjik, in a high, terrified voice, shrinking back into his piece of furniture. "Not the Finger of Truth! I'll talk. I'll tell you everything! Just turn your finger away from me."

"It stays steady upon you until we have heard what you have to say," said Mr. Rejilla.

Tom and Lucy looked at him in admiration.

"Awesome beings, these Oprinkians," chittered Hmmm, barely loud enough to be heard as he floated momentarily between Tom's right ear and Lucy's left one. "What a pity their Finger of Truth, like everything else we've got, seems useless against the Extra-Galactics!"

"—Now, tell me everything," Mr. Rejilla was going on. "Otherwise, you'll tell nothing but the truth to any Being for the rest of your life!"

"No!" cried Mr. Slasjik. "Not that! It would ruin me; and then my fellow Gnassh would eat up what was left of me. Yes, yes, I've dealt with Extra-Galactics; but I never knew what they were like until several came here, a few months ago. What else could I do but deal with them? It was only common sense. They could pay much more for the—" His eyes flickered to Hmmm for a guilt-filled moment. "But I didn't invite them here to our galaxy. Believe me, I didn't. They just came; and I couldn't stop them!"

"None of us are surprised at that," said Mr. Rejilla, coldly. "Stopping an Extra-Galactic invasion is something far beyond the capacity of you Gnassh. They offered you and your kind survival, if you aided them to gain information about our galaxy before they invaded in force—didn't they?"

"Well, yes, but I ask you, what else could I do?" babbled Mr. Slasjik. "I was in their power. If I'd refused, there's no telling what would have happened to me—right then. And, naturally, we Gnassh want to survive, as any Beings would!"

"You were a fool, of course," said Mr. Rejilla. "Didn't you realize that after they had exterminated all life on all other worlds, they would clean off your kind as well?"

"Well, we thought it was a possibility, but . . ."

The trader Shark began to sob, convulsively. Mr. Rejilla lowered his forefinger, for Slasjik was clearly now a broken Being.

"Where are they?" he asked, in a more gentle voice.

"Here!" sobbed Mr. Slasjik. "Here, in my own modest establishment. They even had me construct a special place for them. But I can't even face them there. No one can! There's four of them—like huge gray mountains . . . pyramids. Nothing physical hurts them; and they can reflect back with extra strength any emotion directed at them, so even their psyches are unassailable—"

Mr. Slasjik broke down again.

"So, they're in your home, are they?" said Mr. Rejilla, thoughtfully.

"Yes, do . . . do you really want to see them?" quavered Mr. Slasjik.

"Not quite yet," said Mr. Rejilla.

Chapter 21

They were—abruptly—once more back in Tom and Lucy's room of the night before—Mr. Rejilla, Tom, Lucy and Hmmm.

"It's always wisest never to give one of the Gnassh any clue to what you plan to do," said Mr. Rejilla. "Now, perhaps you and Lucy, Tom, would like to have a moment to yourselves. I have to brief two other honorable Beings. The matter of the Extra-Galactics has been Sector Top Secret until this moment."

He pointed past them, and Tom and Lucy turned to see that two other figures had appeared behind them. One of which was either Drakvil, or a clone of that galactic Assassin, looking unperturbed. A Skikana officer was standing about ten feet away, elaborately ignoring him and looking defiantly unafraid. Tom and Lucy had barely taken in the sight of these two, however, before they found themselves in yet another room, where they were alone.

Tom dropped heavily into one of its human-style overstuffed chairs. Lucy sat down in another one, facing him, and looked at him narrowly.

"What is it?" asked Lucy.

"Lucy," said Tom, "I don't think I can do it."

Lucy looked at him for a long moment. He was sitting with his head supported on his left fist, the elbow of it on the armrest of the chair and staring at the white carpet below his Assassin's boots. She got up, came over and sat down with him (the chair was easily big enough for the two of them) put her arms around him and laid her cheek against his.

"Then, don't," she said. "Let somebody else try to stop these Extra-Galactics if they can; and if they can't, then you and I'll have at least as much time as everyone else they're due to exterminate—instead of being cut off short in the next hour or so. We can be together that much longer."

Tom straightened up. He put his arm around her but looked at her grimly.

"What's this 'we' business?" he asked. "Whatever happens, Lucy, you're not going to be there if I face them. Whatever happens, you're to stay away!"

"No," said Lucy.

"Lucy—"

"No," said Lucy, "and there's no way you can make me stay away. So we won't talk about it. That's settled."

Tom shook his head slowly.

"Oh Lord!" he said, looking at the marble-like wall across from him. "What I got you into!"

"You didn't get me into it."

Lucy had not let go of him and not stirred.

"—We got into it together. Remember?" she said.

Tom opened his mouth and then shut it again.

"Does that mean you do want to be mixed up in this?" he asked.

"I want what you want," said Lucy.

"But if I didn't exist and you were here by yourself—"

"Yes, I'd want to be in on it."

"Blasted Thorsdatter," muttered Tom.

They sat there in silence for a moment that stretched out and out. At last Tom sighed again.

"Well," he said, putting his own arm around her and holding her tight. "I guess we might as well get on with it, then. I wonder how long Mr. Rejilla is going to leave us here?"

"I'll bet, until we want to go back," said Lucy.

The words were hardly out of her mouth, before they and the chair in which they were sitting were once more with Mr. Rejilla, the Assassin and the Ski-kana. Hmmm was nowhere to be seen. Tom and Lucy both looked at Mr. Rejilla angrily. It was as it might have been for any couple bound up in a tender personal moment, suddenly finding the chair they were in sitting in the middle of a busy downtown sidewalk.

They let go of each other. Tom stood up hastily.

"Well?" he said, challengingly, to Mr. Rejilla.

"Well," said Mr. Rejilla, calmly, "I believe you know these two beings. Drakvil, of course; your Master and Trainer in the art of Assassination. And you've met Captain Jahbat of the Eighth Skikana."

"I am honored to face you again!" said Jahbat, bowing stiffly. "May I remind the Ambassador that there is a shot owing from him to me?"

"What are you waiting for, then?" demanded Drakvil, testily, when Tom did not answer at once. "Kill him!"

"Come, come, Drakvil," said Mr. Rejilla in a mildly reproving voice. "This is not a matter that need concern you."

"Oh, very well," said Drakvil. His voice trailed off, muttering something about ". . . Sector Council nonsense . . ."

Mr. Rejilla ignored it.

"Now, you all know what we must do—" he was beginning in a clear voice when he broke off. "Just a moment. The grandfather is missing."

Instantly Rex was also among them. He made a dash

for Tom and Lucy, trying to lick any available skin surface on either one of them as quickly as he could.

"Love Tom!" his telepathic voice roared in their heads. *"Love Lucy. Good Rex? Good dog?"* He began to bark with excitement.

"No, Rex!" said Lucy. When he continued to bark she took hold of his muzzle and held his jaws together. He looked up at her, with his tail momentarily motionless in mid-air and the rest of him a visible question mark. "No, nobody's mad at you. We just don't want any barking right now. *Still*, Rex!"

She let go of his muzzle and patted his head. He whined happily and licked at her hand.

"Rex still," he thought, and did not bark any more.

"Now," went on Mr. Rejilla, "that we really are all together—"

"What does poor old Rex have to do with this?" demanded Lucy.

"His presence, and reactions as representative of a sub-dominate and totally barbaric Race from your world will be highly useful in calibrating the reactions of yourselves—you and Tom," said Mr. Rejilla, courteously switching to English. He reverted to the official Cayahno language to address them as a group. "Does anyone have any reason to delay our confronting these Extra-Galactics at this time?"

"Where's Hmmm?" asked Tom.

"A responsibility has removed him temporarily," Mr. Rejilla answered. "He will join us later."

"Ah," said Tom.

"No other questions?" said Mr. Rejilla. "Then we shall visit them now."

However, it was not wherever the Extra-Galactics were, that they all found themselves next, but in the same room with Mr. Slasjik. A couple of the worm-like beings with fancy hats were fanning him as he lay in his chair; and to Lucy's eye, he seemed definitely more pale than when they had seen him last. As he noticed them he gave a scream.

"It wasn't my fault!" he cried. "I couldn't help it and anyway I had no responsibility. I want my legal advisor—"

"Call him yourself, Mr. Slasjik," said Mr. Rejilla, sternly. "We are not a committee sent to examine you by the Sector Council. We are here to face the Extra-Galactics for ourselves. All that's required is that you give us access to them."

Mr. Slasjik's color darkened immediately.

"Oh is that all—" He caught himself. "Of course, I'll be only too glad to transfer you to their quarters. You won't mind, I suppose, if I don't go along with you. I'm feeling a little unwell at present."

Drakvil snorted in contempt.

"Your presence won't be necessary," said Mr. Rejilla. "Merely do your duty as a citizen of this galaxy."

"Immediately!" said Mr. Slasjik. "Immed—"

They never heard the end of the word he was saying. Suddenly, all of them but Mr. Slasjik were in yet another place.

This one was almost too big to be called a room. It was as large as a hangar for several very large aircraft back on Earth—if not bigger. In fact the ceiling was so high above them that Tom, looking upward, saw a few small clouds floating just beneath it. He was reminded of the fact that the Vehicle Assembly Building for the spacecraft launch site at Cape Canaveral, Florida, had been reputed to be big and tall enough to make its own weather inside it.

"Is this only a part of Mr. Slasjik's home?" Tom asked Mr. Rejilla.

"Yes," answered the Oprinkian. "Unfortunately. Now, where are the Extra-Galactics he was talking about?"

"I think they're right in front of us," said Drakvil,

dryly. "You may have been looking around and between them because of their size, Grandmaster."

"Ah!" said Mr. Rejilla. "You're right; and they seem to be coming this way."

In fact, it was only then that Tom and Lucy identified the huge shapes of the Extra-Galactic Aliens.

They were literally small mountains, roughly pyramidal in shape, and with a light gray skin that reminded Tom, at least, of elephants he had seen in a zoo. But the Extra-Galactics were many times larger than elephants. Only their skin, which looked thick and wrinkled, reminded him of elephants. The highest point of each was either sharp or jagged-looking; and their edges, where two of their sides met, looked sharp. They were now advancing—one of them in the lead, two just behind, and a fourth visible between the tops of the two in the middle—each with one sharp edge forward, like the prow of a ship.

They came slowly, sliding over the floor in a way that produced an odd slurping sound. Except for that, it would have been easy to assume they were not moving at all. But the sound drew attention to the floor, sliding away out of sight under them as they came on.

There was something utterly indifferent about their massive advance; as if all things here were merely ants to be trampled underfoot.

In addition, something came from them that touched a deep, instinctive fear far inside Lucy, like the feel of icy tentacles about her heart, that probed and slid, growing thicker and stronger as the mountains drew closer, bringing a rising panic with it.

Creepy, crawly, inside me, she thought, like a little girl; and like a little girl again, felt the urge to look around for the comforting hand of a tall adult, who would not let any bad thing get her.

But Tom was standing out of reach, even if his hand would have reassured her; and there was no comfort to be found in a hand belonging to Captain Jahbat, Drakvil, or even Mr. Rejilla.

That is ridiculous, her adult self said sternly to the child she had been. But the fear was a real thing; and as the mountains got closer, it continued to grow.

Around her, the others also were not showing any signs of how they were feeling it—if indeed they were. Jahbat was expressionless, inside the thick chitin that was his external body. Drakvil, now fussing with his weapons, seemed no different than usual; and Mr. Rejilla was peaceful and unreadable as always. Even Tom, aside from the fixity of his gaze on the oncoming Extra-Galactics, gave no indication of what he was feeling.

But Lucy found herself moving toward him anyway. She reached him and took, not his hand, but his arm. He glanced at her briefly, patted her hand that held him, and returned his attention to the mountains. There was a tenseness in him she had never felt there before.

They all stood motionless, watching the Extra-Galactics advance. The fear feeling increased steadily. She could not believe it was not doing the same thing to Tom and the others. It had a coldness of its own; and a pressure like that of ever-deepening water, that mounted steadily as the mountains came on. Their advance was slow but without a pause; not even as fast as the walking pace of an adult Human.

Suddenly Captain Jahbat spoke.

"A Skikana always goes first!" His voice rang on Lucy's ears, so loud in that great empty place it almost hurt. "It will be my pleasure to try myself against them before any other of you."

Without waiting for agreement, Jahbat started across the wide floor toward the approaching mountains, into the deepening fear-wave.

Rex was growling, quietly, steadily, deep in his

throat, in a way that was new for him, as well. Lucy put a hand on him to reassure him; but he went on with the low, steady growl as if he had not even noticed he had been touched.

"Remember what I just told you and Drakvil," Rejilla called after Jahbat, barely having to raise his voice to do so, for sound echoed and re-echoed through the enormous chamber, "your weapons are useless! It'll be your will and courage only, bringing them to a halt. Also, remember, they'll reflect against you, with extra power, any emotion you direct at them!"

"I am not concerned," Jahbat's voice came back. He did not turn his head but his advance had slowed. "As a Skikana should, I will win, or fall nobly, in the attempt!"

"He'll fall nobly," growled Drakvil, busy with the items on his weapons harness.

"Drakvil," said Mr. Rejilla severely, "you are a Master Assassin, but I remind you that courtesy has not been abandoned in the Guild that you and I—and, hopefully, Tom—belong to."

"Oh, very well," said Drakvil.

Jahbat was now almost to the mid-point of this enormous room they were in, and his pace, though it had slowed as if the air had thickened and become as heavy as water, was now bringing him very close to a meeting with the leading Extra-Galactic. Suddenly he gave forth a wild battle cry, and tried to run toward that first mountain.

But he would have been better off, thought Lucy now, to shout at a mountain of stone. At least, from that he might have got an echo. But here, his cry only died as if it had gone out into an endless emptiness, and the mountains did not vary their unhurried, sliding advance to meet him.

The nearest one was now only half a dozen meters

from him. He lifted his voice again; but this time what came from him was a shaky cry that carried its own message.

"I . . . am . . . Skikana . . ." His words broke and wavered back to Lucy and the others. "I never. . . ."

He stumbled and fell. For a moment he seemed to be still trying to crawl forward. Then he stopped moving. Lucy's breath stopped, for the sharp point of the leading mountain's edge was still coming at him; and it looked as if the Extra-Galactic intended to slide over the fallen officer. But the mountain did not even show that much interest in him. The point of the huge creature's sharp leading edge missed his body by inches; and the side behind the point merely nudged his motionless body aside, so that as the Extra-Galactic kept coming the unmoving Skikana officer slid and was tumbled down along its length, like a floating bit of trash shoved aside by a vessel.

"Thought so," said Drakvil. "Now, let me see . . . losets, planet-busters . . . yes, all here."

"May I remind you, Drakvil," said Mr. Rejilla, "weapons will not help."

"Depends on how they're used," said Drakvil. "Actually, I intend to make use of my experienced Assassin's strength of will. Has a Galactic Assassin ever been defeated? No. Have I, personally, ever been defeated? Of course not. I'll not be defeated now."

Without another word, he stepped forward in his turn; and began to walk briskly toward the leading mountain, which was still some distance off. The still form of Jahbat had now disappeared behind it.

The leading mountain changed its course to head directly toward the Assassin. Well short of their meeting, however, Drakvil turned and went off at an angle, so that he now looked at all the approaching mountains from the side. He stopped.

The mountains turned also, and moved almost side

by side to meet him; although the one who had been leading was still in advance of the others. By moving aside, the Assassin had lengthened, instead of shortened the distance that would bring them to him. He was now ignoring them, setting up some combination of his harness weapons in what now looked like a tripod, with a surveyor's transit at its top—a narrow tube, pointed toward the mountains.

He seemed to squint through the tube. The mountains came on; but suddenly, on a thin line between Drakvil's instrument and the leading mountain, the air seemed to boil and writhe with turbulence. For a moment this turbulence continued and the mountain touched by it continued to advance. Then it stopped. The other mountains stopped.

"Noble Assassin!" burst out Mr. Rejilla in the Cayahno official language. "Look, Tom. Take note of your Master. He has combined several of his tools to channel his emotions and fighting spirit into a very narrow and fine attack line, and used a planet-busting ray as a carrier for them. By so doing and making small the area on which he attacks one, he has at least checked them momentarily."

"Yes," said Tom, tightly, his gaze riveted on the mountains. "But is it enough to drive them back?"

"We cannot tell," said Mr. Rejilla. "But at least it has obviously hurt the Extra-Galactic it touched; and made the others hesitate. The Council had thought we had nothing that would do it. See now how they are trying to avoid it."

Indeed, Lucy noticed that the other mountains had now moved from beside the leading mountain to behind it, where its bulk shielded them from the effect of Drakvil's attack.

"He's found a weak spot in them!" said Mr. Rejilla. "Perhaps he can win for us, after all. It may be only like sticking a small pin in a very large Being; but perhaps they're hyper-sensitive to resistance that hurts them in any way at all."

"It's draining him, though," said Tom, in a voice that seemed to tear his throat. "Look at him. He can't keep this up much longer. He's weakening!"

It was true. Drakvil was still on his feet, but his head had lowered and his whole body was slumping. The line of turbulence from him to the nearest Extra-Galactic was still straight, holding the mountains back; but he seemed drained and all but exhausted.

"Yay!" said a Xxxytl voice in Lucy's left ear.

Chapter 22

Lucy, a cold fear quenching the sudden hope that had sprung up in her at Drakvil's first apparent success, turned her head and saw the tiny, hummingbird-like shape of Hmmm, hovering in mid-air by the side of her head. The gazes of both Mr. Rejilla and Tom remained fixed on Drakvil and the Extra-Galactics; and neither seemed aware of Hmmm's arrival.

"Sorry to be late," said Hmmm, cheerfully, "we had to do it this way, however. Rejilla was to take you all to face the Extra-Galactics, while I explained our plans to the Sector Council, there not being a moment to lose, because of the timal difference. Should I try to help Drakvil?"

Lucy looked at the little mite with amazement.

"What could you do?" she asked.

"I don't know," said Hmmm. "That's what's so bad about it. I don't even know if I could get as far as he has. Those Extra-Galactics scare me a lot, even back here."

The offer was ridiculous, Lucy thought, her mind spinning. Hmmm could never be any threat to the mountains. But anything—just so it didn't have to be Tom, in case Drakvil failed.

"Hmmm, listen!" she said, urgently. "Mr. Rejilla's a Grandmaster of Assassins. That has to mean he's bet-

ter than any other ordinary Galactic Assassin. Why
doesn't he help Drakvil?"

"Alas," said Hmmm, "with all his virtues, Mr. Rejilla
is a Clinical Philosophical Assassin."

"A what?" demanded Lucy.

"A Clinical Philosophical Assassin," said Hmmm.
"He became interested in the Assassins only because
he is a Clinical Philosopher and they are part of everything in the universe with which a Clinical Philosopher
concerns himself. He therefore took all the Assassin
training and no other living Assassin had ever shown
his excellence. Therefore the other Assassins chose
him as Grandmaster. But I don't think he could do
anything against these Extra-Galactics even if he was
willing to use force against them."

"How about his Finger of Truth?"

"Well," said Hmmm, "it does make whoever it's
pointed at tell the truth for as long as the Oprinkian
wants them to. But do you think making these invaders
tell the truth will stop them?"

"I don't know, but—" began Lucy. A cry from Mr.
Rejilla pulled her attention back to the mountains.

"He's—he's going down!" cried Mr. Rejilla, wring-
ing his long, furry hands.

It was true. Drakvil had dropped to his knees. He
was still managing to point his device at the mountains;
and a certain amount of turbulence showed it was still
working. The mountains were still not coming forward.
But on the other hand, they had not retreated in the
least. They were stopped; but only as long as Drakvil
lasted—and that did not look as if it would be long
now.

Lucy grabbed Tom, just as he started to move.

"*No*, Tom!" she hissed in his ear. "You don't have to
go. Don't go! It's none of our business. Let whatever
happens, happen. It shouldn't be up to us—"

She never finished what she was going to say,

because he turned and seized her so strongly she was sure she felt and heard her ribs crack as he kissed her.

"I love you!" he said fiercely. "But I've got to. Don't you see? I've got to go now!"

He tore himself loose from her and ran toward Drakvil.

"Drakvil!" he shouted. "Hang on! I'm coming!"

He reached the Master Assassin and caught him, just as Drakvil went limp. For a moment he held him and also the instrument that Drakvil had controlled. Then Drakvil dropped out of his arms and lay still on the floor. Tom fumbled with the instrument.

"I don't know how—" he shouted back to Lucy, Hmmm, and Mr. Rejilla—"yes! I do. I can work it!"

He stood behind the instrument on its tripod, with Drakvil still at his feet, and the turbulence sprang into being once more between him and the leading mountain, just as it began to move forward and the others began to follow.

The mountains stopped immediately. This time, they actually recoiled a few feet. Then they stopped again. Tom picked up the instrument, took a stride toward them, put it down and played the turbulence on the leading mountain once more.

Again, the mountains backed up, but this time, not as far.

Tom followed them, taking a long step forward, carrying the instrument Drakvil had built. Again the mountains backed, but certainly no more than they had the second time, possibly a little less. In spite of that, Tom took a second step forward and forced them to back up once more—though, clearly, this time they only backed a fraction of the distance they had backed the first time.

Tom picked up the instrument and stepped forward once more. But this time Lucy saw him stagger slightly; and it was as if she felt something inside her tear open.

She started toward him, nearly fell over backward, and realized the anchor was Rex. She shoved Rex's leash into the hand of Mr. Rejilla.

"Hold him!" she cried; and, turning on her toe like a dancer, ran as fast as she could toward Tom.

Vaguely, she was aware of Mr. Rejilla's voice behind her and of the growling and wild barking of Rex back with Mr. Rejilla. She could also feel the mounting, murderous, icy emotions from the Extra-Galactics trying to freeze the life within her. But now all that they assaulted her with was something outside and unimportant, like the stamping of Shark feet on a clay-hard shore.

The only thing that mattered was the danger to Tom. TOM filled all her consciousness. Everything else was unimportant.

She reached him. Her hands closed on him.

"Come on, Tom!" she cried, trying to pull him away. "Leave that! Come on!"

"No—" he said, thickly, leaning against her like a drunken man. "—Stay . . ."

"No!" she shouted.

She jerked Drakvil's contraption out of his hands. It came easily, as if almost all Tom's strength was gone. Holding the device, she ran to the first mountain and literally jabbed it against the gray skin.

"Take that!" she screamed. "Take that, you—you *bastards*!"

The mountain backed away from her. She followed, keeping the point of the device against its great, gray side. It flinched back, moving away more swiftly now. She burned with fury. This thing would kill her Tom— her TOM! Again and again she jabbed the end of the device right against its body.

"Take that—" she was still shouting, when there was

a roar behind her; and Rex was with her, his leash trailing loose.

Snarling, he flung himself at the edge of the mountain she was attacking and closed his teeth on it, ripping loose a section of gray hide, and revealing pink skin underneath.

"Take that!" cried Lucy, tears streaming down her face. She jabbed the point of the instrument right against the pink flesh; and the mountain before her went back faster than before, but not fast enough to escape the end of the instrument.

She felt the mountain's emanations beating at her, somewhere out on the fringe of her consciousness. But they meant nothing, now. These things would kill Tom if she let them get away. She kept shouting and pushing the tip of the instrument against the one before her . . . and suddenly, without warning, it began to roll over. It rolled all the way over, until it was balanced on its peak; and it began to whimper, audibly.

Rex was still savaging it. She turned the point of the machine toward the three other mountains; but before she could take a step toward them, they too rolled over on their peaks and began to make whimpering noises.

The wildness in her suddenly emptied out, leaving her nothing but a shell. She staggered, and would have fallen, if a pair of arms had not caught her from behind. Tom's voice spoke in her ear.

"Are you all right?" he was asking.

"I'm fine," she said—and collapsed completely, dropping off into a black nothingness.

She opened her eyes to find herself lying on something soft, and Tom sitting beside her, looking down at her concernedly.

"Tom," she said, reaching out to him with one hand. "How are you?"

"I'm fine," said Tom. "The question is, how are you? Hey, you're awake!"

"Of course I am," she said, and started to sit up, but he pushed her back down on what she now perceived to be a very large bed. Tom was sitting beside it, in the one chair in sight, in a room with sunny blue walls and clouds drifting lazily, across them and across the ceiling.

"Where are we?" she asked.

"Oh, in a room that Mr. Rejilla moved us to. You know how he does that," said Tom. "But this is wonderful! You're awake!"

He hugged and kissed her, delightedly.

"Why shouldn't I be awake?" demanded Lucy, coming up for air. "Tom, let me sit up! There's nothing wrong with me!"

Reluctantly, he let her prop herself up against the padded headrest of the bed.

"What happened?" she asked. "How long have I been out?"

"Eight days," said Tom, solemnly.

"Eight days!" she said. "How could I be unconscious that long?"

"Well . . ." Tom cleared his throat. "Mr. Rejilla called in an Oprinkian—I suppose you could call him a doctor . . . anyway, an Oprinkian who could help. He said that according to Human standards, you'd just fainted; but he recommended you stay fainted long enough for your unconscious to completely sort out all the effects of your emotional fugue—"

"My emotional what?"

"Fugue," said Tom. "Apparently you were capable of the best emotional fugue of any of us there. But it puts a tremendous drain on your personal emotional orientation, according to the Oprinkian doctor; so that was why he recommended you sleep until your cognitive sense sorted it all out; then you'd wake naturally."

"But eight days!" said Lucy.

"The Oprinkian doctor said it was for the best," said Tom. "Their medicine's evidently gone far beyond the kind we have. They believe in letting the body heal itself; but sometimes it requires gentle assistance, he said. So he told your unconscious to stay asleep until you'd sorted yourself out, completely."

"I've never heard of such a thing!" said Lucy. "I certainly didn't need eight days' sleep. I was just relieved, that's all, once the Extra-Galactics gave up—they did give up, didn't they?"

"Completely," said Tom. "So completely we could bring in some of our own Galaxy's trans-linguists, who were able to establish communication with them. They begged everybody's pardon most abjectly for venturing into our Galaxy without an invitation. They insisted they had never had any idea of trying to conquer us—but the linguists told us that in their experience and with their instruments, they had no hesitation in pronouncing this a bald-faced lie."

"Of course it was!" said Lucy. "Is Rex all right? He came along and helped."

"Yes," said Tom. "He's fine. But he came along only after he saw you were winning."

"Well, he's only a dog," said Lucy. "And when he did come he helped a lot. He tore off part of one's outer armor, so I was really able to jab it with that thing Drakvil made."

"Yes," said Tom. "But you were the one who really made them give up. Mr. Rejilla said he'd been informed by our own experts that nothing like that had ever been accomplished in all recorded Galactic history. By the way, the experts also testified before the Sector Council that we Humans should have no trouble controlling the former Jaktal Empire, including the Jaktals themselves. However, they did finally send a team to remeasure the latent barbarism level of our

Human population. This was at the demand of one of
the Sector Council Representatives—you remember
the one that looked like a walrus? He insisted we
might be a possible danger to other Civilized Races,
since one of us had been able to conquer the Extra-
Galactic invaders."

"Why, what could make him think we'd be a danger?" said Lucy.

"Well, just between you and me, and judging by our
Human history—anyway," replied Tom, "Hmmm and
Mr. Rejilla, as the incoming Oprinkian Representative,
protested strongly. But the motto of the Council is
'play safe!'—so they sent this team of experts to Earth
to recheck. But one of the team that was going took
me aside privately beforehand. He told me there was
nothing to worry about. Everyone on the team knew
it was unnecessary. They knew they'd just find con-
firming evidence we were past the minimum level
required for a Civilized rating; and this re-examination
was really unnecessary—simply a sort of bureaucratic
endorsement of our Race."

"Good!" said Lucy. "I feel wonderful!"

She swung her legs over the edge of the bed and
stood up. This brought her face to face with a mirror-
section of the blue, cloud-populated wall; and she saw
she was now wearing a regal pink gown with a golden
sash at her waist and a long train, all of which somehow managed to suit exactly with the coloring of her
own skin and hair. In addition, her hair had been elaborately coiffured, high on her head. That, and her
being dressed like this, must have happened while she
was still asleep. Miraculously, hair and dress seemed
not to have been disturbed at all by her lying on them.
Then she noticed that above her hair floated a small
constellation of miniature stars, busily orbiting each
other in a rhythmic dance. As she watched, one of

them swooped down and returned a single stray hair to its proper position.

"What on earth?" she said, turning to Tom—and noticed for the first time that he was wearing a sort of medieval suit of soft red, with a short jacket, and trousers that tapered to a tight fit at his ankles. A long cape hung from his shoulders, scarlet on the inside and white on the outside.

"What are we all dressed up for?" she demanded.

"Well, you see—" Tom began; but before he could finish, Mr. Rejilla and Hmmm both appeared.

"Hay-lo!" said Mr. Rejilla, happily, in English. "So good to see you on your feet and totally conscious, Lucy! All Cayahno has been waiting this moment, the streets decorated for some time. Crowds are already gathered to express thankfulness to you for saving us from the Extra-Galactic invaders. If you are up to it now, we will go ahead with the procession through the streets, up to the special banquet prepared for you and Tom."

"Banquet? Banquet?" said Lucy.

"Yes, indeed," said Hmmm. "It is your human custom, is it not, to celebrate great events with a banquet? All of the individuals of the various races on Cayahno are trying very hard to do things the Human way to honor you."

"They are?" said Lucy, looking around her. Her eyes went back to the mirror surface in the wall directly before her. She studied herself.

"Then shall we go?" asked Hmmm, after a few moments of this.

"Oh, I couldn't possibly go right away," said Lucy, turning to look at herself from the side. The mirror surface immediately produced two extra, flanking mirror surfaces, projecting into the room. Lucy turned for a look at herself from the back. "In a couple of hours, perhaps," she said.

"Of course!" said Mr. Rejilla, immediately. "We will be back in touch with you in two of your hours, then."

He and Hmmm vanished.

"Two hours?" Tom asked.

"Well, of course," said Lucy. "I want to take a shower and—"

She looked at him.

"—did you know when I was going to wake up?" she asked. "And where did they come from, anyway?"

"I didn't know; and I don't know," said Tom. "The clothes just appeared—I found myself wearing mine at the same time when I noticed you suddenly were wearing that dress you've got on now, with those little stars moving around your head."

"And when was that?"

"Well," said Tom, "just before you woke up."

"Well, somebody must have known," said Lucy. "Where can I take my shower? is there a bathroom around here?"

"Right through that door, I think," said Tom.

He had pointed past Lucy; and she turned to look. There was a door in the wall that had not been there a moment before.

"That's the way things are, here," Tom said. "An advanced technology, of course. Things just appear when you need them—or express a want for them. I haven't been through that door; but I'll bet you there's a bathroom beyond it—just like the bathrooms back home."

"Well, I aim to find out," said Lucy, heading for it. But Tom was right, it was a bathroom.

Two hours later, redressed and satisfied with her reflection in the mirror, Lucy was back in the room with Tom who had been dozing, meanwhile, on the bed. At any rate he opened his eyes and got hastily back on his feet when she spoke to him.

"You're ready?" he said, getting up off the bed.

"Come to think of it, how did you take a shower with those little stars zooming around your head?"

"It didn't seem to bother them," said Lucy, "it was probably my imagination, but I could almost swear I heard little tiny voices laughing and saying things like '*whee!*' "

"Are you wearing something different now?" asked Tom, giving her a puzzled look.

"No," said Lucy, defiantly. Her gown was now a deeper shade of pink. Almost provokingly, the mirror in the bathroom had insisted, and the mirror out here agreed, that the outfit still worked beautifully with her skin and hair coloring.

"Anyway," she said, "I'm all ready and we seem to be all right. Shall we call Mr. Rejilla and—"

Immediately Mr. Rejilla and Hmmm were there.

"Were you listening?" demanded Lucy.

"Listening?" said Mr. Rejilla. "Oh, I understand what you mean. No, we were merely reminded that you were now ready to go. Something, perhaps, like your alarm clock—only different."

"I see," said Lucy. "Well, I'm ready. What's next?"

"We go," said Hmmm.

And immediately, as a group they were floating forward along a silver carpet seemingly suspended in mid-air between buildings on either side—all four of them, plus Rex, who had appeared from nowhere and was clearly on his best behavior. He only panted at Tom and Lucy, and gave each a lick on the hand.

The sides of the buildings on either side were stepped back every three or four stories as they rose, leaving level areas, like patios in mid-air, on which were congregated Beings of every shape and description. As their group appeared, a thunderous cheering began and followed along with them as they went.

"Is it not just as you would have it on Earth?" asked Mr. Rejilla, proudly, in Lucy's right ear.

"Well, yes," said Lucy, "I mean—exactly!"

The crowds on either hand were not only cheering but throwing what seemed to be colored lights at them, which arced up into the air and then disappeared before they came down. Among them, also, banners were being held aloft, with words in English painted upon them. The messages they displayed were all in English, but with some small errors.

HOORAY LUCY

—said one in huge letters; and beneath it in smaller printing, were the added words—

ALSO TOM AND REX

—And that was the general tenor of most of the banners they saw, though no two of them exactly agreed with each other. "LUCY, MAGNIFICENT WIF" said one, and another almost right next to it said "MAGNIFICENT WIVE AND CONSORT LUCY. ALL HURRAH!"

"HUMANS FOREVER," announced a third one a little farther along; and even farther yet, a very large one in silver letters against a purple background, upheld by what looked like a group of skinny kangaroos, read "LUCY! DOMINATOR AND DEFENDER OF OUR GALAXY."

At first it had seemed as if they had a very long distance to go to reach a building that looked as if it was built of white stone, at the far end of the silver carpet. But they approached it more quickly than they had expected; and it was not long before they were floating up carpet-covered steps into what looked something like a Greek temple from the outside.

Lucy assumed they were to continue on inside. But to her surprise, they stopped at the top of the steps in the little, open level area between the outer pillars, and a number of other Beings came from inside the building, most of them recognizable as Representatives from the Sector Council—each of which lumbered, swam, hopped or slithered up to Tom and Lucy to offer their personal congratulations and thanks for the defeat of the Extra-Galactics.

Lucy saw Hmmm apparently saying something in Tom's ear; and at almost the same moment she heard Mr. Rejilla speaking in hers, over the noise of the crowd.

"Turn around, now," said Mr. Rejilla.

Tom and Lucy both turned. Unbelievably, but undeniably, the narrow street between the high buildings they had just come up had apparently receded into the far background; and before them was a wide open space, crowded with what must be literally hundreds of thousands of Beings. Banners were everywhere and there was a continual cheering going on, from one part of the audience if not from some other.

"This is just like the way they do it on your Human world, isn't it?" said Mr. Rejilla, delightedly again, in Lucy's ear.

"What's wrong?" asked Tom in her other ear.

"Oh, Tom," said Lucy, almost in tears, "if these were only our own people. But they'd never do this. We can never go back!"

He put an arm around her shoulders and hugged her to him.

"Never mind," he said, "they always say you can't go home again. But we've got you, me, and Rex. We can live anywhere. Maybe in years to come our people will understand—"

He broke off, because at that moment three of the Council Members—the walrus-like Representative and the snake-like Representative, along with the one that looked like a tree—appeared, floating up to her from Mr. Rejilla's other side bearing what looked like a platter—padded and covered with a quilted, silvery, satin-smooth cloth. Underneath the cloth was something about the size and shape of a birthday cake.

The cheering, and other noises from the crowd, quieted immediately. The hush was awe-inspiring, after the constant noise that had followed Tom and Lucy from the time they made their appearance at the beginning of the white carpet. Only a couple of voices, calling Tom and Lucy's names with what might almost have been a Human accent, were to be heard, faint in the distance.

But now the three representatives, carrying whatever it was they had under the silvery cloth, were stopping before Lucy. The tree-like Representative that spoke only by waving its branches let go of the platter and began to wave at her.

"Because of the fact that the translingualphone cannot adequately translate the message of the respected Representative from Wavry," said Mr. Rejilla, "I will translate. You may find what the Member is saying to you a little flowery and also official-sounding; but unfortunately that is the only way it translates into words. It would go much better in music, where it would sound like an anthem of praise by some great composer. However, I will do the best I can."

"I'm sure," said Lucy, graciously, "your translation will do it justice, Mr. Rejilla."

"Thank you," said Mr. Rejilla. "In the usual Human language in which you and Tom normally converse, then, this is what the Representative from Wavry is saying—"

His own voice took on some official overtones.

"—To you, magnificent and resplendent Lucy, for whom the winds on the thousand thousand worlds of this Sector sigh, and the oceans of a thousand thousand planets wave and sparkle in praise—to whom uncounted Beings acknowledge honor and gratitude; we have been advised, valiant and remarkable Lucy, that over the history of your Race on your native world, those for whom cries of praise have ascended most often, and for whom the largest ransoms have been paid, tend to possess an important name and an item of apparel which distinguishes them from other Humans; and so we wish to present you with the name of "First Being of our Galaxy" and a suitable matching item of apparel."

The Council Member from Wavry paused; and Lucy opened her mouth to reply appropriately. But it had evidently been only a ceremonial pause. The branches began to wave again.

"We offer this to you," translated Mr. Rejilla, "with the deep gratitude of all of us in this galaxy whom you have saved—Mr. Rejilla, if you will be so kind—"

He stopped.

"—Those last words, of course," he said in his ordinary voice, "were directed at me." He reached out and pulled the cover off the object on the padded platter.

Lucy found herself looking at a delicately beautiful crown, a circle of several woven bands of gold and silver, widening in front to a much more intricate device, showing a mountain standing on its head. All of it was rich with jewels; and the jewels radiated colors as if there was a light inside each one of them, so that, all together, they created a halo, with every color of the rainbow circling around the crown itself.

Mr. Rejilla took the crown reverently off its platter and lifted it toward Lucy's head.

"—If you'll excuse me," he said to the space just above Lucy's head. A horde of little voices squeaked back agreeably; and Lucy, looking upward, saw the tiny stars that had been dancing around her head flying forward to become a ring in the air, clearly waiting until the crown should be placed on her and they invited to return.

"Why, thank you—" said Lucy, hastily; and as soon as it became evident that Lucy was going to speak, Mr. Rejilla held the crown where it was, waiting for her to make whatever answering speech might be in her mind.

"—It's a very wonderful gift indeed," Lucy went on. "I couldn't have imagined a gift as fine as this; and I can't find the words to tell you how happy I am that you would want to give it to me. But I really don't think I should take it, or the name you gave me. Why don't I accept both in spirit only, but leave the actual gifts themselves with you, to commemorate this moment—"

She broke off, turned her head sideways and hissed at Tom.

"Tom! Will you stop pulling at me!"

"But Lucy!" muttered Tom under his breath. "You can't turn this down! Aside from the fact you've earned it, you'll disappoint them, if you don't take it. Think first—"

Lucy risked a glance about them. Mr. Rejilla, the other Representatives, and everyone else within earshot, were all elaborately looking away, obviously ignoring the private conversation going on between Tom and her.

"Don't you understand, Tom?" she whispered fiercely back at him. "I can't—the way they're thinking about us back on Earth, now. They're all so sure we've both of us just been feathering our own nest at their expense; not giving a hoot for them, but getting everything we can for ourselves. They might still change their minds sometime before we die; but how can they ever accept us back on Earth if I come parading in with a crown like this on my head and calling myself the First Being of our Galaxy! I mustn't accept it!"

"Oh!" said Tom. "Well . . ."

Mr. Rejilla made an awkward, but quiet, sound, next to Lucy's ear. Lucy looked at him swiftly.

"Forgive me," said Mr. Rejilla. "I could not help—that is, I inadvertently overheard—several of the words you spoke to Tom. I don't think you should conclusions-jump so quickly. May I show you something first, before you make your refusal official?"

"Show me what?" asked Lucy.

"If you would just look . . ." said Mr. Rejilla. "Look down toward the front of the audience directly before you. I will arrange a little assistance so that you can see that part more clearly."

Lucy and Tom—for Tom had been leaning in to hear what Mr. Rejilla had to say—both turned their eyes onto the great crowd before them. A sort of magnifying-glass effect seemed to form in the air before them, making a circle perhaps four feet wide. As they looked through this, their viewpoint seemed to zoom in on the audience and particularly on two figures there, holding aloft one more of the kind of banners they had seen so much of on the way here. But this one was lettered in perfectly correct English.

TOM AND LUCY COME HOME
EARTH LOVES YOU!

Holding up the pole that supported one end of the banner, and beaming, was Domango Aksisi. Holding up the other end with one hand was Albert Miles, who was also trying very hard to smile agreeably. In his free hand he waved aloft several newspapers; and with the advantage of the telescopic circle through which they looked Lucy was able to make out part of the headline on one of the papers: "OUR HEROES, LUCY AND TOM!" And below, in only slightly smaller print: "—Earth Readies for Triumphfal Return."

"Earth learned of your victory from our experts sent to recheck the Human Aggression profile," said Mr. Rejilla. "Perhaps a little more magnification—"

The telescopic effect increased its power—so much so that not only was sweat on Miles' face visible, but also tears rolling down Domango's face. As they watched, a Being suspiciously similar to an anonymous, but very Earth-like, spider suddenly ran up from the bottom of the banner to its top, in the center of the banner itself; and it seemed—to Tom at least—that it posed there for a moment, with its two front legs locked together at the tips above its head, like the hands of a boxer congratulating himself on a win.

One of the papers slipped slightly in Miles' frantic grasp, and Lucy read the last two words of another headline that read: "—FOR US."

"Well!" said Lucy; and an inspiration soared up suddenly inside her. She turned to Mr. Rejilla.

"On second thought," she said, "I'll be only too happy to accept, with many, many, heart-felt thanks, the beautiful crown and title you've given me—in the name of all those who ever were or are in our own Human Race, and on behalf of Tom and Rex, as well, without whom I would not be here now to receive it!"

—And the cheers of countless Alien Beings split the Cayahno skies, as Rex, now whining with excitement, leaped into the air above their heads, barking excitedly.

"Mountains! Where Mountains? Kill Mountains! Kill! Kill!" he roared telepathically out at the crowd, dog-paddling around overhead.

"*Rex!*" yelled Tom, furiously. Rex stopped barking, stopped telepathing, and slunk back down through the air to crouch silently at Tom's side.

The Council Members recovered from the stunned immobility into which they had fallen, and proceeded with the presentation of Lucy's gifts.

"When did Rex learn to fly like that?" Tom whispered to Mr. Rejilla, who was standing beside him. But Mr. Rejilla was looking away and refused to answer.

THE END

5/95

FINES 10¢ PER DAY